A RULE OF QUEENS

(BOOK #13 IN THE SORCERER'S RING)

MORGAN RICE

Books by Morgan Rice

THE SORCERER'S RING
A QUEST OF HEROES
A MARCH OF KINGS
A FATE OF DRAGONS
A CRY OF HONOR
A VOW OF GLORY
A CHARGE OF VALOR
A RITE OF SWORDS
A GRANT OF ARMS
A SKY OF SPELLS
A SEA OF SHIELDS
A REIGN OF STEEL
A LAND OF FIRE
A RULE OF QUEENS

THE SURVIVAL TRILOGY
ARENA ONE (Book #1)
ARENA TWO (Book #2)

the Vampire Journals
turned (book #1)
loved (book #2)
betrayed (book #3)
destined (book #4)
desired (book #5)
betrothed (book #6)
vowed (book #7)
found (book #8)
resurrected (book #9)
craved (book #10)
fated (book #11)

"Thus I turn my back:
There is a world elsewhere."

--William Shakespeare
Coriolanus

CHAPTER ONE

Thorgrin's head slammed against rock and mud as he tumbled down the mountainside in free-fall, tumbling hundreds of feet as the mountain collapsed. His world spun end over end, and he tried to stop it, to orient himself, but he could not. Out of the corner of his eye he glimpsed his brothers tumbling, too, flipping end over end, all of them, like Thor, grasping desperately at roots, at rocks—at anything—trying to slow the fall.

Thor realized, with each passing moment, that he was getting farther and farther away from the peak of the volcano, from Guwayne. He thought of those savages up there, preparing to sacrifice his baby, and he burned with fury. He clawed at the mud, shrieking, desperate to get back up there.

But try as he did, there was little he could do. Thor could barely see or breathe, much less shield himself from the blows, as a mountain of dirt thundered down upon him. It felt as if the weight of the entire universe were on his shoulders.

It was all happening so fast, too fast for Thor to even process it, and as he caught a glimpse down below, he saw a field of jagged rocks. He knew that once they hit them, they would all be dead.

Thor closed his eyes and tried to recall his training, Argon's teachings, his mother's words, tried to find calm within the storm, to summon the warrior power within him. As he did, he felt his life flashing before his eyes. Was this, he wondered, his final test?

Please, God, Thor prayed, *if you exist, save me. Do not allow me to die like this. Allow me to summon my power. Allow me to save my son.*

As he thought the words, Thor felt that he was being tested, being forced to draw upon his faith, to summon a stronger faith than he'd ever had. As his mother had warned, he was a warrior now, and he was being put to a warrior's test.

As Thor closed his eyes, the world began to slow, and to his amazement, he began to feel a calm, a sense of peace, within the storm. He began to feel a heat rising within him, coursing through his veins, through his palms. He began to feel bigger than his body.

Thor felt himself outside of his body, looking down, saw himself tumbling down the mountainside. He realized in that moment that he was not his body. He was something greater.

Thor suddenly snapped back into his body, and as he did, he raised his palms high overhead, and watched as a shining white light emanated from them. He directed the light and created a bubble around himself and his brothers, and as he did, suddenly the mudslide stopped in its tracks, a wall of dirt bouncing off the shield and not coming at them any further.

They continued to slide, but now at a much slower rate, easing their way to a gradual stop on a small plateau near the base of the mountain. Thor looked down and saw he had come to a stop in shallow water, and as he stood, he saw it was up to his knees.

Thor looked around in amazement. He looked up the mountain, saw the wall of dirt frozen, hanging there in mid-air, as if ready to come back down at any second, still blocked by his bubble of light. He took it all in, amazed that he had done that.

"Anybody dead?" O'Connor called out.

Thor saw Reece, O'Connor, Conven, Matus, Elden, and Indra, all of them bruised and shaken, getting to their feet, but all miraculously alive, and none with major injuries. They rubbed their faces, covered in black dirt, all of them looking as if they'd crawled through a mine. Thor could see how grateful they were to be alive, and he could see in their eyes that they credited him with saving their lives.

Thor, remembering, turned and immediately looked up at the top of the mountain with only one thing on his mind: his son.

"How are we going to get back up—" Matus began.

But before he could finish his words, Thor suddenly felt something wrap around his ankles. He looked down, startled, and saw a thick, slimy, muscular creature, wrapping around his ankles and up his shins, again and again. He saw in horror that it was a long, eel-like creature, with two small heads, hissing with its long tongues as it looked up at him and wrapped its tentacles around him. Its skin began to burn Thor's legs.

6

Thor's reflexes kicked in, and he drew his sword and slashed, as did the others, also being attacked all around him. Thor tried to slash carefully so as not to slice his own leg, and as he chopped one off, the eel loosened and the horrific pain in his ankles subsided. The eel slithered back into the water, hissing.

O'Connor fumbled for his bow, firing down at them and missing, while Elden shrieked as three eels came upon him at once.

Thor raced forward and slashed the eel making its way up O'Connor's leg, while Indra stepped forward and yelled to Elden: "Don't move!"

She raised her bow and fired off three arrows in quick succession, killing each eel with a perfect shot, and just grazing Elden's skin.

He looked up at her, shocked.

"Are you mad?" he cried out. "You almost took out my leg!"

Indra smiled back.

"But I didn't, did I?" she replied.

Thor heard more splashing and looked all around at the water in shock to see dozens more eels rising up. He realized they had to make a move and get out of there quickly.

Thor felt drained, exhausted, from summoning his power, and he knew there was little of it left within him; he was not yet powerful enough, he knew, to summon his power continuously. Still, he knew he had to draw upon it one last time, whatever the cost. If he did not, he knew they'd never make it back, they would die here in his pool of eels, and there'd be no chance left for his son. It might take all his strength, it might leave him weak for days, but he did not care. He thought of Guwayne, up there, helpless, at the mercy of those savages, and knew he would do anything.

As another group of eels began to slither toward him, Thor closed his eyes and raised his palms to the sky.

"In the name of the one and only God," Thor said aloud, "I command you, skies, to part! I command you to send us clouds to lift us up!"

Thor uttered the words in a deep dark voice, no longer afraid to embrace the Druid he was, and he felt them vibrating in his chest, in the air. He felt a tremendous heat centering in his chest, and as he uttered the words, he felt with certainty that they would come to pass.

There came a great roar, and Thor looked up to see the skies began to change, to morph into a dark purple, the clouds swirling and frothing. There appeared a round hole, an opening in the sky, and suddenly, a scarlet light shot down, and it was followed by a funnel cloud, lowering right down to them.

In moments, Thor and the others found themselves swept up in a tornado. Thor felt the moisture of the soft clouds swirling all around him, felt himself immersed in the light, and moments later, he felt himself hoisted, lifted up into the air, feeling lighter than he'd ever had. He truly felt as one with the universe.

Thor felt himself rising higher and higher, up alongside the mountain, past the dirt, past his bubble, all the way to the top of the mountain. In moments, the cloud took them to the very top of the volcano and then deposited them gently. It then dissipated just as quickly.

Thor stood there with his brothers, and they all looked back at him in complete awe, as if he were a god.

But Thor was not thinking of them; he turned and quickly surveyed the plateau, and there was but one thing on his mind: the three savages standing before him. And the small bassinet in their arms, hovering over the edge of the volcano.

Thor let out a battle cry as he rushed forward. The first savage turned to face him, startled, and as he did, Thor did not hesitate, but rushed forward and decapitated him.

The other two turned to him with a horrified expression, and as they did, Thor stabbed one in the heart, then reached around with the back of his sword and butted the other one in the face, knocking him backwards, shrieking, over the edge of the volcano.

Thor turned and quickly snatched the bassinet before they could drop it. He looked down, his heart pounding with gratitude that he had caught it in time, prepared to lift Guwayne out and hold him in his arms.

But as Thor looked down into the bassinet, his entire world fell apart.

8

It was empty.

Thor's entire world froze, as he stood there, numb.

He looked down inside the volcano, and saw far below, the flames, rising high. And he knew his son was dead.

"NO!" Thor shrieked.

Thor dropped to his knees, shrieking to the heavens, letting out a tremendous cry that echoed off the mountains, the primal scream of a man who had lost everything he had to live for.

"GUWAYNE!"

CHAPTER TWO

High above the lone isle in the center of the sea flew a lone dragon, a small dragon, not yet grown, his cry shrill and piercing, already hinting at the dragon he would one day become. He flew triumphantly, his small scales throbbing, growing by the minute, his wings flapping, his talons clutching the most precious thing he had felt in his short life.

The dragon looked down, feeling the warmth between his talons, and checked on his prized possession. He heard the crying, felt the squirming, and he was reassured to see the baby was still there in his talons, intact.

Guwayne, the man had called out.

The dragon could still hear the shouts echoing off the mountains as he flew high above. He was elated he had saved the baby in time, before those men could bring their daggers downward. He had snatched Guwayne from their hands without a second to spare. He had done well the job he was commanded to do.

The dragon flew higher and higher above the lone isle, into the clouds, already out of sight of all those humans below. He passed over the island, over the volcanoes and mountain ranges, through the mist, further and further away.

Soon he was flying out over the ocean, leaving the small island behind. Before him was a vast expanse of sea and sky, nothing to break up the monotony for a million miles.

The dragon knew exactly where he was going. He had a place to bring this child, this child whom he already loved more than he could say.

A very special place.

CHAPTER THREE

Volusia stood over Romulus's body, looking down at his corpse with satisfaction, his blood, still warm, oozing over her feet, over her sandaled toes. She reveled in the feeling. She could not remember how many men, even at her young age, she had killed, had taken by surprise. They always underestimated her, and displaying just how brutal she could be was one of her greatest delights in life.

And now, to have killed the Great Romulus himself—and by her *own* hand, not by the hand of any of her men—the Great Romulus, man of legend, the warrior who killed Andronicus and who had taken the throne for himself. The Supreme Ruler of the Empire.

Volusia smiled in great delight. Here he was, the supreme ruler, reduced to a pool of blood on her bare feet. And all by her hand.

Volusia felt emboldened. She felt a fire burning in her veins, a fire to destroy everything. She felt her destiny rushing at her. She felt her time had come. She knew, just as clearly as she had known that she would murder her own mother by her own hand, that she would one day rule the Empire.

"You have killed our master!" came a shaky voice. "You have killed the Great Romulus!"

Volusia looked up to see the face of Romulus's commander standing there, staring back at her with a mixture of shock and fear and awe.

"You have killed," he said, despondent, "the Man Who Cannot be Killed."

Volusia stared back at him, hard and cold, and saw behind him the hundreds of Romulus's men, all bearing the finest armor, lined up on the ship, all watching, waiting to see what she would do next. All prepared to attack.

Romulus's commander stood on the docks with a dozen of his men, all awaiting his command. Behind Volusia, she knew, stood thousands of her own men. Romulus's ship, as fine as it was, was outnumbered, his men surrounded here in this harbor. They were

11

trapped. This was Volusia's territory, and they knew it. They knew any attack, any escape, would be futile.

"This is not an act that can come without a response," the commander continued. "Romulus has one million men loyal to his command right now in the Ring. He has one million more loyal to his command in the south, in the Empire capital. When word reaches them of what you've done, they will mobilize, and they will march on you. You may have killed the Great Romulus, but you have not killed his men. And your thousands, even if they outman us here today, cannot stand up to his millions. They will seek vengeance. And vengeance will be theirs."

"Will it?" Volusia said, smiling, taking a step closer to him, feeling the blade crossing in her palm, visualizing herself slicing his throat and already feeling the craving to do it.

The commander looked down at the blade in her hand, the blade that had killed Romulus, and he gulped, as if reading her thoughts. She could see real fear in his eyes.

"Let us go," he said to her. "Send my men on their way. They have done nothing to harm you. Give us a ship filled with gold, and you will buy our silence. I will sail our men to the capital, and I will tell them that you are innocent. That Romulus tried to attack you. They will leave you be, you can have peace here in the north, and they will find a new Supreme Commander of the Empire."

Volusia smiled widely, amused.

"But are not already laying eye upon your new Supreme Commander?" she asked.

The commander looked back at her in shock, then finally burst out into short, mocking laughter.

"You?" he said. "You are but a girl, with but a few thousand men. Because you killed one man, do you really think you can crush Romulus's millions? You'd be lucky to escape with your life after what you've done today. I am offering you a gift. Be done with this foolish talk, accept it with gratitude, and send us on our way, before I change my mind."

"And if I do not wish to send you on your way?"

The commander looked her in the eye, and swallowed.

"You can kill us all here," he said. "That is your choice. But if you do, you only kill yourself and your people. You will be crushed by the army that follows."

"He speaks truly, my commander," whispered a voice in her ear.

She turned to see Soku, her commanding general, coming up beside her, a tall man with green eyes, a warrior's jaw, and short, curly red hair.

"Send them south," he said. "Give them the gold. You've killed Romulus. Now you must broker a truce. We have no choice."

Volusia turned back to Romulus's man. She surveyed him, taking her time, relishing in the moment.

"I will do as you ask," she said, "and send you to the capital."

The commander smiled back, satisfied, and was about to go, when Volusia stepped forward and added:

"But not to hide what I've done," she said.

He stopped and looked at her, confused.

"I will send you to the capital to deliver them a message: that they will know that I am the new Supreme Commander of the Empire. That if they all bow the knee to me now, they just might live."

The commander looked at her, aghast, then slowly shook his head and smiled.

"You are as crazy as your mother was rumored to be," he said, then turned away and began to march back up the long ramp, onto his ship. "Load the gold in the lower holds," he called out, not even bothering to turn back and look at her.

Volusia turned to her commander of the bow, who stood there patiently awaiting her command, and she gave him a short nod.

The commander immediately turned and motioned to his men, and there came the sound of ten thousand arrows being lit, drawn, and fired.

They filled the sky, blackening it, sailing up in a high arc of flame, as the blazing arrows landed on Romulus's ship. It all happened too quickly for any of his men to react, and soon the entire ship was ablaze, men shrieking, their commander most of all, as they flailed about with nowhere to run, trying to put out the flames.

But it was no use. Volusia nodded again, and volley after volley of arrows sailed through the air, covering the burning ship. Men shrieked as they were pierced, some stumbling to the decks, others falling overboard. It was a slaughter, with no survivors.

Volusia stood there and grinned, watching in satisfaction as the ship slowly burned from the bottom to the mast, soon, nothing left but a burning, blackened remnant of a boat.

All fell silent as Volusia's men stopped, all lined up, all looking at her, patiently awaiting her command.

Volusia stepped forward, drew her sword, and chopped the thick cord holding the ship to the dock. It snapped, freeing the ship from shore, and Volusia raised one of her gold-plated boots, placed it on the bow, and shoved.

Volusia watched as the ship began to move, picking up the currents, the currents she knew would carry it south, right into the heart of the capital. They would all see this burnt ship, see Romulus's corpses, see the Volusian arrows, and they would know it came from her. They would know that war had begun.

Volusia turned to Soku, standing beside her, mouth agape, and she smiled.

"That," she said, "is how I offer peace."

CHAPTER FOUR

Gwendolyn knelt on the bow of the deck, clutching the rail, her knuckles white as she mustered just enough strength to lean up and look out over at the horizon. Her entire body was trembling, weak from starvation, and as she looked out, she was dizzy, light-headed. She pulled herself to her feet, somehow finding the strength, and looked out in wonder at the sight before her.

Gwendolyn squinted through the mist and wondered if it was all real or just a mirage.

There, on the horizon, spread an endless shoreline, at its center a busy hub with a massive harbor, two huge, shining gold pillars framing the city behind it, rising up into the sky. The pillars and city took on yellowish-green tint as the sun moved. The clouds moved quickly here, Gwen realized. She did not know if it was due to the sky being so different here in this part of the world, or due to her drifting in and out of consciousness.

In the city's harbor sat a thousand proud ships, all with the tallest masts she'd ever seen, all plated with gold. This was the most prosperous city she had ever seen, built right on the shore and spreading out forever, the ocean breaking up against its vast metropolis. It made King's Court look like a village. Gwen did not know that so many buildings could be in one place. She wondered what sort of people lived here. It must be a great nation, she realized. The Empire nation.

Gwen felt a sudden pit in her stomach as she realized the currents were pulling them in; soon they would be sucked into that vast harbor, surrounded by all those ships, and taken prisoner, if not killed. Gwen thought of how cruel Andronicus had been, how cruel Romulus had been, and she knew it was the Empire way; perhaps it would have been better, she realized, to have died at sea.

Gwen heard a shuffling of feet on the deck, and she looked over and saw Sandara, faint from hunger but standing proudly at the rail and holding up a large golden relic, shaped in a bull's horns, and tilting it so that it caught the sun. Gwen watched the light catch it, again and again, and watched it flashing as it cast an unusual signal to the far shoreline. Sandara did not aim it toward the city, but rather north, toward what appeared to be an isolated copse of trees on the shoreline.

As Gwen's eyes, so heavy, began to close, drifting in and out of consciousness, as she began to feel herself slumping down toward the deck, images flashed through her mind. She was not sure anymore what was real and what was her food-starved consciousness. Gwen saw canoes, dozens of them, emerging from the dense jungle canopy and heading out, on the rolling sea, toward their ship. She caught a glimpse of them as they approached, and she was surprised to see not the Empire race, not massive warriors with horns and red skin, but rather a different race. She saw proud muscular men and women, with chocolate skin and glowing yellow eyes, with compassionate, intelligent faces, all rowing to greet her. Gwen saw Sandara looking at them in recognition, and she realized that these were Sandara's people.

Gwen heard a hollow thumping noise on the ship, and she saw grappling hooks on deck, ropes being cast, locking to the ship. She felt her ship change direction, and she looked down and saw the fleet of kayaks towing their boat, guiding it on the currents in the opposite direction of the Empire city. Gwen slowly realized that Sandara's people were coming to help them. To guide their ship toward another harbor, away from that of the Empire.

Gwen felt their ship veering sharply north, toward the dense canopy, toward a small, hidden harbor. She closed her eyes, filled with relief.

Soon Gwen opened her eyes to find herself standing, leaning over the rail, watching her ship getting towed. Overcome with exhaustion, Gwendolyn felt herself leaning too far forward, losing her grip and slipping; her eyes widened in panic as she realized that she was about to fall overboard. Gwen grasped at the rail, but it was too late, her momentum already carrying her over the edge.

Gwen's heart pounded in a panic; she could not believe that after all she'd been through, she would die this way, plunging silently into the sea when they were so close to land.

16

As she felt herself falling, Gwen heard a sudden snarling, and suddenly, she felt strong teeth biting into the back of her shirt, and she heard a whining noise as she felt herself being yanked backwards by her shirt, pulled back, away from the abyss, and finally back onto the deck. She landed on the wooden deck with a thump, on her back, safe and sound.

She looked up to see Krohn standing over her, and her heart lifted with joy. Krohn was alive, she was overjoyed to see. He looked so much thinner than the last time she'd seen him, emaciated, and she realized she had lost track of him in all the chaos. The last time she'd seen him was when he had descended below deck in a particularly bad storm. She realized now that he must have hidden somewhere below deck, starved himself so that others could eat. That was Krohn. Always so selfless. And now that they were nearing land again, he was resurfacing.

Krohn whined and licked her face, and Gwen hugged him with her last bit of strength. She lay back down, Krohn lying by her side, whining, laying his head on her chest, snuggling with her as if he had no other place left in the world.

*

Gwendolyn felt a liquid, sweet and cold, trickling on her lips, on her tongue, down her cheeks and neck. She opened her mouth and drank, swallowing eagerly, and as she did, the sensation woke her from her dreams.

Gwen opened her eyes, drinking greedily, unfamiliar faces hovering over her, and she drank and drank until she coughed.

Someone pulled her up, and she sat up, coughing uncontrollably, someone patting her on her back.

"Shhhh," came a voice. "Drink slowly."

It was a gentle voice, the voice of a healer. Gwen looked over to see an old man with a lined face, his entire face bunching up into wrinkles as he smiled.

Gwen looked out to see dozens of unfamiliar faces, Sandara's people, staring back at her quietly, examining her as if she were an oddity. Gwendolyn, overcome with thirst and hunger, reached out, and like a crazy woman, grabbed the sack of whatever it was and poured the sweet liquid into her mouth, drinking and drinking, biting down on the tip of it as if she would never drink again.

"Slowly now," came the man's voice. "Or you'll get sick."

Gwen looked over to see dozens of warriors, Sandara's people, occupying her ship. She saw her own people, the survivors of the Ring, lying or kneeling or sitting, each attended to by one of Sandara's people, each given a sack to drink. They were all coming back from the brink. Among them she saw Illepra, holding the baby Gwen had rescued on the Upper Isles, feeding her. Gwen was relieved to hear the baby's cries; she had passed her off to Illepra when she was too weak to hold her, and seeing her alive made Gwen think of Guwayne. Gwen was determined that this baby girl should live.

Gwen was feeling more restored with each passing moment, and she sat up and drank more of the liquid, wondering what was inside, her heart filled with gratitude toward these people. They had saved all of their lives.

Beside Gwen there came a whining, and she looked down and saw Krohn, still lying there, his head in her lap; she reached down and gave him drink from her sack, and he lapped at it thankfully. She stroked his head lovingly; she owed him her life, once again. And seeing him made her think of Thor.

Gwen looked up at all of Sandara's people, not knowing how to thank them.

"You have saved us," she said. "We owe you our lives."

Gwen turned and looked at Sandara, coming over and kneeling beside her, and Sandara shook her head.

"My people don't believe in debts," she said. "They believe it is an honor to save someone in distress."

The crowd parted ways and Gwen looked over to see a stern man, who appeared to be their leader, perhaps in his fifties, with a set jaw and thin lips, approach. He squatted before her, wearing a large turquoise necklace made of shells that flashed in the sun, and bowed his head, his yellow eyes filled with compassion as he surveyed her.

"I am Bokbu," he said, his voice deep and authoritative. "We answered Sandara's call because she is one of us. We have taken you in at the risk of our lives. If the Empire should see us here now, with you, they would kill us all."

Bokbu rose to his feet, hands on his hips, and Gwen herself slowly stood, helped by Sandara and their healer, and faced him. Bokbu sighed as he looked around at all the people, at the sorry state of her ship.

"Now they are better, now they must go," came a voice.

Gwen turned and saw a muscular warrior holding a spear and wearing no shirt, as the others, coming over beside Bokbu, looking at him coldly.

"Send these foreigners back across the sea," he added. "Why shall we shed blood for them?"

"I am of your blood," Sandara said, stepping forward, sternly facing the warrior.

"Which is why you should have never brought these people here and endangered us all," he snapped.

"You bring disgrace on our nation," Sandara said. "Have you forgotten the laws of hospitality?"

"Your bringing them here is the disgrace," he retorted.

Bokbu raised his palms at both sides, and they quieted.

Bokbu stood there, expressionless, and he seemed to be thinking. Gwendolyn stood there, watching it all, and realized the precarious situation they were in. Setting back out on the sea, she knew, would mean instant death; yet she did not want to endanger these people who had helped her.

"We meant you no harm," Gwen said, turning to Bokbu. "I do not wish to endanger you. We can embark now."

Bokbu shook his head.

"No," he said. Then he looked at Gwen, studying her with what seemed to be wonder. "Why did you bring your people here?" he asked.

Gwen sighed.

"We fled a great army," she said. "They destroyed our homeland. We came here to find a new home."

19

"You've come to the wrong place," said the warrior. "This will not be your home."

"Silence!" Bokbu said to him, giving him a harsh look, and finally, the warrior fell silent.

Bokbu turned to look at Gwendolyn, his eyes locking with hers.

"You are a proud and noble woman," he said. "I can see you are a leader. You have guided your people well. If I turn you back to the sea, you will surely die. Maybe not today, but certainly within a few days."

Gwendolyn looked back at him, unyielding.

"Then we shall die," she replied. "I will not have your people killed so that we should live."

She stared at him firmly, expressionless, emboldened by her nobility and her pride. She could see that Bokbu studied her with a new respect. A tense silence filled the air.

"I can see the warrior blood runs in you," he said. "You will stay with us. Your people will recover here until they are well and strong. However many moons it takes."

"But my chief—" the warrior began.

Bokbu turned and gave him a stern look.

"My decision is made."

"But their ship!" he protested. "If it stays here in our harbor, the Empire will see it. We will all die before the moon has waned!"

The chief looked up at the mast, then at the ship, taking it all in. Gwen looked about and studied the landscape and saw they had been towed deep into a hidden harbor, surrounded by a dense canopy. She turned and saw behind them the open sea, and she knew the man was right.

The chief looked at her and nodded.

"You want to save your people?" he asked.

Gwen nodded back firmly.

"Yes."

He nodded back at her.

"Leaders must make hard decisions," he said. "Now is the time for you. You want to stay with us, but your ship will kill us all. We invite your people ashore, but your ship cannot remain. You will have to burn it. Then we shall take you in."

Gwendolyn stood there, facing the chief, and her heart sank at the thought. She looked at her ship, the ship which had taken them across the sea, had saved her people from halfway across the world, and her heart sank. Her mind swirled with conflicting emotions. This ship was her only way out.

But then again, her way out of what? Heading back out into an endless ocean of death? Her people could barely walk; they needed to recover. They needed shelter and harbor and refuge. And if burning this ship was the price of life, then so be it. If they decided to head back out to sea, then they would find another ship, or build another ship, do whatever they had to do. For now, they had to live. That was what mattered most.

Gwendolyn looked at him and nodded solemnly.

"So be it," she said.

Bokbu nodded back to her with a look of great respect. Then he turned and called out a command, and all around him, his men broke into action. They spread out throughout the ship, helping all the members of the Ring, getting them to their feet one at a time, guiding them down the plank to the sandy shore below. Gwen stood and watched Godfrey, Kendrick, Brandt, Atme, Aberthol, Illepra, Sandara, and all the people she loved most in the world pass by her.

She stood there and waited until every single last person left the ship, until she was the last one standing on it, just her, Krohn at her heels, and to her side, standing quietly, the chief.

Bokbu held a flaming torch, handed to him by one of his men. He reached out to touch the ship.

"No," Gwen said, reaching out and clasping his wrist.

He looked over at her in surprise.

"A leader must destroy her own," she said.

Gwen gingerly took the heavy, flaming torch from his hand, then turned and, wiping back a tear, held the flame to a canvas sail bunched up on deck.

Gwen stood there and watched as the flames caught, spreading faster and faster, reaching out across the ship.

She dropped the torch, the heat rising too fast, and she turned, Krohn and Bokbu following, and walked down the plank, heading to the beach, to her new home, to the last place they had left in the world.

As she looked around at the foreign jungle, heard the strange screeches of birds and animals she did not recognize, Gwen could only wonder:

Could they build a home here?

CHAPTER FIVE

Alistair knelt on the stone, her knees trembling from the cold, and looked out as the first light of the first sun of dawn crept over the Southern Isles, illuminating the mountains and valleys with a soft glow. Her hands trembled, shackled to the wooden stocks as she knelt, on her hands and knees, her neck resting over the place where so many necks had lain before her. She looked down and could see the bloodstains on the wood, see the nicks in the cedar where the blades had come down before. She could feel the tragic energy of this wood as her neck touched it, feel the last moments, the final emotions, of all the slain who had lain here before. Her heart dropped in misery.

Alistair looked up proudly and watched her final sun, watched a new day break, having the surreal feeling that she would never live to watch it again. She cherished it this time more than she'd ever had. As she looked out on this chilly morning, a gentle breeze stirring, the Southern Isles looked more beautiful than they'd ever had, the most beautiful place she'd ever seen, trees blossoming in bursts of oranges and reds and pinks and purples as their fruit hung abundantly in this bountiful place. Purple morning birds and large, orange bees were already buzzing in the air, the sweet fragrance of flowers wafting toward her. The mist sparkled in the light, giving everything a magical feel. She had never felt such an attachment to a place; it was a land, she knew, she would have been happy to live in forever.

Alistair heard a shuffling of boots on stone, and she glanced over to see Bowyer approaching, standing over her, his oversized boots scraping the stone. He held a huge double ax in his hand, loosely at his side, and he frowned down at her.

Beyond him, Alistair could see the hundreds of Southern Islanders, all lined up, all men loyal to him, arranged in a huge circle around her in the wide stone plaza. They were all a good twenty yards away from her, a wide clearing left just for her and Bowyer alone. No one wanted to be too close when the blood sprayed.

Bowyer held the ax with itchy fingers, clearly anxious to finish the business. She could see in his eyes how badly he wanted to be King.

Alistair took satisfaction in at least one thing: however unjust this was, her sacrifice would allow Erec to live. That meant more to her than her own life.

Bowyer stepped forward, leaned in close, and whispered to her, low enough that no one else could hear:

"Rest assured your death stroke will be a clean one," he said, his stale breath on her neck. "And so will Erec's."

Alistair looked up at him in alarm and confusion.

He smiled down at her, a small smile reserved just for her, that no one else could see.

"That's right," he whispered. "It may not happen today; it may not happen for many moons. But one day, when he least expects it, your husband will find my knife in his back. I want you know, before I ship you off to hell."

Bowyer took two steps back, squeezed his hands tight around the shaft of the ax, and cracked his neck, preparing to strike the blow.

Alistair's heart pounded as she knelt there, realizing the full depth of evil in this man. He was not only ambitious, but a coward and a liar.

"Set her free!" demanded a sudden voice, piercing the morning stillness.

Alistair turned as well as she could and saw the chaos as two figures suddenly came bursting through the crowd, to the edge of the clearing, until the beefy hands of Bowyer's guards held them back. Alistair was shocked and grateful to see Erec's mother and sister standing there, frantic looks across their faces.

"She's innocent!" Erec's mother yelled out. "You must not kill her!"

"Would you kill a woman!?" Dauphine cried out. "She's a foreigner. Let her go. Send her back to her land. She need not be involved in our affairs."

Bowyer turned to them and boomed:

"She is a foreigner who aspired to be our Queen. To murder our former King."

24

"You are a liar!" Erec's mother yelled. "You would not drink from the fountain of truth!"

Bowyer scanned the faces of the crowd.

"Is there anyone here who dares defy my claim?" he shouted, turning, meeting everyone's gaze, defiant.

Alistair looked about, hopeful; but one by one, all the men, all brave warriors, mostly from Bowyer's tribe, looked down, not one of them willing to challenge him in combat.

"I am your champion," Bowyer boomed. "I defeated all opponents on tournament day. There is no one here who could beat me. Not one. If there is, I challenge you to step forward."

"No one, save Erec!" Dauphine called out.

Bowyer turned and scowled at her.

"And where is he now? He lies dying. We Southern Islanders shall not have a cripple for a King. *I* am your King. I am your next best champion. By the laws of this land. As my father's father was King before Erec's father."

Erec's mother and Dauphine both lunged forward to stop him; but his men grabbed them and pulled them back, detaining them. Alistair saw beside them, Erec's brother, Strom, wrists bound behind his back; he struggled, too, but could not break free.

"You shall pay for this, Bowyer!" Strom called out.

But Bowyer ignored him. Instead, he turned back to Alistair, and she could see from his eyes he was determined to proceed. Her time had come.

"Time is dangerous when deceit is on your side," Alistair said to him.

He frowned down at her; clearly, she had struck a nerve.

"And those words will be your last," he said.

Bowyer suddenly hoisted the ax, raising it high overhead.

Alistair closed her eyes, knowing that in but a moment, she would be gone from this world.

Eyes closed, Alistair felt time slow down. Images flashed before her. She saw the first time she had met Erec, back in the Ring, at the Duke's castle, when she had been a serving girl and had fallen in love with him at first sight. She felt her love for him, a love she still felt to

25

this day, burning inside her. She saw her brother, Thorgrin, saw his face, and for some reason, she did not see him in the Ring, in King's Court, but rather in a distant land, on a distant ocean, exiled from the Ring. Most of all, she saw her mother. She saw her standing at the edge of a cliff, before her castle, high above an ocean, before a skywalk. She saw her holding out her arms and smiling sweetly at her.

"My daughter," she said.

"Mother," Alistair said, "I will come to join you."

But to her surprise, her mother slowly shook her head.

"Your time is not now," she said. "Your destiny on this earth is not yet complete. You still have a great destiny before you."

"But how, Mother?" she asked. "How can I survive?"

"You are bigger than this earth," her mother replied. "That blade, that metal of death, is of this earth. Your shackles are of this earth. Those are earthly limitations. They are only limitations if you believe in them, if you allow them to have authority over you. You are spirit and light and energy. That is where your real power is. You are above it all. You are allowing yourself to be held back by physical constraints. Your problem is not one of strength; it is one of faith. Faith in yourself. How strong is your faith?"

As Alistair knelt there, trembling, eyes shut, her mother's question rang in her head.

How strong is your faith?

Alistair let herself go, forgot her shackles, put herself in the hands of her faith. She began to let go of her faith in the physical constraints of this planet, and instead shifted her faith to the supreme power, the one and only supreme power over everything else in the world. A power had created this world, she knew. A power had created all of this. That was the power she needed to align herself with.

As she did, all within a fraction of a second, Alistair felt a sudden warmth coursing through her body. She felt on fire, invincible, bigger than everything. She felt flames emanating from her palms, felt her mind buzzing and swarming, and felt a great heat rising up in her forehead, between her eyes. She felt herself stronger than everything, stronger than her shackles, stronger than all things material.

Alistair opened her eyes, and as time began to speed again, she looked up and saw Bowyer coming down with the ax, a scowl on his face.

In one motion, Alistair turned and raised her arms, and as she did, this time her shackles snapped as if they were twigs. In the same motion, lightning fast, she rose to her feet, raised one palm toward Bowyer, and as his ax came down, the most incredible thing happened: the ax dissolved. It turned to ashes and dust and fell at a heap at her feet.

Bowyer swung down, nothing in his hand, and he went stumbling, falling to his knees.

Alistair wheeled and her eyes were drawn to a sword on the far side of the clearing, in a soldier's belt. She reached out her other palm and commanded it come to her; as she did, it lifted from his scabbard and flew through the air, right into her outstretched palm.

In a single motion, Alistair grabbed hold of it, spun around, raised it high, and brought it down on the back of Bowyer's exposed neck.

The crowd gasped in shock as there came the sound of steel cutting through flesh and Bowyer, beheaded, collapsed to the ground, lifeless.

He lay there, dead, in the exact spot where, just moments before, he had wanted Alistair dead.

There came a cry from the crowd, and Alistair looked out to watch Dauphine break free of the soldier's grip, then grab the soldier's dagger from his belt and slice his throat. In the same motion, she spun around and cut loose Strom's ropes. Strom immediately reached back, grabbed a sword from a soldier's waist, spun and slashed, killing three of Bowyer's men before they could even react.

With Bowyer dead, there was a moment of hesitation, as the crowd clearly didn't know what to do next. Shouts rose up all amongst the crowd, as his death clearly emboldened all those who had been allied with him reluctantly. They were re-examining their alliance, especially as dozens of men loyal to Erec broke through the ranks and came charging forward to Strom's side, fighting with him, hand-to-hand, against those loyal to Bowyer.

The momentum quickly shifted in the favor of Erec's men, as man by man, row by row, alliances formed; Bowyer's men, caught off guard, turned and fled across the plateau to the rocky mountainside. Strom and his men chased closed behind.

Alistair stood there, sword still in hand, and watched as a great battle rose up, up and down the countryside, shouts and horns echoing as the entire island seemed to rally, to spill out to war on both sides. The sound of clanging armor, of the death cries of men, filled the morning, and Alistair knew a civil war had broken out.

Alistair held up her sword, the sun shining down on it, and knew she had been saved by the grace of God. She felt reborn, more powerful than she'd ever had, and she felt her destiny calling to her. She welled with optimism. Bowyer's men would be killed, she knew. Justice would prevail. Erec would rise. They would wed. And soon, she would be Queen of the Southern Isles.

CHAPTER SIX

Darius ran down the dirt trail leading from his village, following the footprints toward Volusia, a determination in his heart to save Loti and murder the men who took her. He ran with a sword in his hand— a *real* sword, made of *real* metal—the first time he'd ever wielded real metal in his life. That alone, he knew, would be enough to have him, and his entire village, killed. Steel was taboo—even his father and his father's father feared to possess it—and Darius knew he had crossed a line in which there was now no turning back.

But Darius no longer cared. The injustice of his life had been too much. With Loti gone, he cared about nothing but retrieving her. He had hardly had a chance to know her, and yet paradoxically, he felt as if she were his whole life. It was one thing for he himself to be taken away as a slave; but for *her* to be taken away—that was too much. He could not allow her to go and still consider himself a man. He was a boy, he knew, and yet he was becoming a man. And it was these very decisions, he realized, these hard decisions that no one else was willing to make, that were the very things that made one a man.

Darius charged down the road alone, sweat blurring his eyes, breathing hard, one man ready to face an army, a city. There was no alternative. He needed to find Loti and bring her back, or die trying. He knew that if he failed—or even if he succeeded—it would bring vengeance on his entire village, his family, all his people. If he stopped to think about that, he might have even turned around.

But he was driven by something stronger than his own self-preservation, his family's and people's preservation. He was driven by a desire for justice. For freedom. By a desire to cast off his oppressor and to be free, even if for just one moment in his life. If not for himself, than for Loti. For her freedom.

Darius was driven by passion, not by logical thought. It was the love of his life out there, and he had suffered one time too many at the hands of the Empire. Whatever the consequences, he no longer cared. He needed to show them that there was one man amongst his people, even if it was just one man, even if just a boy, who would not suffer their treatment.

Darius ran and ran, twisting and turning his way out past the familiar fields, and into the outskirts of Volusian territory. He knew that just being found here, this close to Volusia, would alone merit his death. He followed the tracks, doubling his speed, seeing the zerta prints close together, and knowing they were moving slowly. If he went fast enough, he knew, he could catch them.

Darius rounded a hill, gasping, and finally, in the distance, he spotted what he was looking for: there, perhaps a hundred yards off, stood Loti, chained by her neck with thick iron shackles, from which led a long chain, a good twenty feet, to the back harness of a zerta. On the zerta rode the Empire taskmaster, the one who had taken her away, his back to her, and by his side, walking beside them, two more Empire soldiers, wearing the thick black and gold armor of the empire, glistening in the sun. They were nearly twice the size of Darius, formidable warriors, men with the finest weapons, and a zerta at their command. It would, Darius knew, take a host of slaves to overcome these men.

But Darius did not let fear get in his way. All he had to carry him was the strength of his spirit, and his fierce determination, and he knew he would have to find a way to make that be enough.

Darius ran and ran, catching up from behind on the unsuspecting caravan, and he soon caught up to them, racing up to Loti from behind, raising his sword high, and as she looked over at him with a startled expression, slashing down on the chain affixing her to the zerta.

Loti cried out and jumped back, shocked, as Darius severed her chains, freeing her, the distinctive ring of metal cutting through the air. Loti stood there, free, the shackles still around her neck, the chain dangling at her chest.

Darius turned and saw equal looks of astonishment on the face of the Empire taskmaster, looking down from his seat on the zerta. The soldiers walking on the ground beside him stopped, too, all of them stunned at the sight of Darius.

Darius stood there, arms trembling, holding out his steel sword before him and determined not to show fear as he stood between them and Loti.

"She does not belong to you," Darius called out, his voice shaky. "She is a free woman. We are all free!"

The soldiers looked up to the taskmaster.

"Boy," he called out to Darius, "you've just made the biggest mistake of your life."

He nodded down to his soldiers, and they raised their swords and charged Darius.

Darius stood his ground, holding his sword in trembling hands, and as he did, he felt his ancestors looking down on him. He felt all the slaves who had ever been killed looking down on him, supporting him. And he began to feel a great heat rising up within him.

Darius felt his hidden power deep within beginning to stir, itching to be summoned. But he would not allow himself to go there. He wanted to fight them man to man, to beat them as any man would, to apply all of his training with his brothers in arms. He wanted to win as a man, fight like a man with real metal weapons, and defeat them on their own terms. He had always been faster than all of the older boys, with their long wooden swords and muscular frames, even boys twice his size. He dug in, and braced himself as they charged.

"Loti!" he called out, not turning, "RUN! Go back to the village!"

"NO!" she yelled back.

Darius knew he had to do something; he could not stand there and wait for them to reach him. He knew he had to surprise them, to do something they would not expect.

Darius suddenly charged, choosing one of the two soldiers and racing right for him. They met in the middle of the dirt clearing, Darius letting out a great battle cry. The soldier slashed his sword at Darius's head, but Darius raised his sword and blocked it, their swords sparking, the impact of metal on metal the first Darius had ever felt. The blade was heavier than he thought, the soldier's blow stronger, and he felt a great vibration, felt his entire arm shaking, up to his elbow and into his shoulder. It caught him off guard.

The soldier swung around quickly, aiming to strike Darius from the side, and Darius spun and blocked. This did not feel like sparring with his brothers; Darius felt himself moving slower than usual, the blade so heavy. It was taking some getting used to. It felt as if the other soldier were moving twice as fast as he.

The soldier swung again, and Darius realized he could not beat him blow for blow; he had to draw on his other skills.

Darius stepped sideways, ducking the blow instead of meeting it, and he then threw an elbow into the soldier's throat. He caught it perfectly. The man gagged and stumbled back, hunched over, grasping his throat. Darius raised the butt of his sword and brought it down on his exposed back, sending him face down into the dirt.

At the same time the other soldier charged, and Darius spun, raised his sword, and blocked a mighty blow as it came down for his face. The soldier kept charging, though, driving Darius back and down to the ground, hard.

Darius felt his rib cage being crushed as the soldier lay on top of him, both of them landing on the hard dirt in a big cloud of dust. The soldier dropped his sword and reached out with his hands, trying to gouge out Darius's eyes with his fingers.

Darius grabbed his wrists, holding them back with shaking hands, but losing ground. He knew he needed to do something fast.

Darius raised a knee and turned, managing to spin the man onto his side. In the same motion, Darius reached down and extracted the long dagger he spotted in the man's belt—and in the same motion, raised it high and plunged it into the man's chest, as they rolled on the ground,

The soldier cried out, and Darius lay there on top of him, and watched him die before his eyes. Darius lay there, frozen, shocked. It was the first time he had killed a man. It was a surreal experience. He felt victorious yet saddened at the same time.

Darius heard a cry from behind, snapping him out of it, and he turned to see the other soldier, the one he had knocked out, back on his feet, racing for him. He raised his sword and swung it for his head.

Darius waited, focused, then ducked at the last second; the soldier went stumbling past him.

Darius reached down and drew the dagger from the dead man's chest and spun around, and as the soldier turned back and charged again, Darius, on his knees, leaned forward and threw it.

He watched the blade spin end over end, then finally lodge itself into the soldier's heart, piercing his armor. The Empire's own steel, second to none, used against them. Perhaps, Darius thought, they should have crafted weapons less sharp.

The soldier sank to his knees, eyes bulging, and he fell sideways, dead.

Darius heard a great cry behind him, and he jumped to his feet and wheeled to see the taskmaster dismounting from his zerta. He scowled and drew his sword and bore down on Darius with a great cry.

"Now I shall have to kill you myself," he said. "But not only will I kill you, I shall torture you and your family and your entire village slowly!"

He charged for Darius.

This Empire taskmaster was obviously a greater soldier than the others, taller and broader, with greater armor. He was a hardened warrior, the greatest warrior Darius had ever fought. Darius had to admit he felt fear at this formidable foe—but he refused to show it. Instead, he was determined to fight through his fear, to refuse to allow himself to be intimidated. He was just a man, Darius told himself. And all men can fall.

All men can fall.

Darius raised his sword as the taskmaster bore down on him, swinging his great sword, flashing in the light, with both hands. Darius shifted and blocked; the man swung again.

Left and right, left and right, the soldier slashed and Darius blocked, the great clang of metal ringing in his ears, sparks flying everywhere. The man drove him back, further and further, and it took all of Darius's might just to block the blows. The man was strong and quick, and Darius was preoccupied with just staying alive.

Darius blocked one blow just a bit too slowly, and he cried out in pain as the taskmaster found an opening and slashed his bicep. It was a shallow wound, but a painful one, and Darius felt the blood, his first wound in battle, and was stunned by it.

It was a mistake. The taskmaster took advantage of his hesitation, and he backhanded him with his gauntlet. Darius felt a great pain in his cheek and jaw as the metal met his face, and as the blow knocked him backwards, sent him stumbling several feet, Darius took a mental note to never stop and check a wound anytime in battle.

As Darius tasted blood on his lips, a fury washed over him. The taskmaster, charging him again, bearing down on him, was big and strong, but this time, with pain ringing in his cheek and blood on his tongue, Darius didn't let that intimidate him. The first blows of battle had been struck, and Darius realized, as painful as they were, they were not that bad. He was still standing, still breathing, still living.

And that meant he still could fight. He could take blows, and he could still go on. Getting wounded was not as bad as he had feared. He might be smaller, less experienced, but he realized his skill was as sharp as any other man's—and it could be just as deadly.

Darius let out a guttural cry and lunged forward, embracing battle this time instead of shying away from it. No longer fearing being wounded, Darius raised his sword with a cry, and slashed down at his opponent. The man blocked it, but Darius did not give up, swinging again and again and again, driving the taskmaster back, despite his greater size and strength.

Darius fought for his life, fought for Loti, fought for all of his people, his brothers in arms, and, slashing left and right, faster than he'd ever had, not letting the weight of the steel slow him down any longer, he finally found an opening. The taskmaster screamed out in pain as Darius slashed his side.

He turned and scowled at Darius, first surprise, then vengeance in his eyes.

He shrieked like a wounded animal, and charged Darius. The taskmaster threw down his sword, raced forward, and embraced Darius in a bear hug. He heaved Darius up off the ground, squeezing him so tight, Darius dropped his sword. It all happened so fast, and it was such an unexpected move, that Darius could not react in time. He had expected his foe to use his sword in battle, not his fists.

34

Darius, dangling off the ground, groaning, felt as if every bone in his body was going to crack. He cried out in pain.

The taskmaster squeezed him harder, so hard Darius was sure he was going to die. He then leaned back and head-butted Darius, smashing his forehead into Darius's nose.

Darius felt blood gushing out, felt a horrible pain shoot through his face and eyes, stinging him, blinding him. It was a move he had not expected, and as the taskmaster leaned back to head-butt him again, Darius, defenseless, was certain he would be killed.

The noise of chains cut through the air, and suddenly the taskmaster's eyes bulged wide open, and his grip loosened on Darius. Darius, gasping, confused, looked up, wondering why he'd let go. Then he saw Loti, standing behind the taskmaster, wrapping her dangling shackles around his neck, again and again, and squeezing with all her might.

Darius stumbled back, trying to catch his breath again, and he watched as the taskmaster stumbled back several feet, then reached back over his shoulder, grabbed Loti from behind, leaned over, and flipped her over his head. Loti landed on her back, on the hard ground, in the dirt, with a cry.

The taskmaster stepped forward, lifted his leg, aimed his boot over her face, and Darius saw he was about to bring it down and crush her face. The taskmaster was a good ten feet away by now, too far for Darius to reach him in time.

"NO!" Darius yelled.

Darius thought quickly: he reached down, grabbed his sword, stepped forward, and in one swift motion, he threw it.

The sword went flying through the air, end over end, and Darius watched, transfixed, as the point pierced the taskmaster's armor, impaling him right through his heart.

His eyes bulged wide open again and Darius watched as he stumbled and fell, sinking to his knees, then to his face.

Loti quickly gained her feet, and Darius rushed to her side. He draped a reassuring hand over her shoulder, so grateful to her, so relieved she was okay.

Suddenly, a sharp whistle cut through the air; Darius turned and saw the taskmaster, lying on the ground, raise a hand to his mouth and whistle again, one last time, before he died.

A horrific roar shattered the silence, as the ground shook.

Darius looked over, and was terror-stricken to see the zerta suddenly charging right for them. It sprinted for them in a rage, lowering its sharp horns. Darius and Loti exchanged a look, knowing they had nowhere to run. Within moments, Darius knew, they would both be dead.

Darius looked all around, thinking quick, and he saw beside them the steep slope of the mountainside, littered with rocks and boulders. Darius raised his arm, his palm out, and draped his other arm around Loti, holding her close. Darius did not want to summon his power, but he knew that now, he had no choice, if he wanted to live.

Darius felt a tremendous heat rush through him, a power he could barely control, and he watched as a light shot forth through his open palm, onto the steep slope. There came a rumbling, gradual at first, then greater and greater, and Darius watched as boulders began tumbling down the steep mountainside, gaining steam.

An avalanche of boulders all rushed down on the zerta, crushing it just before it reached them. There was a huge cloud of dust, a tremendous noise, and finally, all was still.

Darius stood there, nothing but silence and dust swirling in the sun, hardly understanding what he had just done. He turned and saw Loti looking at him, saw the look of horror in her face, and he knew everything had changed. He had unleashed his secret. And now, there was no turning back.

CHAPTER SEVEN

Thor sat erect at the edge of their small boat, legs crossed, palms resting on his thighs, his back to the others as he stared out at the cold, cruel sea. His eyes were red from crying, and he did not want the others to see him like this. His tears had dried up long ago, but his eyes were still raw as he stared out, baffled, at the sea, wondering at the mysteries of life.

How could a son have been given to him, only to have been taken away? How could someone he loved so much disappear from him, be snatched away with no warning and no chance of return?

Life, Thor felt, was too relentlessly cruel. Where was the justice in it all? Why couldn't his son return to him?

Thor would give anything—*anything*—walk through fire himself, die a million deaths—to have Guwayne given back to him.

Thor closed his eyes and shook his head as he tried to blot out the image of that burning volcano, the empty bassinet, the flames. He tried to block out the idea of his son dying such a painful death. His heart burned with fury, but most of all, sorrow. And shame, for not reaching his little boy sooner.

Thor also felt a deep pit in his stomach as he tried to imagine his encounter with Gwendolyn, his telling her the news. She would surely never look him in the eyes again. And she would never be the same person again. It was as if Thorgrin's entire life had been snatched away from him. He did not know how to rebuild, how to pick up the pieces. How does one, he wondered, find another purpose for living?

Thor heard footsteps and felt the weight of a body beside him as the boat shifted, creaking. He looked over and was surprised to see Conven take a seat at his side, staring out. Thor felt as if he hadn't talked to Conven in ages, not since his twin's death. He welcomed seeing him here. As Thor looked at him, studied the sorrow in his face, for the first time, he understood. He really understood.

Conven didn't say a word. He didn't need to. His presence was enough. He sat beside him in sympathy, brothers in grief.

They sat there in silence for a long time, no noise but the sound of the wind ripping through, the sound of the waves lapping gently against the boat, this small boat of theirs adrift in an endless sea, their quest to find and rescue Guwayne taken away from all of them.

Finally Conven spoke:

"Not a day goes by when I don't think of Conval," he said, his voice somber.

They sat again silence for a long time. Thor wanted to reply, but he could not, too choked up to speak.

Finally, Conven added: "I grieve for you for Guwayne. I would have liked to see him become a great warrior, like his father. I know he would have been. Life can be tragic and cruel. It can give only to take away. I wish I could tell you I have recovered from my sorrow— but I have not."

Thor looked at him, Conven's brutal honesty somehow giving him a sense of peace.

"What keeps you living?" Thor asked.

Conven looked out at the water for a long time, then finally sighed.

"I think it was what Conval would have wanted," he said. "He would have wanted me to go on. And so I go on. I do it for him. Not for myself. Sometimes we live a life for others. Sometimes we don't care enough to live it for ourselves, so we live it for them. But, I am coming to realize, sometimes that must be enough."

Thor thought of Guwayne, now dead, and he wondered what his son would have wanted. Of course, he would have wanted Thorgrin to live, to take care of his mother, Gwendolyn. Thor knew that logically. But in his heart, it was a hard concept to grasp.

Conven cleared his throat.

"We live for our parents," he said. "For our siblings. For our wives and sons and daughters. We live for everybody else. And sometimes, when life has beaten you down so much that you don't want to go on for yourself, that has to be enough."

"I disagree," came a voice.

Thor looked over to see Matus coming up on his other side, sitting and joining them. Matus looked out at the sea, stern and proud.

"I believe there is another thing we live for," he added.

"And what is that?" Conven asked.

"Faith." Matus sighed. "My people, the Upper Isle men, they pray to the four gods of the rocky shores. They pray to the gods of the water and wind and sky and rocks. Those gods have never answered my prayers. I pray to the ancient god of the Ring."

Thor looked at him, surprised.

"I have never known an Upper Isle men to share the faith of the Ring," Conven said.

Matus nodded.

"I am unlike my people," he said. "I always have been. I wanted to enter the monastic order when I was young, but my father would never hear of it. He insisted I take up arms, like my brothers."

He sighed.

"I believe we live for our faith, not for others," he added. "That is what carries us through. If our faith is strong enough, *really* strong enough, then anything can happen. Even a miracle."

"And can it return my son to me?" Thor asked.

Matus nodded back at him, unflinching, and Thor could see the certainty in his eyes.

"Yes," Matus answered flatly. "Anything."

"You lie," Conven said, indignant. "You give him false hope."

"I do not," Matus retorted.

"Are you saying faith will return my dead brother to me?" Conven urged, angry.

Matus sighed.

"I am saying that all tragedy is a gift," he said.

"A gift?" Thor asked, horrified. "Are you saying the loss of my son is a gift?"

Matus nodded back confidently.

"You are being given a gift, as tragic as that sounds. You can't know what it is. You might not for a long time. But one day, you will see."

Thor turned and looked out at the sea, confused, unsure. Was this all a test? he wondered. Was it one of the tests his mother had spoken of? Could faith alone bring his son back? He wanted to believe it. He really did. But he did not know if his faith was strong enough. When his mother had spoken of tests, Thor had been so sure he could pass anything that was thrown his way; yet now, feeling as he did, he did not know if he was strong enough to go on.

The boat rocked on the waves, and suddenly the tides turned, and Thor felt their small boat turning around and heading the opposite direction. He snapped out of it and checked back over his shoulder, wondering what was happening. Reece, Elden, Indra, and O'Connor were all still rowing and manning the sail, a confused look across their face, as their small sail flapped wildly in the wind.

"The Northern Tides," Matus said, standing, hands on his hips and looking out, studying the waters. He shook his head. "This is not good."

"What is it?" Indra asked. "We can't control the boat."

"They sometimes pass through the Upper Isles," Matus explained. "I have never seen them myself, but I have heard about them, especially this far north. They are a riptide. Once you're caught in them, they take you where they please. No matter how much rowing or sailing you try to do."

Thor looked down, and saw the water below them rushing by at twice the speed. He looked out and saw they were heading toward a new, empty horizon, purple and white clouds spotting the sky, both beautiful and foreboding.

"But we're heading east now," Reece said, "and we need to head west. All of our people are west. The Empire is west."

Matus shrugged.

"We head where the tides take us."

Thor looked out in wonder and frustration, realizing that each passing moment was taking them further from Gwendolyn, further from their people.

40

"And where does it end?" O'Connor asked.

Matus shrugged.

"I know only the Upper Isles," he said. "I have never been this far north. I know nothing of what lies beyond."

"It does end," Reece spoke up, darkly, and all eyes turned to him. Reece looked back, grave.

"I was tutored on the tides years ago, at a young age. In the ancient book of Kings, we had an array of maps, covering every portion of the world. The Northern Tides lead to the eastern edge of the world."

"The eastern edge?" Elden said, concern in his voice. "We'd be on the other end of the world from our people."

Reece shrugged.

"The books were ancient, and I was young. All I really remember was that the tides were a portal to the Land of Spirits."

Thor looked at Reece, wondering.

"Old wives' tales and fairytales," O'Connor said. "There is no portal to the Land of Spirits. It was sealed off centuries ago, before our fathers walked the earth."

Reece shrugged, and they all fell silent as they turned and stared out at the seas. Thor examined the fast-moving waters, and he wondered: Where on earth were they being lead?

*

Thor sat alone, at the edge of the boat, staring into the waters as he had been for hours, the cold spray hitting him in the face. Numb to the world, he barely felt it. Thor wanted to be in action, to be hoisting sails, rowing—anything—but there was nothing for any them to do now. The Northern tides were taking them where they would, and all they could do was sit idly by and watch the currents, their boat rolling in the long waves, and wonder where they would end up. They were in the hands of the fates now.

As Thor sat there, studying the horizon, wondering where the sea would end, he felt himself drifting into nothingness, numb from the cold and the wind, lost in the monotony of the deep silence that hung over all of them. The seabirds that had at first circled them had disappeared long ago, and as the silence deepened, as the sky fell darker and darker, Thor felt as if they were sailing into nothingness, into the very ends of the earth.

It was hours later, as the last light of day was falling, that Thor sat upright, spotting something on the horizon. At first he was certain it was an illusion; but as the currents became stronger, the shape became more distinct. It was real.

Thor sat up straight, for the first time in hours, then rose to his feet. He stood there, boat swaying, hands on his hips, looking out.

"Is it real?" came a voice.

Thor looked over to see Reece stepping forward beside him. Elden, Indra, and the rest soon joined them, all staring out in wonder.

"An island?" O'Connor wondered aloud.

"Looks like a cave," Matus said.

As they approached, Thor began to see the outline of it, and he saw that it was indeed a cave. It was a massive cave, an outcropping of rock that rose up from the sea, emerging here, in the midst of a cruel and endless ocean, rising hundreds of feet high, the opening shaped in a big arch. It looked like a giant mouth, ready to swallow all the world.

And the currents were taking their boat right toward it.

Thor stared at in wonder, and he knew it could only be one thing: the entrance to the Land of the Spirits.

CHAPTER EIGHT

Darius walked slowly down the dirt path, Loti by his side, the air filled with the tension of their silence. Neither had said a word since their encounter with the taskmaster and his men, and Darius's mind swarmed with a million thoughts as he walked beside her, accompanying her back to their village. Darius wanted to drape an arm around her, to tell her how grateful he was that she was alive, that she had saved him as he had saved her, how determined he was to never let her leave his side again. He wanted to see her eyes filled with joy and relief, he wanted to hear her say how much it meant to her that he had risked his life for her—or at the very least, that she was happy to see him.

Yet as they walked in the deep, awkward silence, Loti said nothing, would not even look at him. She had not said a word to him since he had caused the avalanche, had not even met his eyes. Darius's heart pounded, wondering what she was thinking. She had witnessed him summoning his power, had witnessed the avalanche. In its wake, she had given him a horrified look, and had not looked at him again since.

Perhaps, Darius thought, in her view, he had broken the sacred taboo of her people in drawing on magic, the one thing her people looked down upon more than anything. Perhaps she was afraid of him; or even worse, perhaps she no longer loved him. Perhaps she thought of him as some sort of freak.

Darius felt his heart breaking as they walked slowly back to the village, and wondered what it was all for. He had just risked his life to save a girl who no longer loved him. He would pay anything to read her thoughts, anything. But she would not even speak. Was she in shock?

Darius wanted to say something to her, anything to break the silence. But he did not know where to begin. He had thought he'd known her, but now he was not so sure. A part of him felt indignant, too proud to speak, given her reaction, and yet another part of him was somewhat ashamed. He knew what his people thought of the use of magic. Was his use of magic such a terrible thing? Even if he'd saved her life? Would she tell the others? If the villagers found out, he knew, they would surely exile him.

They walked and walked, and Darius finally could stand it no longer; he had to say something.

"I'm sure your family will be happy to see you back safely," Darius said.

Loti, to his disappointment, did not take the opportunity to look his way; instead, she just remained expressionless as they continued to walk in silence. Finally, after a long while, she shook her head.

"Perhaps," she said. "But I should think they will be more worried than anything. Our entire village will be."

"What do you mean?" Darius asked.

"You've killed a taskmaster. *We've* killed a taskmaster. The entire Empire will be out looking for us. They'll destroy our village. Our people. We have done a terrible, selfish thing."

"Terrible thing? I saved your life!" Darius said, exasperated.

She shrugged.

"My life is not worth the lives of all of our people."

Darius fumed, not knowing what to say as they walked. Loti, he was beginning to realize, was a difficult girl, hard to understand. She had been too indoctrinated with the rigid thought of her parents, of their people.

"So you hate me then," he said. "You hate me for saving you."

She refused to look at him, continued to walk.

"I saved you, too," she retorted proudly. "Don't you remember?"

Darius reddened; he could not understand her. She was too proud.

"I don't hate you," she finally added. "But I saw how you did it. I saw what you did."

Darius found himself shaking inside, hurt at her words. They came out like an accusation. It wasn't fair, especially after he had just saved her life.

"And is that such an awful thing?" he asked. "Whatever power it was that I used?"

Loti did not reply.

"I am who I am," Darius said. "I was born this way. I did not ask for it. I do not entirely understand it myself. I do not know when it comes and when it leaves. I do not know if I shall ever be able to use it again. I did not want to use it. It was as if…it used me."

Loti continued to look down, not responding, not meeting his eyes, and Darius felt a sinking feeling of regret. Had he made a mistake in rescuing her? Should he be ashamed of who he was?

"Would you rather be dead than for me to have used…whatever it was I used?" Darius asked.

Again Loti did not reply as they walked, and Darius's regret deepened.

"Do not speak of it to anyone," she said. "We must never speak of what happened here today. We will both be outcasts."

They turned the corner and their village came into view. They walked down the main pathway and as they did, they were spotted by villagers, who let out a great shout of joy.

Within moments there was a great commotion as villagers swarmed out to meet them, hundreds of them, excitedly rushing to embrace Loti and Darius. Breaking through the crowd was Loti's mother, joined by her father and two of her brothers, tall men with broad shoulders, short hair, and proud jaws. They all looked down at Darius, summing him up. Standing beside them was Loti's third brother, smaller than the others and lame in one leg.

"My love," Loti's mother said, rushing through the crowd and embracing her, hugging her tight.

Darius hung back, unsure what to do.

"What happened to you?" her mother demanded. "I thought the Empire took you away. How did you get free?"

The villagers all fell grave, silent, as all eyes turned to Darius. He stood there, not knowing what to say. This should be a moment, he felt, of great joy and celebration for what he did, a moment for him to take great pride, for him to be welcomed home as a hero. After all, he alone, of all of them, had had the courage to go after Loti.

Instead, it was a moment of confusion for him. And perhaps even shame. Loti gave him a meaningful look, as it to warn him not to reveal their secret.

"Nothing happened, Mother," Loti said. "The Empire changed their mind. They let me go."

"Let you go?" she echoed, flabbergasted.

Loti nodded.

"They let me go far from here. I was lost in the woods, and Darius found me. He led me back."

The villager, silent, all looked skeptically back and forth between Darius and Loti. Darius sensed they did not believe them.

"And what is that mark on your face?" her father asked, stepping forward, rubbing his thumb on her cheek, turning her head to examine it.

Darius looked over and saw a large black and blue welt.

Loti looked up at her father, unsure.

"I…tripped," she said. "On a root. As I said, I am fine," she insisted, defiant.

All eyes turned to Darius, and Bokbu, the village chief, stepped forward.

"Darius, is this true?" he asked, his voice somber. "You brought her back peacefully? You had no encounter with the Empire?"

Darius stood there, his heart pounding, hundreds of eye staring at him. He knew if he told them of their encounter, told them what he had done, they would all fear the reprisal to come. And he would have no way to explain how he killed them all without speaking of his magic. He would be an outcast, and so would Loti—and he did not want to strike panic in all of the people's hearts.

Darius did not want to lie. But he did not know what else to do.

So instead, Darius merely nodded back to the elders, without speaking. Let them interpret that as they would, he thought.

Slowly, the people, relieved, all turned and looked to Loti. Finally, one of her brothers stepped forward and draped an arm around her.

"She's safe!" he called out, breaking the tension. "That's all that matters!"

There came a great shout in the village, as the tension broke, and Loti was embraced by her family and all the others.

Darius stood there and watched, receiving a few halfhearted pats of approval on his back, as Loti turned alone with her family, and was ushered off into the village. He watched her go, waiting, hoping she would turn around to look at him, just once.

But his heart dried up within him as he watched her disappear, folded into the crowd, and never turning back.

CHAPTER NINE

Volusia stood proudly atop her golden carriage, mounted atop her golden vessel gleaming in the sun, as she drifted her way slowly down the waterways of Volusia, her arms outstretched, taking in the adulation of her people. Thousands of them came out, rushed to the edge of the waterways, lined the streets and alleys, and shouted her name from all directions.

As she drifted down the narrow waterways that wound their way through the city, Volusia could almost reach out and touch her people, all hailing her name, crying and screaming in adulation as they threw torn-up shreds of scrolls of all different colors, sparkling in the light as they rained down on her. It was the greatest sign of respect their people could offer. It was their way of welcoming a returning hero.

"Long live Volusia! Long live Volusia!" came the chant, echoed down one alleyway after the next as she passed through the masses, the waterways taking her straight through her magnificent city, its streets and buildings all lined with gold.

Volusia leaned back and took it all in, thrilled that she had defeated Romulus, had slaughtered the Supreme Ruler of the Empire, and had murdered his contingent of soldiers. Her people were one with her, and they felt emboldened when she felt emboldened, and she had never felt stronger in her life—not since the day she'd murdered her mother.

Volusia looked up at her magnificent city, at the two towering pillars leading into it, shining gold and green in the sun; she took in the endless array of ancient buildings erected in her ancestors' time, hundreds of years old, well worn. The shining, immaculate streets were bustling with thousands of people, guards on every corner, the precise waterways cut through them in perfect angles, connecting everything. There were small footbridges on which could be seen horses clomping, bearing golden carriages, people dressed in their finest silks and jewels. The entire city had declared a holiday, and all had come out to greet her, all calling her name on this holy day. She was more than a leader to them—she was a goddess.

It was even more auspicious that this day should coincide with a festival, the Day of Lights, the day in which they bowed to the seven gods of the sun. Volusia, as leader of the city, was always the one to initiate the festivities, and as she sailed through, the two immense golden torches burned brightly behind her, brighter than the day, ready to light the Grand Fountain.

All the people followed her, hurrying along the streets, chasing after her boat; she knew they would accompany her all the way, until she reached the center of the six circles of the city, where she would disembark and set fire to the fountains that would mark the day's holiday and sacrifices. It was a glorious day for her city and her people, a day to praise the fourteen gods, the ones that were rumored to circle her city, to guard the fourteen entrances against all unwanted invaders. Her people prayed to all of them, and today, as on all days, thanks was due.

This year, her people would be in for a surprise: Volusia had added a fifteenth god, the first time in centuries, since the found of the city, that a god had been added. And that god was herself. Volusia had erected a towering golden statue of herself in the center of the seven circles, and she had declared this day her name day, her holiday. As it was unveiled, all her people would see it for the first time, would see that she, Volusia, was more than her mother, more than a leader, more than a mere human. She was a goddess, who deserved to be worshipped every day. They would pray and bow down to her along with all the others—they would do it, or she would have their blood.

Volusia smiled to herself as her boat drifted ever closer to the city center. She could hardly wait to see their expressions, to have them all worship her just as the other fourteen gods. They did not know it yet, but one day, she would destroy the other gods, one by one, until all that was left was her.

Volusia, excited, checked back over her shoulder and she saw behind her an endless array of vessels following, all carrying live bulls and goats and rams, shifting and noisy in the sun, all in preparation of the day's sacrifice to the gods. She would slaughter the biggest and best one before her own statue.

Volusia's boat finally reached the open waterway to the seven golden circles, each one wider than the next, wide golden plazas that were separated by rings of water. Her boat made its way slowly through the circles, ever closer towards the center, passing each of the fourteen gods, and her heart pounded in excitement. Each god towered over them as they went, each statue gleaming gold, twenty feet high. In the very center of all this, in the plaza that had always been kept empty for sacrifice and congregation, there now stood a newly constructed golden pedestal, atop of which was a fifty-foot structure covered in a white silk cloth. Volusia smiled: she alone of all her people knew what lay beneath that cloth.

Volusia disembarked, her servants rushing forward to help her down, as they reached the innermost plaza. She watched as another vessel was brought forward, and the largest bull she had ever seen was taken off and led right to her by a dozen men. Each held a thick rope, leading the beast carefully. This bull was special, procured in the Lower Provinces: fifteen feet high, with bright red skin, it was a beacon of strength. It was also filled with fury. It resisted, but the men held it in place as they led it before her statue.

Volusia heard a sword being drawn, and she turned and saw Aksan, her personal assassin, standing beside her, holding out the ceremonial sword. Aksan was the most loyal man she'd ever met, willing to kill anyone she asked him with just so much as a nod of her head. He was also sadistic, which was why she liked him, and he had earned her respect many times. He was one of the few people she allowed to stay close to her side.

Aksan stared back at her, with his sunken, pockmarked face, his horns visible behind his thick, curly hair.

Volusia reached out and took the long, golden ceremonial sword, its blade six feet long, and tightened her grip on the hilt with both hands. A hushed silence fell over her people as she wheeled, raised it high, and brought it down on the back of bull's neck with all her might.

The blade, as sharp as could be, as thin as parchment, sliced right through, and Volusia grinned as she heard the satisfying sound of sword piercing flesh, felt it cutting all the way through, and felt its hot blood spraying her face. It gushed everywhere, a huge puddle oozing onto her feet, and the bull stumbled, headless, and fell at the base of her still-covered statue. The blood gushed all over the silk and the gold, staining it, as her people let out a great cheer.

"A great omen, my lady," Aksan leaned over and said.

The ceremonies had begun. All around her, trumpets sounded, and hundreds of animals were brought forth, as her officers began slaughtering them on all sides of her. It would be a long day of slaughtering and raping and gorging on food and wine—and then doing it all over again, for another day, and another. Volusia would make sure she joined them, would take some men and wine for herself, and would slit their throats as a sacrifice to her idols. She looked forward to a long day of sadism and brutality.

But first, there was one thing left to do.

The crowd quieted as Volusia ascended the pedestal at the base of her statue and turned and faced her people. Climbing up on the other side of her was Koolian, another trusted advisor, a dark sorcerer wearing a black hood and cloak, with glowing green eyes and a wart-lined face, the creature who had helped guide her to her own mother's assassination. It was he, Koolian, who had advised her to build this statue to herself.

The people stared at her, silent as could be. She waited, savoring the drama of the moment.

"Great people of Volusia!" she boomed. "I present to you the statue of your newest and greatest god!"

With a flourish Volusia pulled back the silk sheet, to a gasp of the crowd.

"Your new goddess, the fifteenth goddess, Volusia!" Koolian boomed to the people.

The people let out a hushed sound of awe, as they all looked up at it in wonder. Volusia looked up at the shining golden statue, twice as high as the others, a perfect model of her. She waited, nervous, to see how her people would react. It had been centuries since anyone had introduced a new god, and she was gambling to see if their love for her was as strong as she needed it to be. She didn't just need them to love her; she needed them to worship her.

To her great satisfaction, her people, as one, all suddenly dropped to their faces, bowing down, worshiping her idol.

"Volusia," they chanted sacredly, again and again. "Volusia. Volusia."

Volusia stood there, arms out wide, breathing deep, taking it all in. It was enough praise to satisfy any human. Any leader. Any god.

But it was still not enough for her.

*

Volusia walked through the wide, open-air arched entrance to her castle, passing marble columns a hundred feet high, the halls lined with gardens and guards, Empire soldiers, standing perfectly erect, holding golden spears, lined up as far as the eye could see. She walked slowly, the golden heels of her boots clicking, accompanied, on either side Koolian, her sorcerer, Aksan, her assassin, and Soku, the commander of her army.

"My lady, if I could just have a word with you," Soku said. He'd been trying to talk to her all day, and she'd been ignoring him, not interested in his fears, in his fixation on reality. She had her own reality, and she would address him when the time suited her.

Volusia continued marching until she reached another entrance to another corridor, this one bedecked with long strips of emerald beads. Immediately, soldiers rushed forward and pulled them to the side, allowing a passage for her.

As she entered, all the chanting and cheering and reveling of the sacred ceremonies outdoors began to fade away. She'd had a long day of slaughtering and drinking and raping and feasting, and Volusia wanted some time to collect herself. She would recharge, then go back for another round.

Volusia entered the solemn chambers, dark and heavy, just a few torches lighting it. What lit the room mostly was the sole shaft of green light, shooting down from the oculus high above in the center of the hundred-foot-high ceiling, straight down to a singular object that sat alone in the center of the room.

The emerald spear.

Volusia approached it, in awe, as it sat there, as it had for centuries, pointing straight up into the light. With its emerald shaft and emerald spear point, it glistened in the light, aimed straight up at the heavens, as if challenging the gods. It had always been a sacred object for her people, one that her people believed sustained the entire city. She stood before it in awe, watching the particles swirl about it in the green light.

"My lady," Soku said softly, his voice echoing in the silence. "May I speak?"

Volusia stood a long time, her back to him, examining the spear, admiring its craftsmanship as she had every day of her life, until finally she felt ready to hear her councilor's words.

"You may," she said.

"My lady," he said, "you have killed the ruler of the Empire. Surely, word has spread. Armies will be marching for Volusia right now. Massive armies, larger than we could ever defend against. We must prepare. What is your strategy?"

"Strategy?" Volusia asked, still not looking at him, annoyed.

"How will you broker peace?" he pressed. "How will you surrender?"

She turned to him and fixed her eyes on him coldly.

"There will be no peace," she said. "Until I accept their surrender and their oath of fealty to me."

He looked back, fear in his face.

"But my lady, they outnumber us a hundred to one," he said. "We cannot possibly defend against them."

She turned back to the spear, and he stepped forward, desperate.

"My Empress," he persisted. "You've achieved a remarkable victory in usurping your mother's throne. She was not loved by the people, and you are. They worship you. None will speak to you frankly. But I shall. You surround yourself by people who tell you what you wish to hear. Who fear you. But I shall tell you the truth, the reality of our situation. The Empire will surround us. And we will be crushed. There will be nothing left of us, of our city. You must take action. You must broker a truce. Pay whatever price they want. Before they kill us all."

Volusia smiled as she studied the spear.

"Do you know what they said about my mother?" she asked.

Soku stood there and looked back at her blankly, and shook his head.

"They said she was the Chosen One. They said she would never be defeated. They said she would never die. Do you know why? Because no one had wielded this spear in six centuries. And she came along and wielded it with one hand. And she used it to kill her father and take his throne."

Volusia turned to him, her eyes aglow with history and destiny.

"They said the spear would only be wielded once. By the Chosen One. They said my mother would live a thousand centuries, that the throne of Volusia would be hers forever. And do you know what happened? I wielded the spear myself—and I used it to kill my mother."

She took a deep breath.

"What does that tell you, Lord Commander?"

He looked at her, confused, and shook his head, puzzled.

"We can either live in the shadow of other people's legends," Volusia said, "or we can create our own."

She leaned in close, scowling, glaring back at him in fury.

"When I have crushed the entire Empire," she said, "when everyone in this universe bends their knee to me, when there is not a single living person left that doesn't know and scream and cry my name, you will know then that I am the one and only true leader—and that I am the one and only true god. I am the Chosen One. Because I have chosen myself."

CHAPTER TEN

Gwendolyn walked through the village, accompanied by her brothers Kendrick and Godfrey, and by Sandara, Aberthol, Brandt and Atme, with hundreds of her people trailing her, as they all were welcomed here. They were led by Bokbu, the village chief, and Gwen walked beside him, filled with gratitude as she toured his village. His people had taken them in, had provided them safe harbor, and the chief had done so at his own risk, against some of his own people's will. He had saved them all, had pulled them all back from the dead. Gwen did not know what they would have done otherwise. They would probably all be dead at sea.

Gwen also felt a rush of gratitude for Sandara, who had vouched for them with her people, and who'd had the wisdom to bring them all here. Gwen looked about, taking in the scene as all the villagers swarmed them, watching them arrive like things of curiosity, and she felt like an animal on display. Gwen saw all the small, quaint, modeling clay cottages, and she saw a proud people, a nation of warriors with kind eyes, watching them. Clearly, they'd never seen anything like Gwen and her people. Though curious, they were also guarded. Gwen could not blame them. A lifetime of slavery had molded them to be cautious.

Gwen noticed all the bonfires being erected everywhere, and she wondered.

"Why all the fires?" she asked.

"You arrive at an auspicious day," Bokbu said. "It is our festival of the dead. A holy night for us, it arrives but once a sun cycle. We burn fires to honor the gods of the dead, and it is said that on this night, the gods visit us, and speak to us of what is to come."

"It is also said that our savior will arrive on this day," chimed in a voice.

Gwendolyn looked over to see an older man, perhaps in his seventies, tall, thin with a somber look to him, walk up beside them, carrying a long, yellow staff and wearing a yellow cloak.

"May I introduce you to Kalo," Bokbu said. "Our oracle."

Gwen nodded, and he nodded back, expressionless.

"Your village is beautiful," Gwendolyn remarked. "I can see the love of family here."

55

The chief smiled.

"You are young for a queen, but wise, gracious. It is true what they say about you from across the sea. I wish that you and your people could stay right here, in the village, with us; but you understand, we must hide you from the prying eyes of the Empire. You will be staying close, though; that will be your home, there."

Gwendolyn followed his gaze and looked up and saw a distant mountain, filled with holes.

"The caves," he said. "You will be safe there. The Empire will not look for you there, and you can burn your fires and cook your food and recover until you're well."

"And then?" Kendrick asked, joining them.

Bokbu looked over at him, but before he could respond, he suddenly came to a stop as before him there appeared a tall, muscular villager holding a spear, flanked by a dozen muscular men. It was the same man from the ship, the one that protested their arrival—and he did not look happy.

"You endanger all of our people by allowing the strangers here," he said darkly. "You must send them back to where they came from. It is not our job to take in every last race that washes up here."

Bokbu shook his head as he faced him.

"Your fathers are ashamed of you," he said. "The laws of our hospitality extend to all."

"And is it the burden of a slave to extend hospitality?" he retorted. "When we cannot even find it ourselves?"

"How we are treated has no bearing on how we treat others," the chief retorted. "And we shall not turn away those who need us."

The villager sneered back, glaring at Gwendolyn, Kendrick, the others, then back to the chief.

"We do not want them here," he said, seething. "The caves are not far away enough, and every day they are here, we are a day closer to death."

"And what good is this life you cling to if it is not spent justly?" the chief asked.

The man stared him down for a long time, the finally turned and stormed off, his men following him.

Gwendolyn watched them go, wondering.

"Do not mind him," the chief said, as he continued walking and Gwen and the others fell in beside him.

"I do not wish to be a burden on you," Gwendolyn said. "We can leave."

The chief shook his head.

"You will not leave," he said. "Not until you are rested and ready. There are other places you can go in the Empire, if you choose. Places that are also well hidden. But they are far from here, and dangerous to reach, and you must recover and decide and stay here with us. I insist on it. In fact, for this night only, I wish for you to join us, to join our festivities in the village. It is already nightfall—the Empire will not see you—and this is an important day for us. I would be honored to have you as our guests."

Gwendolyn noticed dusk was falling, saw all the bonfires being lit, the villagers dressed in their finest, gathering around; she heard a drumbeat start to rise up, soft, steady, then chanting. She saw children running around, grabbing treats that looked like candies. She saw men passing around coconuts filled with some sort of liquid, and she could smell the meat in the air from the large animals roasting on the fires.

Gwen liked the idea of her people having a chance to rest and recover and have a good meal before they ascended to the isolation of the caves.

She turned to the chief.

"I'd like that," she said. "I would like that very much."

*

Sandara walked by Kendrick's side, overcome with emotion to be back home again. She was happy to be home, to be back with her people on familiar land; yet she also felt restrained, felt like a slave again. Being here brought back memories of why she had left, why she had volunteered to be in service to the Empire and cross the seas with them as a healer. At least it had gotten her out of this place.

Sandara felt so relieved that she had been able to help save Gwendolyn's people, to bring them all here before they died at sea. As she walked beside Kendrick, more than anything, she wanted to hold his hand, to proudly display her man to her people. But she could not. There were too many eyes on them, and she knew her village would never condone a union between the races.

Kendrick, as if reading her thoughts, reached up and slipped an arm around her waist, and Sandara quickly brushed it away. Kendrick looked at her, hurt.

"Not here," she replied softly, feeling guilty.

Kendrick frowned, baffled.

"We have spoken of this," she said. "I told you my people are rigid. I must respect their laws."

"Are you ashamed of me then?" Kendrick asked.

Sandara shook her head.

"No, my lord. On the contrary. There is no one I am more proud of. And no one I love more. But I cannot be with you. Not here. Not in this place. You must understand."

Kendrick's expression darkened, and she felt awful for it.

"Yet this is where we are," he said. "There is no other place for us. Shall we not be together then?"

She spoke, her heart breaking at her own words: "You will stay in the caves of your people," she said. "I shall stay here, in the village. With my people. It is my role. I love you, but we cannot be together. Not in this place."

Kendrick looked away, hurt, and Sandara wanted to explain further when suddenly a voice interrupted.

"Sandara!?" called out the voice.

Sandara turned, shocked to recognize the familiar voice, the voice of her only brother. Her heart leapt as she saw him, pushing out from the crowd, walking toward her.

Darius.

He looked much bigger and stronger and older than when she had left him, filled with a confidence she had not seen before. She left him as a boy, and now, while young, he appeared to be a man. With his long, unruly hair hanging down, tied behind his back, still never cut, his face as proud as ever, he looked exactly like their father. She could see the warrior in his eyes.

Sandara was overwhelmed with joy to see him, to see that he was alive, had not died or been broken like all the other slaves, his proud spirit still leading the way. She rushed forward and embraced him, as he embraced her back. It felt so good to see him again.

"I feared you were dead," he said.

She shook her head.

"Just across the sea," she said. "I left you a boy—and you have become a man."

He smiled back proudly. In this small oppressive village, in this awful place in the world, Darius had been her one source of solace, and she his. They had both suffered together, especially since the disappearance of their father.

Kendrick approached and Sandara saw him and stood there, frozen, unsure how to introduce him as she saw Darius looking at him. She knew she had to make some sort of introduction.

Kendrick beat her to it. He stepped forward, reaching out a hand.

"I am Kendrick," he said.

"And I am Darius," he replied, shaking hands.

"Kendrick, this is my brother," Sandara said, nervous, stumbling. "Darius, this is…well…this is…"

Flustered, Sandara paused, unsure what to say. Darius held out a hand.

"You don't have to explain to me, my sister," he said. "I'm not like the others. I understand."

Sandara could see in Darius's eyes that he *did* understand, and that he did not judge her. Sandara loved him for it.

They all turned and walked together, falling in with the others as they toured the village.

"You have chosen quite a tumultuous time to return," Darius said, tension in his voice. "Much has happened here. Much *is* happening."

"What do you mean?" she asked, nervous.

"We have much catching up to do, my sister. Kendrick, you shall join us too. Come, the fires have begun."

CHAPTER ELEVEN

Godfrey sat in the village before the raging bonfire in the starry night, nearby his sister Gwendolyn, his brother Kendrick, Steffen, Brandt, Atme, Aberthol, and nearly all the people he remembered from the Ring. Seated beside him were Akorth and Fulton, and as he saw them it reminded him that more than ever he desperately needed a drink.

Godfrey stared into the flames, wondering how he had ended up here, trying to process everything that had happened, everything feeling like a blur in a long series of blurs. First there was the death of his father; then the death of his brother, Gareth; then the invasion of the McClouds; then invasion of the Ring; then the Upper Isles; then the long journey across the sea…. It felt like one tragedy, one journey, after the next. His life had devolved to nothing but war and chaos and exile. It felt good to finally stop moving. And he sensed that it was all just beginning.

"What I wouldn't do for a pint right now," Akorth said.

"Surely they must have something to drink around here," Fulton said.

Godfrey rubbed his aching head, wondering the same thing. If ever he needed a drink, it was now. This last voyage across the sea was the worst he could remember, so many days without food or ale, so often on the brink of starvation…. He had been sure, too many times, that he had died. He closed his eyes and tried to shut out the awful pictures, his memories of his fellow Ring members turning to stone and falling over the rail.

It had been an endless voyage, a voyage through hell and back, and Godfrey was surprised that it had not led to any sort of epiphany or enlightenment for him. It had not led him to change his ways. It had merely led him to want to drink more, to want to blot it all out. Was there something wrong with him? he wondered. Did it make him less profound than the others? He hoped not.

Now here they were, in the Empire no less, surrounded by a hostile army that wanted them dead. How long, he wondered, before they were discovered? Before Romulus's million men hunted them down? Godfrey had a sinking feeling that their days were numbered.

"I see a sight for sore eyes," Akorth said.

Godfrey looked up.

"There," Fulton said, elbowing him in the ribs.

Godfrey looked over and saw the villagers passing around a bowl filled with a clear liquid. Each took it carefully in his palms, took a sip, and passed it on.

"That doesn't exactly look like the Queen's ale," Akorth commented.

"And do you want to wait for a better vintage to come around?" Fulton replied.

Fulton leaned forward and took the bowl before Akorth could grab it, and took a long drink himself, the liquid pouring down his cheeks. He wiped his mouth with the back of his hand and groaned in delight.

"That burns," he said. "You're right. Sure isn't the Queen's ale. It's a hell of a lot stronger."

Akorth snatched it, took a long drink, and then nodded in agreement. He began coughing as he handed it to Godfrey.

"My God," Akorth said. "It's like drinking fire."

Godfrey leaned over and smelled it, and he recoiled.

"What is it?" he asked one of the villagers, a tough-looking warrior with broad shoulders wearing no shirt, sitting next to him, looking serious and wearing a necklace of black stones.

"We call it the heart of the cactus," he said. "It is a drink for men. Are you a man?"

"I doubt it," Godfrey said. "Depends who you ask. But I'll be whatever I have to be to drown out my sorrows."

Godfrey raised the bowl to his lips and drank, and he felt the liquid going down his throat like fire, burning his belly. He coughed, too, and the villagers laughed as the next one took the bowl from him.

"Not a man," they observed.

"So my father used to say," Godfrey agreed, laughing with them.

Godfrey felt good as the drink went to his head, and as the villager who insulted him began to drink from the bowl, Godfrey reached out and snatched it from his hands.

"Wait a minute," Godfrey said.

Godfrey drank, this time in several long gulps, taking it without coughing.

The villagers all looked at him in surprise. Godfrey turned to them in satisfaction, a smile returning to his face.

"I may not be a man," he said, "and you might be better with your weapons. But don't challenge me to drink."

They all laughed, the villagers passed the bowl, and Godfrey sat back on his elbows in the dirt, already feeling lightheaded, feeling good for the first time. It was a strong drink, and he felt dizzy, never having had anything like it before.

"I see you've turned over a new leaf," came a woman's disapproving voice.

Godfrey turned and looked up to see Illepra standing over him, hands on her hips, looking down, frowning.

"You know, I spent the afternoon healing our people," she said, disapprovingly. "Many still suffer the effects of starvation. And what have you done to help? Here you are, sitting by the fire and drinking."

Godfrey felt his stomach turning; she always seemed to find the worst in him.

"I see many of my people sitting here drinking," he replied, "and god bless them for it. What's the harm in that?"

"They're not *all* drinking," Illepra said. "At least not as much as you."

"And what is it to you?" Godfrey retorted.

"With half our people sick, do you think now is the time to drink and laugh the night away?"

"What better time?" he retorted.

She frowned.

"Wrong," she said. "It is time for repentance. A time for fasting and prayer."

Godfrey shook his head.

"My prayers to the gods have always gone unanswered," he replied. "As for fasting—we did enough of that aboard ship. Now is the time to eat."

He reached over, grabbing a chicken bone being passed around, and took a big bite, chewing defiantly in her face. The grease ran down his chin, but he did not wipe it and did not look away as she stared down at him in icy disapproval.

Illepra looked down on him with scorn, and slowly shook her head.

"You were a man once. Even if briefly. Back in King's Court. More than a man—you were a hero. You stayed behind and protected Gwendolyn in the city. You helped save her life. You kept back the McClouds. I thought you had…become someone else.

"But here you are. Making jokes and drinking the night away. Like the boy you've always been."

Godfrey was upset now, his buzz and sense of relaxation quickly fading.

"And what would you have me do?" he retorted, annoyed. "Get up from my spot here and run off into the horizon and defeat the Empire alone?"

Akorth and Fulton laughed, and the villagers laughed with him.

Illepra reddened and shook her head.

"You haven't changed," she said. "You've crossed half the world and you still haven't changed."

"I am who I am," Godfrey said. "An ocean voyage won't change that."

Her eyes narrowed in rebuke.

"I loved you once," she said. "Now, I feel nothing for you. Nothing at all. You are a disappointment to me."

She turned and stormed off, and the men laughed and grunted around Godfrey.

"I see women are no different even on the other side of the sea," one villager said, and they all broke out into laughter.

But Godfrey was not laughing. She had hurt him. And he was starting to realize, even in his drunken haze, that perhaps Illepra meant something to him after all.

Godfrey reached over, snatched the bowl, and took another long swig.

"Here's to heroes!" he said. "God knows I'm not one of them."

*

Gwendolyn sat before the bonfire, joined by Kendrick, Brandt, Atme, Aberthol, and a dozen knights of the Silver; alongside them sat Bokbu, along with the dozen elders and dozens of villagers. The elders were engaged in a long discussion with Gwen, and as she stared into the flames, she tried to be polite and listen, Krohn laying his head in her lap as she fed him small pieces of meat. The elders had been going on for hours, seemingly thrilled with the chance to talk to an outsider, venting about their problems with the Empire, their village, their people.

Gwendolyn tried to concentrate. But a part of her was distracted, thinking of nothing but Thor and Guwayne, hoping and praying for their safety, for their return to her. On this night of the fires, she prayed with all their heart for them to come back to her, for her to have another chance. She prayed for a message, a sign, anything to let her know that they were safe.

"My lady?"

Gwen turned to see Bokbu staring back at her.

"Your thoughts on the matter?" he asked.

Gwen snapped out of it.

"I'm sorry," she said. "Can you ask me again?"

Bokbu cleared his throat, clearly compassionate and understanding.

"I had been explaining the ways of my people. Of our life here. You had asked me what a day is like. A day begins in the fields and ends when the sun falls. The taskmasters of the Empire take us as slaves, as they do every other city in the Empire not of their race. They work us until we die."

"Haven't you tried to escape?" Kendrick asked.

Bokbu turned to him.

"Escape where exactly?" he asked. "We are slaves in the service of Volusia, the great northern city by the sea. There is no free province of the Empire, nowhere to run to within hundreds of miles of here. We have Volusia to one side, the ocean on the other, and the vast desert behind us."

"And what lies on the other side of the desert?" Gwen asked.

"The entire rest of the Empire," another chieftain chimed in. "Endless lands. More provinces and regions than you can dream of. All under the thumb of the Empire. Even if we managed to cross the great desert, we know little of what lies beyond."

"Except slavery and death," another chimed in.

"Has anyone ever tried to cross it?" Gwen asked.

Bokbu turned to her somberly.

"Every day some of our people try to flee. Most are killed quickly, an arrow or spear in the back as they try to run. Those who escape, disappear. Sometimes the Empire brings them back days later, corpses for us to see, to hang from the highest tree. Other times, they bring back mere bones, eaten by some animal. Other times, they never bring them back at all."

"Have any survived?" Gwen asked.

Bokbu shook his head.

"The Great Waste is merciless," he said. "Surely they were taken by the desert."

"But maybe some survived?" Kendrick pressed.

Bokbu shrugged.

"Perhaps. Perhaps only to make it to another region and become enslaved elsewhere. Slaves have it worse than us in other Empire regions. They are killed randomly and routinely every day, just for the amusement of the taskmasters. Here, at least, we're not torn apart from our families and sold off for fun. We're not shipped from city to city and town to town; here, at least, we have a home. They allow us to live as long as we labor."

"It is not much of a life," another chieftain added. "It is a life of bondage. But it is a life nonetheless."

"Can you not raise arms and fight back?" Kendrick asked.

Bokbu shook his head.

"There have been other times, other generations, in other cities, that have tried. They have never won. We are outmanned, out armed. The Empire have superior armor, weaponry, animals, enforced walls, organization…and most of all, they have steel. We have none. It is outlawed here."

"And if a slave rises up and loses, the entire village is killed."

"They outnumber us vastly," another chieftain chimed in. "What are we to do? Are a few hundred of us, with our wooden weapons, to attack a hundred thousand of them, while they wear steel armor?"

Gwendolyn contemplated their predicament. She understood, and she felt compassion for them. They had given up on who they were, on their proud warrior spirit, to try to protect their families. She could not blame them. She wondered if she would have done the same in their position. If her father would have.

"Subjugation is a terrible thing," she said. "When one man thinks he is greater than another, because of his race or his weapons or his power or his numbers or his riches—or whatever reason—then he can become cruel for no reason."

Bokbu turned to her.

"You have experienced it yourself," he said. "Or you would not be here."

Gwendolyn nodded, looking into the flames.

"Romulus and his million men invaded our homeland and burned it to the ground," she said. "There are but a few hundred of us now, all that remains of what was once the most glorious nation. At its center, a city of such prosperity that it put any other to shame. It was a land overflowing with abundance of every sort, with a Canyon that protected us from all sorts of evil. We were invincible. For generations, we were invincible."

"And yet, even the great fall," Bokbu prodded.

Gwen nodded, seeing he understood.

"And what happened?" another chieftain asked.

As she reflected on their fall, Gwendolyn wondered the same thing.

"The Empire," she said. "The same as you."

They all fell into a gloomy silence.

66

"What if we were to join you?" Atme said, breaking the silence. "What if we were to attack them with you?"

Bokbu shook his heads.

"The city of Volusia is well-fortified, well-manned. And they outnumber us a thousand to one."

"Surely, there must be something that could bring down the Empire?" Brandt asked.

The elders looked at each other cautiously, then after a long pause, Bokbu said:

"The Giants, perhaps."

"The Giants?" Gwen asked, intrigued.

Bokbu nodded.

"There are rumors of their existence. In the far reaches of the Empire."

Aberthol spoke up:

"The Land of the Giants," he said. "A land with creatures so tall, their feet could crush a thousand men. The Land of the Giants is a land of myth. A convenient myth. It was disproved in our fathers' fathers' time."

"Whether you are right or wrong, no one knows," Bokbu said. "But one thing we do know is that the Giants, at one time, existed. And that they are fickle. You might as well try to tame a wild beast. They might just as easily kill you as the Empire. They do not seek justice; they do not seek to take sides. They only seek bloodshed. Even if they still existed, even if you found them, you would more likely end up dead by visiting them than by invading Volusia."

A long silence fell over them all as Gwen studied the flames, pondering it all.

"Is there no other place?" Gwendolyn asked, as all eyes turned to her. "Once our people heal, is there no other place in the Empire we can go where we can be safe? Where we can start again?"

The elders exchanged a long look, and finally, they nodded to each other.

Bokbu raised his staff, reached out, and began to draw in the dirt. Gwendolyn was surprised at how skilled he was, as she watched an intricate map unfold before her, and all her people crowded around.

She watched as the contours of the Empire took shape, and was in awe at how vast and complex it was.

"Do you recognize it?" he asked her as he finally finished.

Gwendolyn examined it, all the different regions and provinces, dozens and dozens of them. She looked at the odd shape of the Empire lands, it center rectangular, and in each of its four corners, a long, curved peninsula jutting out in opposite directions. They each looked like a bull's horn. *The four horns of the Empire*, her father used to say. Now she understood.

"I do," she said. "I once spent an entire moon in the house of the scholars, studying ancient maps of the Ring and of the Empire. The four corners are the four horns for the four directions and those two spikes are of the North and the South. In the center is the Great Waste."

Bokbu looked back at her, wide-eyed, impressed.

"You are the only outsider who has ever known this," he said. "Your learning must be great indeed."

He paused.

"Yes, the very shape of the Empire belies its nature. Horns. Spikes. Waste. They are vast lands, with many regions in between. Not to mention the islands, which I've not even drawn here. There is much that is uncharted and unknown. Much is rumor. Some wishful thinking passed down from those who were enslaved too long. We no longer know what's true. Maps are living things, and mapmakers lie as much as kings. All maps are politics. And all maps are power."

There came a long silence, nothing save the crackling of the fire, as Gwen pondered his words.

"Before the time of Antochin," Bokbu finally continued, "before the time of my father's and your father, there was a time when the Ring and the Empire were one. Before the Great Divide. Before the Canyon. Your men of armor, of steel, legend has it, split from each other. Half left for the Ring and half stayed behind. If it is true, then somewhere, in the midst of these Empire lands, the kingdom of the Second Ring lives."

Gwendolyn paused, her mind racing.

"The Second Ring?" she asked, under her breath, growing with excitement. It was all coming back to her, all her reading. It was hazy, and she could not quite remember all of it; she had thought it was a children's fable.

"More myth than fact," Aberthol chimed in, his old voice cutting into the air as he stepped forward to look at the map. "*Between the four horns and the two spikes,*" he began to recite, "*between the ancient shores and the Twin Lakes, north of the Althu—*"

"*—and south of the Reche,*" Bokbu finished, "*the Second Ring resides.*"

Aberthol and the chief locked eyes with each other, each recognizing the old writings by heart.

"A myth from centuries past," Aberthol said. "You trade old wives' tales and myths here. That is your currency."

"Some call it myth," Bokbu said. "And some, fact."

Aberthol shook his head doggedly.

"The chances of an alternate Ring are remote," Aberthol said. "To stake the hopes of our people on such a venture would be to stake our future on death."

Gwen studied Bokbu and she could see the seriousness on his face, and she felt he truly believed that the Second Ring existed. He studied the map he had drawn, his face grave.

"Years ago," Bokbu finally continued, his voice grave, "when I was a young boy, I saw a sword of steel, and a breastplate, brought into this village. It was found, my father said, in the desert, on a dying man. A man who looked like your people, with pale skin. A man who wore a suit of steel, who had armor with the same markings as yours. He died before he could tell us where he was from, and we hid the armor on fear of death."

Bokbu sighed.

"I believe the Second Ring exists," he added. "If you can find it, if you can reach it, perhaps you can find a home, a true home, in the Empire."

"Another place to hide from the Empire?" Kendrick said, derisively.

"If the Second Ring exists," Bokbu said, "it is so well-hidden that they are not hiding. They are living. It is a remote chance, my lady," he concluded, "but a chance nonetheless."

Before Gwen could process it all, a shrill voice suddenly cut through the night. At first it was a shriek, and then it morphed into a long cry, and then a sustained chanting.

Gwen turned as all the men fell silent and sat back and watched, as there stepped forward a woman with long black hair falling down to her waist, palms up by her side, and a red silk scarf wrapped about her neck. She leaned back, raised her hands to the heavens, and chanted a solemn song. She chanted louder and louder, and as she did, the flames on all the bonfires leapt higher.

"Spirits of the flames!" she chanted. "Visit us. Let us pay our respects. Tell us what you have to tell us. Let us see what we cannot!"

Gwendolyn flinched and jumped back as the fire before her began to spark and grow brighter. She looked and was shocked to see shapes swirling within it. She felt her hairs stand on end.

The seer's chanting slowed, then stopped, as she came over and stood over Gwendolyn. Gwen felt fear as the seer's glowing yellow eyes stared back at her.

"Ask me what you will," the seer said, her voice inhumanly dark.

Gwen sat there, trembling inside, wanting to ask, wanting to know, but afraid to. What if it was not the answer she sought?

Finally, she summoned the courage.

"Thorgrin," Gwendolyn said, barely getting out the words. "Guwayne. Tell me. Do they live?"

There was a long silence, as the seer turned her back on her and faced the fire. She reached down and threw two fistfuls of dirt into the flames. The fire sparked and shot up, and the seer, her back to Gwendolyn, began muttering dark words Gwen did not understand.

Finally, she turned to her, her glowing yellow eyes fixed on hers. Gwen could not look away if she wanted to.

"Your baby will not return as you know him," she pronounced darkly. "And your husband, as we speak, is entering the Land of the Dead."

70

"NO!" Gwendolyn wailed, her cry rising above the incessant crackling of the flames.

She stood in outrage, felt her heart beating too fast, felt her whole body go weak. The world began to spin, and the last thing she saw was Steffen and Kendrick behind her, getting ready to catch her, and she fell into their arms and her world went black.

CHAPTER TWELVE

Thorgrin stood on the edge of the boat and looked up in wonder as the current carried them slowly forward, drifting into the immense cave at the edge of the world. He looked up at the ancient arched ceiling a hundred feet above, the gnarled black rock dripping, covered in moss and strange scurrying animals. A cold draft arose as they entered, and the temperature dropped ten degrees. Behind him, Reece, Conven, Elden, Indra, O'Connor, and Matus all stood, looking out in wonder as they drifted deeper and deeper into the darkness of the immense cave. Thor felt as if they were being swallowed whole, never to return, and his sense of foreboding increased.

As they went, Thor looked down and saw the waters change, begin to glow, phosphorescent, a soft blue lighting up the darkness, reflecting off the walls, giving just enough light to see by. The walls and the creatures clinging to them were reflected in grotesque shadows, and the deeper they went the more the sounds amplified, the screeching insects, the fluttering of wings, and the strange low moans. Thor tightened his grip on his sword, on guard.

"What is this place?" O'Connor said aloud, asking the question that was on all their minds.

Thor peered into the darkness, wondering. On the one hand, he was relieved to be out of the ocean and into a harbor of sorts, a place where they could all rest and regroup. On the other hand, Thor felt a chill in the air, and sensed something that made the hairs on his arms stand on end. His instincts were telling him to turn around, to head back to open sea. But their provisions were so low, they all needed rest, and most of all, Thorgrin had to explore this place in case it was truly the land of the dead. What if Guwayne were here? Now that Guwayne was dead, Thorgrin no longer cared about danger or darkness or even death; a part of him wanted death, would even embrace it. And if Guwayne was here, then, Thor felt, it was worth coming here to see him, even if he could never escape.

An eerie moan pierced the darkness, setting them all on edge.

"I wonder if we'd be safer risking the sea," Matus said softly, his voice echoing off the cave walls.

The waters twisted and turned, and as they went deeper and deeper into this place, the currents dragging them in as if dragging them to their fates, Thor turned and glanced back, and he saw that the ocean was already gone from view. They were embraced by the darkness, by the glowing waters, and they were now at the mercy of wherever the tides should take them.

"The current runs only one way," Reece said. "Let's hope it also leads us out of this place."

They floated in the blackness, turning a narrow bend, and as they went, Thor looked out and examined the walls, and all along them, he saw pairs of small, yellow eyes blinking in the darkness, belonging to some unknown creatures. They blinked and scurried, and Thor wondered what they were. Were they watching them? Were they waiting to strike?

Thor tightened his grip on his sword. He was on alert as they turned and turned.

Finally, they turned a corner and Thor saw, up ahead in the distance, the waters came to an abrupt end. They stopped at a beach of black sand, giving way to a new terrain of black rock.

Thor and the others looked out, baffled, as the boat came to a stop, bumping gently against the sand. They all looked at each other, then out at the wide rocky expanse before them. The cave disappeared in blackness.

"Is this where the ocean ends?" Indra asked.

"Only one way to find out," Conven said, stepping out of the boat and onto the beach.

The others followed, Thor going last, and as they stood on the beach, Thor looked back at their boat, rocking gently on the soft currents. Thor looked out at the glowing water, saw where the cave twisted, and saw the exit no more.

He turned back around, and peered into the darkness, darker here without the glowing of the water, and felt a cold draft rise out of somewhere.

"We can camp here at least," Elden said. "We can wait out the night."

"Assuming nothing eats us in the darkness," O'Connor said.

Suddenly, in the distance, a torch was lit—then another, and another. Dozens of torches lit up the darkness, and Thor, grabbing the hilt of his sword, looked out and saw people facing them, small people, half his height, their bodies way too thin, looking emaciated, with long, pointy fingers, long pointy noses, and small beady eyes. Their heads were rose to a point.

One of them stepped forward, clearly their leader, held up his torch and broke into a grin, revealing hundreds of small, sharp black teeth.

"You stand at a crossroads," the creature replied.

The leader was not like the others. He was three times their height, twice as tall as Thorgrin and his men, with a big belly, a long brown beard, and carrying a staff. The man rubbed his long beard as he stared down at them in the tense silence.

"A crossroads to what?" Thor asked.

"The land of the living and the land of the dead," he replied. "It is where the ocean ends. We are the keepers of the gate. Beyond us lie the gates to the land of the dead."

Thor looked beyond, over his shoulder, and in the distance he saw massive gates, a hundred feet high, made of iron ten feet thick. His heart leapt with excitement and hope.

"It is true then?" Thor asked, filled with hope for the first time since Guwayne's death. "There is a land of the dead?"

The creature nodded back solemnly.

"You can stay here for the night," he replied. "We shall provide you harbor, provisions, and send you on your way. You can go back from where you came and continue wherever the ocean takes you."

"Why should you give us your hospitality?" Reece asked, cautious.

The creature turned to him.

"That is the duty of the Keepers," he said. "It is our job to keep the gates closed. We do not accept people into the land of the dead— we keep them out. Those who have lost loved ones come here, searching, grieving, and we reject them. It is not yet their time. They struggle and strive to see them the ones they love, and we must send them away. As we must send you away."

Thor frowned and stepped forward.

"I want to enter," he said, without hesitating, thinking of Guwayne. "I want to see my boy."

The creature stared back at him, cold and hard.

"You do not understand," he said. "There is but one entrance, and there is no exit. To enter those gates means to never leave."

Thor shook his head, determined, filled with grief.

"I do not care," Thorgrin said firmly. "I will see my son."

"Thorgrin, what are you saying?" Reece said, coming up beside him. "You can't enter."

"He does not mean his words," Matus called out.

"Yes I do," Thorgrin insisted, filled with sorrow and a longing to see Guwayne. "Every one of them."

The creature stared back at Thor for a long time, as if summing him up, then shook his head.

"You are very brave," he said, "but the answer is no. You will stay here for the night, then you will set back out for the ocean. The morning tides will take you away. Stay on them long enough, and over the course of a moon, you'll reach the eastern shores of the Empire. This is no place for men to stay."

"I will enter those gates!" Thor demanded darkly, drawing his sword. The sound of the metal leaving the scabbard echoed loudly off the cave's walls, and the cave came alive with the sounds of insects and creatures scrambling to get out of the way, as if they knew a storm were coming.

Immediately, the dozens of creatures behind their leader drew their swords, too, white swords made of bone.

"You disgrace our hospitality," the leader sneered at Thor.

"I don't want your hospitality," Thor said. "I want my boy. I will see him. And not you, or any creatures of this world, will stop me. I will walk through the gates of hell to do so. I want enter the land of the dead. I will go alone. My men can accept your provisions and head back out to sea. But not I. I will enter here. And no one and nothing of this earth will stop me."

The leader shook his head.

"Every once in a while we encounter someone like you," he said. He shook his head again. "Foolish. You should have accepted my offer the first time."

Suddenly, all of the creatures behind him charged Thorgrin, dozens of them, swords held high, racing toward him.

Thor felt such a determination to see his son that something overcame him: his body suddenly welled up with heat, and his palms felt on fire, as he felt more powerful than he'd ever had. He replaced his sword, raised his palms, and as he did, an orb of light shot forth and flashed through the cave, lighting it up. He moved his hands in a semicircular motion, and as he did, the beams of light struck the creatures on the chest, knocking them all down.

They all collapsed, moaning, writhing on the ground, stunned but not dead.

Their leader's eyes opened wide in shock as he looked Thor over carefully.

"It is you," he said, in awe. "The King of the Druids."

Thor stared back calmly.

"I am king of no one," he replied. "I am just a father who wishes to see his son."

The leader stared back at him with a new respect.

"It was told there would come a day when you would arrive," he said. "Of a day when the gates would open. I did not think it would be so soon."

The leader looked Thorgrin over long and hard, as if looking at a living legend.

"To enter those gates," he said, "it is not the price of gold. But the price of life."

Thor stepped forward and nodded solemnly.

"Then that is the price I shall pay," he said.

The leader stared back for a long time, until finally he was satisfied. He nodded, and his dozens of men slowly gained their feet and stepped aside, creating a path for Thor to pass. Dozens more of them rushed forward to the gates, and, all of them grabbing hold of the iron, they yanked on it with all their might.

With a great groaning and creaking noise, the gates of death, protesting, opened wide.

Thor looked up in awe and watched the hundred-foot high gates swing. It was like looking at a portal to another world.

As they held their torches out toward the gate, it was lit up, and standing beyond them, on the other side, Thor saw a man in a long black robe, holding a long staff, wearing a black cloak and hood pulled over his face. He stood near a small boat, which sat at the edge of a bobbing river.

"He will be your shepherd to the land of death," the leader said. "He will take you across the river. On the other side of it lies the ladder down to the center of the world. It is a one-way boat ride."

Thor nodded back gravely, realizing it was permanent, and grateful for the chance.

Thorgrin began to walk, past the leader, past the rows of his creatures lined up, creating a passage for him, and toward the open gates of death, prepared to take the long march alone.

Suddenly, he heard a shuffling of feet all around him, and he turned and was surprised to see all of his brothers standing beside him, looking back solemnly.

"If you are going to the land of the dead," Reece said, "you're going to need some company."

Thor looked back at them, confused; he had never expected them to give up their lives for his sake.

O'Connor nodded.

"If you're not coming back, then neither are we," O'Connor said.

Thor looked into their eyes and saw their seriousness, saw that there would be no changing their minds. They were standing there with him, at his side, brothers in arms, prepared to march through the gates of hell with him.

Thor nodded back, more grateful than he could say. He had found his true brothers. His true family.

As one, they all turned and began to walk, Thor leading the way as they marched through the gates and through the entrance to another world, a world from which, Thor knew, they were never coming back.

CHAPTER THIRTEEN

Alistair stood guard before the vast doors to the royal house of the sick, standing before the building as war raged all around her, determined not to let anyone in to kill Erec. Shouts pierced the air alongside the clang of metal, as the Southern Islanders fought furiously against each other. It had become a civil war. Half the island, led by Erec's brother, Strom, fought the other half, led by Bowyer's men.

As dawn began to break over the hillside, Alistair recalled what an intense night of fighting it had been. The battle had broken out as soon as she had killed Bowyer, and it had not stopped since. All over the Southern Isles, men raged against each other, fighting on foot, on horseback, up and down the steep mountain slopes, killing each other face-to-face, hand to hand, throwing each other off of horses and cliffs, all fighting to see who would hold the crown.

As soon as the fighting broke out, Alistair rounded up two dozen of Erec's most loyal watchmen, and headed with them for the House of the Sick. She knew that no matter where the battle raged, eventually Bowyer's men would attempt to come here to kill Erec, so that they could end the fighting and claim the throne for themselves. She was determined that, in all the chaos that ensued, no matter who won, Erec would not be harmed.

Alistair had watched the fighting from her vantage point here all throughout the night, and had seen thousands of dead bodies piling up, up and down the hillsides, littering the city grounds. It was an island made up of great warriors, and great warriors fought against great warriors, needlessly killing each other. As hour blended into hour during the horrible night, Alistair didn't even know who or what they fought for anymore. The tide of battle was impossible to gauge, as it had been all throughout the night, the tug-of-war going back and forth as one group battled the next.

As dawn broke, Alistair looked up and saw that the cliffs were filled with Bowyer's men and that the battle was now much closer to the city walls, raging just outside of it. Momentum was giving way, and she sensed that soon they would be through the gates, overriding the city. After all, this city was the center of power on the island, and whoever was victorious would want to claim it first, to raise the banner high and proclaim himself the next King.

Alistair looked up and down the mountainside and watched Strom's men, holding their ground, using long pikes, waiting patiently, disciplined, behind rocks. As Bowyer's men charged down on horseback, Strom's men, on foot, jumped up and thrust them up. One at a time, the horses reared and neighed, impaled with pikes. Bowyer's men swung back, but the pikes were too long, the distance too far for the swords to reach.

Horses reared and fell, and men tumbled off them, rolling down the cliffs and rocks.

Alistair watched Strom, out in front of his men, rush forward, grab a man, and throw him off his horse headfirst, sending him falling, shrieking, down the steep mountainside. Yet at the same moment, Strom was kicked in the back of the head by a horse, and he fell onto his side.

A soldier, seeing an opportunity, rushed forward with his sword and swung for Strom's head; Strom whirled out of the way and chopped off the man's legs at the last moment.

The battle raged, the fighting went on and on, brutal, vicious, and Alistair, filled with a sense of foreboding, determined to keep Erec safe, stood her ground, waiting, wanting to join Strom's men, but knowing her place was here, by Erec's side. So far, it was quiet within the city walls. Eerily quiet. Too quiet.

As soon as she thought it, suddenly, that all changed. Alistair heard a great battle shout, and charging around the corner of the house of the sick there poured out hundreds of Bowyer's men, charging right for the doors.

They stopped but feet away, as they saw Alistair there, proudly, unyielding, her dozen watchmen behind her. Alistair knew instantly that they were all well outnumbered by Bowyer's men, and from the smug look on his face, she saw that Bowyer's lead knight, Aknuf, knew it, too.

A thick silence fell over them as Aknuf stepped forward and faced off against Alistair.

"Out of the way, witch," he said. "And I will kill you quickly. Stand there, and it will be slow and painful."

Alistair stood her ground, unwavering.

"You will not pass through these doors," she said firmly. "Unless I am dead at your feet."

"Very well, woman," he replied. "Just remember: you brought this on yourself."

Aknuf raised his sword high, and as he did, her dozen watchmen rushed forward to protect her. They all met in battle but ten yards before her. There arose a great clash of arms, as the watchmen fought valiantly, going blow for blow with Bowyer's men.

But they were vastly outnumbered, and soon Bowyer's men closed in on her. Alistair knew that in but moments they would lose the battle, and she could not stand to see these men die on her watch, protecting her and Erec.

Alistair closed her eyes and raised her palms up high overhead, towards the sky. She used all of her might to summon her power.

Please, God. Let it come to me.

She slowly felt a great power rising up within her, and as she did, a brilliant white light, like a streak of lightning, burst through the dawn sky, came shooting down at her from the clouds high above. She pulled her arms down and aimed her palms at Bowyer's men, and as she did, a great noise erupted as chaos ensued.

Hail the size of rocks began falling from the sky; the sound of ice cracking armor filled the air. Alistair directed the hail to the other side of the battle line, missing her own men and pounding down on Bowyer's men, one man at a time, with such force that it knocked them down, shrieking. It freed up her watchmen, one at a time, who fought back, killing them left and right.

Bowyer's men, terrified, unable to raise their swords, pounded by the ice, turned and ran for the city gates, her watchmen chasing after them.

There came another great battle shout from behind her, and Alistair turned to see Strom pouring into the city with all his men. She looked up and saw the hillsides filled with dead soldiers, heard the trumpet sounding out three times for victory, and she realized Strom had won.

Alistair looked out and saw the hundreds of Bowyer's men, still fleeing from the house of the sick, running for the open city gates. They were trying to escape, surely to regroup on another day, on another field of battle. Alistair was determined that would not be.

Alistair redirected her palm, and as she did, a white light shot forth and the huge iron portcullis, a foot thick, came slamming down at the city gates, stopping Bowyer's men from leaving.

Aknuf turned, trapped with his men, and watched, terrified, as Strom's men closed in.

Strom, sitting proudly on his horse, turned to her, as if to ask for her approval.

Alistair, thinking of Erec, nodded gravely.

With one final battle cry, Strom charged with his men, closing in on the men at the gates from all directions.

Alistair stood there and watched, satisfied, as their shouts arose.

Finally, it was over. Finally, the island was safe. Finally, justice had been done.

*

Alistair stood at Erec's bedside in the dim chamber, watching the morning sunrise, feeling an immense sense of relief. Victory was theirs, the drama was all behind them, and all that remained was for her and Erec to be as they once were, for Erec to rise, to be well again, to be by her side.

Alistair held her hand to his forehead and prayed silently, as she had since the battle had ended.

Please, God. Allow Erec to waken. Allow this all to be over.

Alistair felt a subtle shift in the air, and she watched, elated, as Erec opened his eyes, slowly. His eyes were bright, a bright blue in the early morning, and he smiled as he looked up at her. The color had returned to his face, and he looked more alert than he'd ever had. She could see that he was finally healed, back to himself.

Erec sat up and embraced her, and she leaned forward and rushed into his arms, tears falling from her eyes as she held him tight. It felt so good to be in his arms again, so good to have him back to life.

"Where am I?" he asked. "What has happened?"

"Shhh," she said, smiling, putting a finger to his lips. "All is well now."

He blinked, alarmed, as if remembering.

"Our wedding day," he said. "I was…stabbed. Are you safe? Is the kingdom safe?"

"I am fine, my lord," she answered calmly. "And your kingdom is ready for your ascent."

He hugged her, and she hugged him back, and she wept, not thinking this day would ever come, overwhelmed with joy to have him back at her side. She wanted to tell him everything. How she had sacrificed herself for him. Her imprisonment. How she had almost died. How he had almost died. The battles that had raged. Everything that happened.

But none of that mattered now. All that mattered was that he was alive, safe, that they would be back together again. Words could not explain how she felt. So instead, she held him tight, and let her embrace speak for her.

Their life was just beginning, she knew. And nothing—*nothing*— would ever keep her away from him again.

CHAPTER FOURTEEN

Darius raised his sledgehammer with both hands and brought it down hard, smashing a boulder to bits under the sun of another bright, hot Empire morning. Surrounded by all his friends in the dusty working fields, he felt the sweat on his brow rolling down into his eyes, but he did not bother to wipe it away. Instead he raised his sledgehammer and grunted as he smashed another rock. And another.

Darius relived in his mind, again and again, the events of the day before, images flashing through his head. He was confused and frustrated as he thought of Loti. Why had she reacted the way she had? Was there no part of her that was grateful? How had she managed to turn his heroic acts into something he should be ashamed of? Did she really never want to see him again?

And after the way she'd reacted, did he ever really even want to see her?

Darius set down his hammer and caught his breath, the green dust rising up and settling in his face and hair and nose. He thought also about what he had done, killing those Empire soldiers, drawing upon his powers, and he wondered if the dead men would be found on that remote field. Surely, eventually, they would, even if it took one moon cycle or two. Perhaps when the rains came and washed away that avalanche. What would happen then? Would the Empire then come for retribution, as Loti said? Had he just signed a death sentence for them all?

Or was it possible, buried as deep beneath that avalanche as they were, that they would never be found? That the wild animals, notorious for roaming that area, would eat their corpses before they were discovered?

As Darius picked up his hammer and smashed rock under the watchful eyes of the Empire taskmasters, his thoughts drifted to the arrival of his sister, Sandara, and of the new people she had brought with her. The arrival of those people from the Ring had been a day unlike any other for his village. He thought of Sandara's new people hiding out in the caves, and he wondered if they would all be seen by the Empire. Surely, it was only a matter of time until they were, when conflict with the Empire would be inevitable. Unless they fled beforehand.

But to where?

To Darius's continued frustration, the village elders—indeed, the entire village—seemed to hold firm in their belief that confrontation with the Empire was not inevitable, that life could keep marching on the way it was. Darius saw it differently. He felt that things were changing. Wasn't this a sign from the gods, the arrival of all these warriors from across the sea, who too had cause to fight the Empire? Shouldn't they be harnessed, shouldn't they all fight together, to overthrow Volusia? Wasn't this the gift they'd all been waiting for?

The others didn't see it that way. Instead, they wanted to turn them away, to send them off. They saw it as another reason to keep a low profile in the Empire, to do everything they could to keep their pathetic little lives as steady as they were now.

Darius recalled the last time he had seen Sandara, as she had departed for the Ring. He had not thought he would ever see her again. Seeing her again now had both surprised and inspired him. Sandara had managed to cross the great sea, to survive amongst the Empire army, and to come back. Partly it was because she was a great healer—and yet, in her heart, she was also a warrior. After all, they shared the same father. It made Darius feel that anything was possible. It made him feel that he, too, could one day get out of this place.

Darius thought back warmly to the night before, during the festivities, when he had spent half the night catching up with his sister, talking to her around the fires. He had witnessed firsthand her love for Kendrick, that fine warrior. They had taken an instant liking to each other, each recognizing the warrior spirit in one another, and he seemed to Darius to be a leader of men. Darius had encouraged his big sister to follow her passion, to be with Kendrick, regardless of whatever the elders had to say. He did not understand how she, so fearless in every other part of our life, could be so afraid to declare her love for him, to spur tradition, to spur the taboo of marrying another race. Was she like everyone else here, so afraid of the elders, of others' opinions? Why did it matter so much what they all thought?

Darius blinked sweat from his eyes as he smashed another rock, and another. He could feel the eyes of all of his friends on him on this day. Since the day before, when he had arrived with Loti, he felt the entire village looked upon him differently. They had all watched him run off to bring Loti back, had all witnessed him run off to face the Empire, alone, without fear of consequence. And they had seen him return, with her. He had gained great respect in their eyes.

He also seemed to have gained their skepticism: no one seemed to believe their story, to believe that Loti had gotten lost, that they had merely found each other and walked back. Perhaps they all knew Darius too well. They looked on him with different eyes, as if they knew that something had happened, knew he was holding a great secret. He wanted to tell them, but he knew that he could not. If he did, he would have to explain how he did it, how he, the youngest and smallest of the bunch, the one no one thought would amount to anything, had alone killed three Empire warriors with superior weapons and armor—and a zerta. It would come out that he used his power. And he would be an outcast. They would exile him. As they had, Darius suspected, his father.

"So are you going to tell me?" came a voice.

Darius looked over to see Raj standing beside him, a mischievous smile on his face. Nearby, also looking his way, were Desmond and Luzi, each smashing rock, glancing over at Darius.

"Tell you what?" Darius asked.

"How you did it," Raj said. "Come on. You didn't find Loti wandering alone. You did something. Did you kill the soldiers? Did she?"

Darius looked over and saw the other boys coming over, looking at him, and he could see they all had this question burning in their minds. Darius raised his hammer, took aim at a rock, and smashed it again.

"Come on," Raj said. "I gave you a zerta ride. You owe me."

Darius laughed.

"You didn't give it to me," he replied. "I chose to go with you."

"Okay," Raj conceded, "but tell me all the same. I need a story. I live for stories of valor. And this day is going on way too long."

"The day has barely begun," Luzi said.

"Precisely," Raj said. "Too long. Like every other day."

"Why don't *you* tell us a story of valor?" Luzi said to Raj, seeing that Darius would not reply.

"Me?" Raj replied. "I don't think you shall find one amongst our people."

"You are quite wrong about that," Desmond said. "There are always stories of valor, even amongst the oppressed."

"*Especially* amongst the oppressed," Luzi added.

They all turned to him, his deep, commanding voice filled with confidence.

"Do you have one, then?" Raj pressed, leaning on his hammer, breathing hard.

Desmond raised his hammer and smashed rock, and was silent for so long, Darius was sure he would not reply. They all settled back into the rhythm of smashing rock, when finally Desmond surprised them all by speaking up, looking down and smashing rock all the while.

"My father," Desmond said. "The elders will tell you he died in a mine. That is the story they would like you to believe. To know otherwise would cause too much dissent, foment too much revolution. I will tell you: he died in no mine."

Darius studied Desmond with the others as a heavy silence fell over them, and he could see his furrowed brow, the seriousness in his face, as if he were struggling with something internally.

"And how should you know?" Desmond asked.

"Because I was there," Desmond replied, looking him in the eyes, cold and hard, defiant. With his commanding presence, several other boys began crowding around, too. They all wanted to hear his tale, which commanded attention. The air of truth was ringing out, such a rare thing amongst his villagers.

"One day," Desmond continued, "the taskmaster whipped him too hard. My father snatched the whip from the man's hands and choked him to death with it. I remember watching, being so young, so proud of him.

"When it was done, when we were both standing there looking down at the lifeless body, I asked my father what was next. Was it time to revolt? But he had no answer. I could see it in his eyes: he did not know what was next. He had given in to a moment of passion, a moment of justice, of freedom, and in that moment he had risen above it all. But after that, he did not know what to do. Where does life go from there?"

Desmond paused, smashing several rocks, wiping sweat from his brow, until he continued again.

"That moment passed. Life went on. Within the hour, horns of warning sounded, and I was with my father as he was surrounded by a dozen taskmasters. He had urged me to hide in the woods, but I would not leave his side. Until he smacked me so hard with the whip across my mouth, that finally, I did.

"I hid behind a tree, not far, and I watched it all. The taskmasters...they did not kill him quickly," Desmond said, his voice choked with emotion as he stopped hammering and looked away. "He fought back valiantly. He even managed to whip several of them. He left marks on them which I am sure are still there to this day.

"But he was one man with a big heart and a whip. They were dozens of professional soldiers, with steel weapons, in armor. And they enjoyed to kill."

Desmond shook his head, quiet for several minutes, the boys riveted, all silent, all stopping their work.

"I can still hear my father's screams, to this day," Desmond said. "When I go to sleep at night, I hear them. I see him struggling. In my dreams, I wish I was older, armed, and try to see myself fighting back, killing them all, saving him. But I was too young. There was nothing I could do."

He finally stopped, the work fields completely silent. Finally, he raised a hammer and brought it down with all his might, smashing a large boulder into pieces.

"He died in no mine," he concluded softly. And then he fell silent, going back to work.

Darius's heart was heavy as he contemplated the tale, all the boys quiet now, a somber air over all of them. Raj's smile had long faded, and Darius wondered if that was the tale of valor he'd hoped to hear.

After a long while of smashing rock, Raj came up beside Darius.

"Now it's your turn," Raj said to him quietly, out of earshot of the others. "What happened out there?"

Darius continued smashing rock, shaking his head, silent.

"They changed their mind," Darius insisted. "They let her go."

"And the soldiers who changed their mind," Raj said, a mischievous smile on his face, "would they be back in Volusia now? Or shall we never be seeing them again?"

Darius turned to see Raj smiling back at him knowingly, admiringly.

"It's a long road back to Volusia," Darius said. "Stronger men have been known to get lost themselves."

*

Darius stood in the small dirt field behind his cottage, the click-clacks of his wooden sword filling the air as he attacked the well-worn wooden target. It was a large cross he had made out of layers of bamboo, tied together and stuck into the ground, one which he had been swinging at since the time he could walk. In the dirt, his footprints were well-worn, embedded in the ground before it.

The cross was crooked by now, nearly falling over, but Darius didn't care. It served its purpose. He slashed at it again and again, left and right, ducking an imaginary enemy, spinning around, slashing its stomach. He lunged forward, jabbed, turned his sword sideways and blocked an imaginary blow. In his mind, he saw a great many enemies coming at him, an entire army approaching, and he fought and fought in the sunset, at the end of his day shift, until he was dripping with sweat.

The persistent sounds of his swordplay filled the air, and while his neighbors yelled out to complain, he didn't stop. He didn't care. He would slash away the day's memories, every day's memories, until he was spent with exhaustion.

Darius heard the occasional bark at his feet, and he did not need to look down to know it was Dray, the neighbor's dog, sitting loyally by his side, watching him as he always did, barking and getting excited as Darius struck the target. A medium-size dog with scarlet hair that grew too long, like his master's untamed hair, Dray had unofficially become Darius's dog long ago. He belonged to one of the neighbors, but whoever owned it had stopped feeding it long ago. Darius had encountered Dray whining one day, and had given him one of his scarce meals. Ever since, Darius had had a friend for life. Since that day, they had developed a ritual: Dray watched Darius fight, and Darius ate only half of his dinner, giving the other half to Dray. Dray rewarded him by always seeking out his company, especially when he was at home, sometimes even sleeping in his cottage.

Dray lunged forward and bit the bamboo, playing along with Darius's imagination, snarling and tearing at in imaginary enemy, as if it were a true foe coming for Darius. Darius often wondered what would happen if he faced an enemy with Dray at his side. Like Darius, Dray was not the biggest of the bunch, or the strongest, or the most loved. But he had a great heart, and he was the most loyal animal in the universe. Over the last few moons, he had even taken to sleeping curled up before Darius's door, snarling if Darius's grandfather even dared to approach.

"Are you tired of swinging at sticks?" came a voice.

Darius looked over to see Raj and Desmond standing there, each holding long wooden swords, looking back with a mischievous grin.

Darius stopped, breathing hard, wondering; they lived on the other side of the village and had never come by his cottage before.

"It's time you sparred with *men*," Desmond said, his voice dark, serious. "If you strive to become a warrior, you are going to need to hit targets that hit back."

Darius was surprised and grateful that they had stopped by. They were several classes older than him, much bigger and stronger, and well respected amongst the boys. They had many older, stronger boys to spar with.

"Why would you waste your time on me?" Darius asked.

"Because my sword needs sharpening," Desmond said. "And you look like a good target."

Desmond charged for Darius, and Darius held up his wooden sword and at the last minute, blocked the blow. It was a mighty blow, strong enough to shake his hands and arms, and to send him stumbling back several feet.

Darius, caught off guard, saw Desmond standing there, waiting for him.

Darius raised his sword and lunged forward, slashing down. Desmond blocked it easily. Darius kept swinging, slashing left and right, again and again, and the click-clacks of their wooden swords filled the air. He was thrilled to have a real, moving target, even if he could not overpower the bigger and stronger Desmond.

Dray snarled and barked at Raj and Desmond, running alongside Darius, snapping at Desmond's heels.

"You're quick," Desmond said, between blows. "I will give you that. But you don't use it to your advantage. You're not half as strong as I—and yet you fight as if you're trying to cut through me. You cannot fight a man my size. Fight as if you're *your* size. Be quick and nimble. Not strong and direct."

Darius swung with all his might and Desmond stepped back, and Darius went circling through the air, stumbling forward, landing on the ground.

Darius looked up and saw Desmond standing over him, reaching out, giving him a hand, pulling him up.

"You fight for the kill," Desmond said. "Sometimes you just need to fight to survive. Let your opponent fight for the kill. If you are patient, if you avoid him, and watch him, he will overreach; he will expose himself."

"You'd be surprised at how easy it is to kill a man," said Raj, coming over. "You don't need a strong blow—just a precise one. I believe it's my turn."

Raj raised his sword high, aiming for Darius's head, and Darius spun, raised his sword sideways, and barely blocked the blow. Then Raj leaned back, put his foot in Darius's chest, and shoved him, and Darius stumbled backwards.

Dray barked and barked, snarling at Raj.

"That's not fair," Darius said, indignant. "This is a swordfight!"

"Fair!?" Raj yelled out with derisive laughter. "Tell that to your enemy after he has stabbed you between the legs and you lay dying. This is combat—and in combat all is fair!"

Raj swung his sword again, before Darius was ready, and he knocked the sword from Darius's hands. Raj then dropped to the ground, swung his legs, and kicked out Darius's knees from under him.

Darius, not expecting it, landed hard on his back in a cloud of dust, winded; Raj then pulled a wooden dagger out of nowhere, dropped down, and held it to Darius's throat.

Darius conceded, raising his hands, pinned to the ground.

"Again, unfair!" Darius complained. "You cheated. You pulled a hidden dagger. These are not honorable actions."

Dray rushed forward, snarling, and leaned in close to Raj's face, showing his teeth, close enough to make Raj drop his dagger, raise his hands, and slowly get up.

Raj roared with laughter as he jumped to his feet, grabbed Darius, and pulled him up.

"What is honor?" Raj said. "Honor is what we, the victors, name it to be. When you are dead, there is no honor."

"What is battle without honor?" Darius said.

"He who speaks of honor is he who never lost," Desmond said. "Lose once, lose a leg, an arm, a loved one—and you will think twice of honor next time you face your foe on the field. Surely, he is not thinking of honor. He is thinking of winning. Of life. Whatever the cost."

"You'd be surprised how much a man is willing to throw away—including honor—when he is staring death in the face," Desmond said.

"I would rather die with honor," Darius countered, defiant, "than live in dishonor."

"Wouldn't we all," Desmond said. "Yet what you think and what you do in a moment of life and death do not always match."

Raj stepped forward and shook his head.

"You are young yet," Raj said. "Naïve. What you still don't see is that honor comes in victory. And victory comes in expecting everything. Even dishonorable actions. You can fight with honor if you choose. If you are able. But don't expect your enemy to."

Darius thought about that—when suddenly a strident voice cut through the air, interrupting him.

"DARIUS!" yelled the harsh voice.

Darius turned to see his grandfather standing at the door of his cottage, scowling down at him. "I don't want you with these boys!" he snapped. "Get inside now!"

Darius scowled back.

"These are my friends," Darius said.

"They're trouble," Darius's grandfather replied. "Inside now!"

Darius turned to Raj and Desmond apologetically.

"I'm sorry," Darius said. He felt bad, as he'd truly enjoyed fighting with them. He already felt his skills sharpened from just their small bout, and he wanted to fight again.

"Tomorrow," Raj said, "after training."

"And every day after that," Desmond said. "We are going to make a warrior out of you."

They turned to go, and Darius realized he'd made two close friends in the group for the first time. Older friends, great fighters. He wondered again why they'd taken an interest in him. Was it because of what he'd done for Loti? Or was it something else?

"Darius!" snapped his grandfather.

Darius, Dray at his heels, turned and walked to his grandfather, who stood at the door, scowling. Darius knew he'd face his grandfather's wrath; his grandfather never wanted him sparring at all.

"You should not have been rude," Darius said as he walked through the door. "Those are my friends."

"Those are boys who do not know the cost of war," he retorted. "Boys who embolden each other to revolt. Have you any idea what happens in a revolt? The Empire would kill us. All of us would die. Every last one of us."

Today, Darius, emboldened, was in no mood for his grandfather's fear.

"And what of it?" Darius asked. "What is so wrong with death, when it is from fighting for our lives? Would you call what we have now life? Slaving away all day? Cringing at the hand of the Empire?"

Darius's grandfather smacked him hard across the face.

Darius, shocked, stood there, feeling the sting. It was the first time he had ever struck him.

"Life is sacred," his grandfather said harshly. "That is what you and your boy friends have yet to learn. Your grandparents and mine sacrificed so that we should have life. They put up with slavery so that their children, and their children's children, could have a life of safety. And all of the reckless actions of you teenage boys will undo generations of their work."

Darius glowered, ready to argue, not agreeing with anything he'd said, but his grandfather turned his back and snatched a cauldron of soup and crossed the cottage with it, preparing it before a flame. Something Darius's grandfather said made him think. Something clicked within him, and for some reason he had a sudden burning desire to know.

"My father," Darius said coldly, standing his ground. "Tell me about him."

His grandfather froze, his back to him, holding the pot where he stood.

"You know all there is to know," he said.

"I know nothing," Darius replied firmly. "What happened to him? Why did he leave us?"

Darius's grandfather stood there, his back to him, and remained silent. Darius knew he was on to something.

"Where did he go?" Darius pressed, stepping forward. "Why did he leave?" he asked again.

His grandfather shook his head slowly, as he turned. He looked a thousand years older as he did, saddened.

"Like you, he was rebellious," he said, his voice broken. "He could stand it no more. One day, he made a run for it. And he was never seen again."

Darius stared at his grandfather, and for the first time in his life, he felt certain he was lying.

94

"I don't believe you," Darius said. "You are hiding something. Was my father a warrior? Did he defy the Empire?"

His grandfather stared into space, as if staring into lost years.

"Speak no more of your father."

Darius frowned.

"He is my father and I will speak of him as much as I wish."

Now it was his grandfather's turn to scowl.

"Then you shall not be welcome in my house."

Darius glowered.

"It was my father's house before you."

"And your father is here no longer here, is he?"

Darius studied his grandfather's face, seeing it in a different light for the first time. He could see how different of a man he was from him. They were cut from different cloths, and they would never understand each other.

"My father wouldn't run," Darius insisted. "He wouldn't leave me. He would *never* leave me. He loved me."

As he spoke them, Darius for the first time sensed the truth of his words. He sensed also that there was some great secret that was being hidden from him, that had been hidden from him his whole life.

"He would not abandon me," Darius insisted, desperate for the truth.

His grandfather stepped forward, seething with anger.

"And who are you to think you are so great as to not be abandoned?" Darius's grandfather said sharply. "You are just a boy. Just another boy. Just another slave in a village of slaves. There is nothing special about you. You fancy yourself to be a great warrior. You play with sticks. Your friends play with sticks. The Empire, they play with steel. Real steel. You cannot rise up against them. You never can. You will end up dead like the rest of them. And then where have your precious sticks gotten you?"

Darius frowned, hating his grandfather for the first time, hating everything he was and everything he stood for.

"I might end up dead," Darius said back, his voice steel, "but I'll never end up like you. You are already dead."

Darius turned and began to storm from the cottage—but he stopped at the door, turned, and faced his grandfather one last time.

"I am special," Darius said, wanting his grandfather to hear the words. "I am the son of a great warrior. I am a warrior myself. And one day, you, and the entire world, should know it."

Darius, fed up, unable to withstand another moment, turned and stormed from the cottage.

Darius burst outside into the late afternoon light, no longer wanting to see his grandfather's face, to face his lies. He walked quickly out through the back fields, and looked out at the horizon, at all the slaves still filtering back from a day's work. He studied the horizon, the endless sky, lit up in pinks and purples. His father, he knew, was out there somewhere. He was a great warrior. He had risen above all this.

One day, somehow, he would find him.

CHAPTER FIFTEEN

Gwendolyn sat in the cave with the others, before a fire, staring at the flames here in her new home, and feeling hollowed out. It was late at night, most of the others fast asleep, the cave walls punctuated by their snoring and by the crackle of flames. Nearby sat her brothers Kendrick and Godfrey, their backs to the wall, along with Steffen, his newlywed wife, Arliss, Brandt, Atme, Aberthol, Illepra—still holding the rescued baby—and a half a dozen others. At Gwen's feet lay Krohn, his head curled in her lap, fast asleep. She had fed him well all night, all throughout the festivities, and he looked as if he could sleep a million years. Even he was snoring.

Throughout the rest of the endless cave, going so deeply into the mountainside, were hundreds of people, what remained of the Ring, all spread out, all finally sated from the food and wine. They had all come here, led by the village elders, after the long night of festivities, and had been shown their new home. It was a far cry from what she was used to at King's Court, and yet still, Gwendolyn was grateful. At least they were alive, had a place to stay, to rest and recover.

And yet hanging over her like a dark cloud were those words from the seer at the night's festivities, ringing in her ears. Thorgrin, in the land of the dead. If the seer was true, then that meant he was dead. How? she wondered. Somewhere in his search for Guwayne? Eaten by a sea monster? Blown off course? Caught in a storm? Dying of starvation, as she almost had?

The possibilities were endless, and each anguished her to no end as she contemplated them. Each made her want to curl up and die. And with Thor dead and gone, that meant Guwayne was gone to her forever, too.

Gwen stared into the flames and wondered what she had left to live for. Without Thorgrin, without Guwayne, she had nothing. She hated herself for letting Guwayne go on that fateful day on the Upper

Isles; she hated herself for the decisions she had made that had led her people to this place. Deep down, she knew she was not to blame. She had done the best she could to defend and save her people from the million attacks on her troubled kingdom that had been left to her by her father. And yet still, she blamed herself. It was hard to feel anything but grief.

"My sister," came a voice.

Gwen looked over to see Kendrick sitting beside her, arms crossed over his knees, face reflected by the flames, somber, tired. His eyes were filled with compassion and respect, and he wore the look that he always wore when he wanted to console her.

"Not all seers see clearly," he said. "Perhaps Thorgrin returns for you as we speak. And your child with him."

Gwendolyn wanted to believe his words, but she knew he was just trying to console her. The seer's words still rang in her head with more authority.

She shook her head.

"I wish I could believe it was so," she said. "But this is the night of the dead. The night when the spirits speak the truth."

Gwendolyn sighed as she stared into the flames. She wanted his words to be true. She really did. But she sensed they were just the words of a kind brother trying to console her.

Krohn shifted in her lap, whining softly, as if he sensed her sadness. Gwen reached out and stroked his head and offered him another strip of beef. But Krohn would not take it. Instead, he lay in her lap and whined again.

Kendrick sighed. He spoke again, softly, his voice cracked with exhaustion:

"I had always taken such pride in my lineage," he said. "I had always known myself to be father's firstborn son. The King's first son. The next in line to rule. Not that I cared to rule. Yet I took pride in knowing who I was in the family. I looked at all of you as my little brothers and sisters, as I still do today. Everyone always said how I looked exactly like Father, and indeed I did. I thought I knew my place in the world."

Kendrick took a deep breath.

98

"We were young, just kids, maybe ten or eleven, and one day I came home from sparring with the Legion. I encountered Gareth, younger than me, but already looking for trouble wherever he could find it. He was standing there with Luanda, and the two of them faced me, and Gareth uttered the words that would change my life forever: 'You are not our mother's son.'

"I could not comprehend what he was talking about. I thought it was just another one of his schemes, his imagination run wild, another cruel trick. He enjoyed meanness, after all. But Luanda, who never lied, nodded along with him. 'You don't belong in our family,' she said. 'You are not mother's.' 'You are the son of a whore,' Gareth said. 'You are just a bastard.'

"Luanda had stared at me disapprovingly. I can still see that look in her eyes today. 'I do not wish to see you anymore,' she said. Then she turned and walked off. I do not know who had hurt me more, Gareth or Luanda."

Kendrick sighed, and Gwen could see the pain on his face as he stared into the flames, reliving the scene.

"I confronted Father, and he admitted the truth. At that moment, my world spun. It all fell into place: Father's never speaking of my being King after him. Others being distant from me; the way the staff looked at me. I never really fit in, and from that day onward, I noticed it everywhere. It was as if I were a visitor in my own home. But not family. Not true family. As if I didn't really belong. Do you know what it feels like? To feel like a stranger in your own home?"

Gwen sighed, pained by his story, overwhelmed with compassion for him.

"I'm sorry," she said. "You did not deserve that. You, of all people. I'm sorry I wasn't there to shield you from that. Gareth and Luanda were cruel as children."

"As they were as adults," he added. "You become more of what you are as you age."

Gwendolyn thought about that, and realized there was some truth to it.

Kendrick sighed.

"I don't need sympathy," he said. "That is not why I tell you this story. It was the worst day of my life; I had been told news from which I was certain I would never recover. And yet here I am. I have recovered. Life is incredibly resilient."

Gwen thought about that in the silence, the crackling flames.

Life is incredibly resilient.

"You're stronger than you think," he added, clasping her hand. "You have overcome tremendous things. And you can overcome anything. Even this. Even whatever has happened to Thorgrin and Guwayne."

Gwen looked back at him, tears falling down her cheeks.

"You are a true brother," she said, and turned away, too choked up to say any more. She squeezed his hand, and in silence, she sent him her gratitude.

"There is the irony," she finally said. "You would have been the greatest ruler of them all. A greater ruler than I have been."

Kendrick shook his head.

"I could not lead in the way you have done," he said. "I could not have survived what you have survived. I might be a great warrior. But you are a great leader. That is something else entirely. Look over there, at the fruit of your labors."

Gwen turned and followed his gaze, and saw the baby girl in Illepra's arms close by, the girl she had rescued on the Upper Isles.

"You snatched that girl from the dragons' breath," Kendrick said. "I'll never forget how brave you were. You, the only one of all of us willing to leave our hiding spot from underneath the earth, to run out there all alone and save that child. She is alive because of you. Because of your valor."

"I was not in my right mind," Gwen said.

"Oh yes you were," he said. "It is precisely moments of crisis that bring out who we are. And that is you."

Gwen, touched by Kendrick's words, looked at the sleeping infant, and she wondered.

"Who do you think her parents were?" she asked.

Kendrick shook her head.

100

"You are her parents now," he said. "You are her whole world. If nothing else, you have saved this child. You have saved this one life. That is more than most people do in a lifetime."

Gwen stared into the flames, pondering. Maybe he was right. Maybe she shouldn't be so hard on herself. After all, another queen might have given in a long time ago. She, at least, had managed to rescue some of her people, had managed to go on. To survive.

Gwen thought of her father, of what he would have done, what he would have wanted. He was a hard man to know. Would he be proud of her? Would he have done things differently?

It made Gwen think of her ancestors, and she reached down, hoisted the ancient, heavy, leather-bound book sitting by her side and placed it on her lap. It was as thick as ten books, and three times the size, and the weight of it was disarming. She was surprised Aberthol had managed to salvage it from the House of Scholars, to bring it all this way. She loved him for it. She remembered it fondly from her years of study, and having it here now with her was like reuniting with an old friend.

"What is it?" Kendrick asked, looking over.

She reached over, struggling with the weight of it, and placed it in his lap. He looked down in wonder.

"*The History of the Empire, in Seven Parts*," she said. "It is one of the few books we salvaged, one of the few precious artifacts that remains of our homeland."

He looked at her in awe.

"Have you read it all?" he asked.

"Not all of it," she admitted. "And it was when I was younger."

Gwen turned and called out: "Aberthol!"

Aberthol, dozing, opened his eyes, his back against the cave wall.

"Come here," she said.

He got up lazily, groaning, and made his way over to the fire, sitting down between them, joining them.

"Yes, my lady?" he asked.

"Tell us," she said. "All that talk of a second Ring—is it true?"

His eyes followed hers and they lit up as they focused on the volume in Kendrick's lap.

He sighed.

"It is alluded to many times, for certain," he said slowly, clearing his throat, his voice hoarse. "Whether it's true or not is another thing entire. To understand it, one must put it into context. It was a different time, before our father's time. A time when the Ring and the Empire were one. Before even the Canyon. Such a place might exist; it has certainly been hinted at for centuries. If so, it would certainly be well hidden, deep within the Empire. And who knows if it ever existed, if it still survives this day? It might be just a ruin, a ghost of the past."

Aberthol's arrival brought the attention of the others, all of whom, Gwen realized now, had been awake, like she, unable to sleep. They all seemed to welcome a distraction, and they all rose and ambled over—Steffen, Brandt, Atme, and Godfrey—who seemed a bit drunk. They all joined them beside the fire, Godfrey with a sack of spirits in hand, taking a long swig.

"We cannot go chasing ghosts of the past, my lady," Aberthol said. "We must find a way to return to our homeland, to the Ring."

"The Ring is no more, old man," Brandt said.

"To return there is to return to death," Atme said. "Even if we could rebuild, even if we could start again, have you forgotten Romulus's million men?"

"If we remain here, they will find us," Steffen said. "We cannot stay here in this cave forever. This is no home."

"No," Gwendolyn said. "But we can recover here. Look around: our people are still weak, some still sick. They need time to mourn. Time to eat and drink and sleep. This cave will suit us just fine for now."

"And then what, my lady?" Godfrey asked.

Gwen stared into the flames, that very same question swimming in her head. And then what? She saw all their eyes looking to her hopefully, as if she were their god, some long-lost messiah leading a people to salvation. She desperately wanted to give them the right answer, a definitive, confident answer that would set them all at ease.

But she did not know it herself. All she knew was that she desperately wanted Thorgrin and Guwayne back by her side. She wanted to return home, to the Ring. She wanted her father back, here with her, as he was in days of old.

But all that, she knew, was gone. That was her old life. And she needed to imagine a new one.

"I don't know," she finally answered, honestly. "Time, and only time, will tell."

CHAPTER SIXTEEN

Thor sat in the small vessel with his Legion brothers, as the man in the cloak and hood silently rowed them across the phosphorus waters, the only sound that of the dripping water echoing off the cave walls. Down below, Thor watched the murky waters change colors, from a glowing green to an aqua blue, and saw something swirling beneath the surface, he was not sure what, teeming as if it were alive with creatures. Before them, the air swirled with mist, scarlet, thick, drifting in and out. With each gentle splash of the water, their boat glided deeper and deeper into the cave, toward the blackness on the other side. Thor felt a finality with each row, felt as if he were entering another realm, never to turn back. As long as Guwayne was up ahead, he would venture anywhere.

Thor could feel the anxiety and tension amongst all his brothers, all of them silent, one hand clutching the edge of the boat, the other on their weapons. They had ventured to the ends of the earth together, but never into a realm like this. He could sense their fear. They could battle anything—but could they battle death?

The rowing finally stopped, and their boat continued to glide, all of them silent, until it came to a stop on the far shore with a gentle bump. Thor looked out and saw a small strip of black rock, perhaps twenty feet wide, and beyond that, a narrow footbridge, leading across a great divide, inside of which swirled the mist, even thicker here.

Thor turned and looked at the man, who kept his head down, his cloak covering his face. Thor could not see his face, and wondered what sort of creature lurked behind it.

"The path to death lies before you," the man said, his voice dark, ancient. "Cross the Canyon of Blood, and if you dare to enter, knock three times on the Gates of Death. They will open for you—once. And they will never open for you again."

Thor felt a sense of apprehension, all of his friends looking to him, all pale. He knew it was now or never.

Thor took the step off the vessel and onto the black rock, and his friends followed.

The boat pushed off, the riverkeeper returning from where he'd come, and as he did, he called out for the last time: "If you pass through those gates, beware: our sense of time here is not as yours. A few steps can last many moons."

With that, the man rowed one last time, and disappeared into the blackness.

Thor and his brothers exchanged a worried look.

Thor looked out and could see a footbridge in the mist. It looked precarious, a narrow bridge of rotting wooden planks, leading across a great abyss, perhaps fifty feet. All around it hung a swirling red mist, reflecting some light source far below. Thor did not want to know what lay at the bottom.

Conven stepped forward to go first, but Thor held out a hand.

"You are brave," Thorgrin said, "but I will go first. The bridge might give. And if it does, I shall go down alone."

"I do not fear death," Conven said, looking at him with hollowed eyes.

"Nor do I," Thor said, meaning it.

Conven nodded, seeing the seriousness on Thor's face, and as the others watched, Thor took the first step onto the narrow footbridge, only a few feet wide, with no handrails. It would be a balancing act.

Thor hesitated, as he could feel the wood wobbling beneath his feet. He took another step, then another, trying to keep his eyes fixed before him, and not on the drop below.

He felt the wood shake and he knew that, one by one, his Legion brothers were following behind him.

As he crossed the bridge, the hairs rose on Thor's neck as he began to hear the awful sound of planks cracking.

He turned and saw that the last person, O'Connor, was walking quickly, and with every step he took, the planks, one at a time, fell behind him, hurling down into the abyss. With each step they took more planks fell. It was a one-way bridge, a bridge that would never appear again. Somehow, the bridge magically stayed stable, and they were continue to cross, each step erasing another plank forever.

Thor knew there was no turning back. Ever.

Thor stepped onto the black rock on the far side of the canyon, and he looked up to see himself standing before a massive arched entrance, carved out of black rock: the entrance rose a hundred feet high, and it was blocked by huge gates, the largest iron gates Thor had ever seen, putting even the other ones to shame.

Before it stood two creatures, trolls, perhaps, twice the size of Thor, wearing black hoods and cloaks, scowling back, their faces disfigured. Each held a long, scarlet trident, with black shafts and short silver spikes, pointing straight up to the sky.

Thor looked up and saw the iron knocker, as large as he, in the center of the gates, and he knew what he had to do.

He stepped forward and grabbed the knocker.

The trolls stood there silently, staring out, as if Thor and his brothers were not even there.

With all his might, Thor pulled on the knocker. As he struggled, his brothers rushed forward and grabbed it, helping him. Together, with all their might, they all managed to pull it back, this knocker on the gates of death.

Finally, they could pull it back no longer, and they all let go and sent it flying forward. It crashed into the metal, and the reverberation nearly knocked them all off their feet.

They all did it again.

And again.

The ground trembled beneath them, Thor's ears ringing with the noise, his hands shaking from the vibration. But he had knocked three times, as instructed, and now all he had to do was wait.

Slowly, there came a tremendous groaning noise, and the massive gates began to open inward, a few inches at a time, until finally, they opened the entire way.

Thor saw, lying before them, a massive cave lit by sporadic torches, filled with the sound of a million screeching bats. The entrance to the land of death. A threshold beyond which he could never return.

Thinking only of Guwayne, Thor took a fateful step forward, across the threshold.

Then another.

He stood inside, and beside him, his brothers appeared, one by one, until he heard a great groan and the massive doors slowly, definitively, slammed shut behind them.

As it echoed and echoed, and as he looked before him at the endless tunnel leading into the earth, he knew he would never return to the land of the living again.

CHAPTER SEVENTEEN

Alistair stood beside Erec, holding his hand, the two of them standing on the highest plateau of the Southern Isles, looking out together at the dazzling vista, at the morning sun spreading out over the isles. Alistair was elated to have Erec back, on the road to healing, and to be standing by his side again. Erec was finally like his old self, clutching her hand with the strength of the warrior she once knew.

As Alistair stood there, greeting another day with him, all the chaos and bloodshed behind them, she felt her own life being restored to her again, and felt so grateful to God for answering her prayers.

The two of them stood there, looking out, and as Alistair surveyed the landscape of her new home, this home she had already come to love, she could already see all the rebuilding taking place, up and down the isles. Like she and Erec, this entire nation was picking up the pieces, getting ready to rebuild, to start again. In the distance, Alistair could hear the soft, soothing noise of distant chisels, hammering away, rebuilding.

"The hammers and chisels never cease," Erec said, "and yet there remains much to do."

The land was in ruins, destroyed from the civil war. But with the men finally united again under Erec's rule, there was now a joy, a purpose in the air, and they all set about rebuilding with alacrity, as one. Houses were already beginning to rise again, as bodies were dragged from the streets, buried in the hills, and bells were tolled to commemorate the losses. Alistair could hear them even now, distant, ringing from one village to the next.

It was a peaceful air, a calm after the storm.

"You saved my life," Erec said. "Don't think I don't know that. It is a very sacred thing. Our lives are bound. Mine to yours, and yours to mine. Until the day I die, I shall owe you."

Alistair smiled and squeezed his hand.

"You are back to life," she replied. "That's payment enough."

He draped an arm around her shoulder and Alistair leaned into him. She looked out, overwhelmed with the beauty of this place, the sun shining off of everything, the beauty of her future before her. She and Erec would wed soon. They would have a child. She would rule this magnificent place with him.

Her dreams were finally coming true. It was time to start again.

ONE MOON LATER

CHAPTER EIGHTEEN

Gwen, slumped against the wall of the cave near its entrance, heard the exotic birds tweeting, and she opened her eyes to look out at the breaking dawn of yet another day here in the Empire. She had been awake most of the night, unable to sleep yet again, staring most of the night into the flames of a dying fire, beset with grief. Another day on this earth without Thorgrin. Without Guwayne.

Gwen looked out on yet another day here in this Empire, the arid landscape desert landscape spread out below, and she could hardly believe an entire moon had passed. And still no sign of Thorgrin, of Guwayne. Each day she had woken up expecting them to arrive here, knowing with all her heart that they would. After all, how could they not? Thorgrin was her husband. Guwayne her child. There was no way they could stay away from her for long. It was all just one long nightmare waiting to be over.

And yet each day she had awoken, and they had never arrived, and no news had arrived. Now that an entire moon cycle had passed, the reality of it was starting to sink in. Gwen was finally beginning to realize that they might not ever come back to her.

The realization made her feel crushed, hollowed out, lower than she'd ever had in her life. Perhaps that seer had been right: perhaps Thorgrin had truly gone into the land of the dead. And perhaps her baby would never return.

Gwen had tried desperately to rouse Argon during the past moon cycle, and the few times that she had, he had spoken weakly, barely conscious, and had been unable to give her any insight into their whereabouts. It all felt increasingly foreboding to her.

Gwen had sat inside this cave day after day, depressed, frozen with immobility, with indecision. She was a Queen, she knew, but now she found herself unable to make choices even for the smallest things. Each day, Kendrick and Aberthol and Steffen and Godfrey had come to her with the myriad of small things her people in exile needed—and she been unable to make even the smallest decision. She was a Queen, she knew, frozen by grief. Frozen in depression.

111

Gwendolyn looked around and saw her people lying about, scattered by the embers, most asleep, and the few who were awake, staring hopelessly into the flames. Most had wine sacks in their hands, empty from another long night of drinking. She could see in their eyes what they were thinking. They were thinking of home. Of the Ring. Possibly of family and friends lost or killed along the way. They were thinking of how much they had given up, how much they had lost. Of how they were all living like moles here, hiding, wasting away in this cave, not really living at all.

Gwen knew it was better than the alternative: being captured by the Empire and taken as slaves. At least they were alive, and safe.

Gwen kicked the embers with her boot and watched the sparks. She could not imagine her life had come to this. It seemed like only yesterday she was in King's Court, in the most beautiful castle, in the most abundant landscape, preparing for her wedding with her most devoted husband. Holding her baby. Everything had been perfect in the universe, and she hadn't appreciated it. Everything had seemed indestructible.

Now here she was, stripped of her husband and her son, night after night staring into flames in a lost land.

Gwen snapped out of it as she heard a sudden scream, the sound of a woman crying out, followed by hurried footsteps coming from deep inside the massive cave. Gwen turned and peered into the cave, and there suddenly appeared, in the predawn light, a girl, perhaps Gwen's age, stumbling toward her, half dressed, her shirt torn. She had a frantic look in her eye, and she was weeping as she ran toward Gwen and threw herself down at her feet, clutching her ankles in hysterics.

"My lady!" she cried out. "Please, you must do something! You must help me!"

Gwendolyn stared at her, pulled from her reverie, wondering what could have put the girl in such a state.

The girl sobbed, and Gwen placed a reassuring hand on her shoulder.

"Tell me what happened," she said, her voice compassionate, queenly. It carried a strength she had not heard in a while. Caring for someone else made her forget her own troubles.

"I was accosted, my lady!" the girl yelled. "He came upon me in the cave. In the black of night. While I was sleeping. He attacked me!"

She wept.

"Justice must be done!" she cried out. "Whether we are in the Ring or not, justice must be done!"

She sobbed at Gwen's feet, and Kendrick, Godfrey, Brandt, Atme, Aberthol, and several others roused, coming over, their boots crunching on the gravel.

Gwendolyn looked down at the girl and raised her to her feet and hugged her, her heart breaking. Gwen could not help but feel that somehow this was all her fault. Her people had become too restless here in this cave, with nothing to do but sit here day after day in the blackness, drinking. Order was beginning to fall apart, chaos was beginning to rule. Gwendolyn hated herself for this girl's suffering.

"His name?" Gwen demanded. "What was his name?" she asked, remembering her own attack at the hand of McCloud and feeling a new indignation rising within her.

"It was Baylor, my lady," she said.

Baylor. The name struck a nerve in Gwendolyn. Baylor was one of the survivors of the Ring, a minor captain in one of the King's guards, who had survived, unfortunately, with the others here in exile. He had been a rabble-rouser from the start, constantly expressing dissatisfaction with the Queen's rule, perpetually drunk and instigating others. She should have known trouble was coming from him.

Gwendolyn held the girl's face in her palm, and made her look in the eyes.

"I promise you justice shall be done. Do you hear me? Justice shall be yours."

The girl finally began to calm, nodding through her tears.

Gwendolyn looked over to see Kendrick nodding back at her in understanding. On her other side stood Godfrey, drunk, wobbly, but standing there by her side in solidarity.

There came from the far side of the cave a sudden shuffling of feet, followed by a low, chaotic murmur, and Gwendolyn stood with the others and peered into the blackness of the cave, dimly lit by sporadic fires. The shuffling grew louder, and finally she spotted Baylor marching toward her, leading an unruly mob of men. He was clearly drunk, slovenly, unshaven, a portly man in his fifties, with a wild beard, a balding head, and scowling eyes.

He didn't concern Gwendolyn; what concerned her were the hundreds of men marching behind men, all with a wild, cooped-up look to their faces.

"Nor shall we stand it one more day!" Baylor yelled out, and there came a cheer behind him. They all marched threateningly toward the entrance of the cave, toward Gwendolyn, and as they did, all around Gwendolyn her circle loyal to her got to their feet, including Brandt and Atme, and stood by her side.

Gwen stood her ground, blocking them, knowing she could not allow them to leave. Baylor came to a stop ten feet away from her, glaring back at her.

Gwendolyn looked over to see Kendrick, Steffen, and the others by her side, and took comfort in their presence. At her feet, she looked down and saw Krohn standing beside her, hairs standing on end as he faced the mob.

"Out of my way, girl!" Baylor yelled to Gwendolyn.

Gwendolyn merely shook her head, standing in place, not about to give in.

Krohn snarled back at the man, and the man looked down, nervous.

"And where do you plan to go with these men?" she asked.

"We plan to go outside, into daylight, to live as free men, not as refugees hiding in a cave!"

There rose up another great cheer behind him, and Gwen realized she was facing a full-fledged revolt. She realized she had allowed herself to be out of it for too long, to drown in her own sorrows, and she had not been perceptive enough of all that had been going on around her. She had allowed her people to become restless for far too long—and for a queen, restlessness was a very dangerous thing.

114

Gwen blamed herself. This last moon cycle, as they'd recovered, there had been day after day of her indecision, of lack of direction.

"And then where would you go?" Gwen asked calmly.

"Anywhere but here!"

Another cheer.

"We will not live as captives or as slaves!" came another shout, followed by a cheer.

"We will go out and buy ships, and sail back home!" Baylor yelled, to another cheer.

Gwendolyn shook her head, realizing how misguided they were.

"If you leave this cave in daylight," she said, "not only will you all get spotted and killed, but you will get all of us killed, too. Even if by some miracle you reached the shore and bought a ship, you would get killed before you even set sail. You would never make it out of the harbor."

"It beats rotting to death in here!" Baylor yelled.

The crowd cheered.

Baylor stepped forward, but Gwen sidestepped and blocked his path.

"I am sorry," she said, "but you are not leaving this cave." She raised her voice, and for the first time in weeks, assumed a Queenly tone: "None of you are."

Kendrick, Steffen, Brandt, Atme, and Godfrey all drew their swords beside her, and a tense silence fell over the group.

"I am not going to tell you to get out of my way again, woman," Baylor seethed, scowling at Gwendolyn.

"You will do as the Queen commands," Kendrick said, stepping forward, "whatever that command should be."

"She has not commanded us a thing!" Baylor boomed out. "She sits here, frozen, day after day, while we all rot!"

There came a cheer.

"She is no Queen to us anymore!" Baylor continued.

Another cheer.

"*You* should have been King, like your father!" Baylor yelled to Kendrick. "But you stepped aside and let a girl take it for you. It's too late for you now. I'm leading this group—and I'm telling you to get out of our way, or we'll kill you, too!"

There arose yet another cheer, and Baylor began to step forward, reaching out to shove Gwen out of the way.

Krohn snarled, and Gwen could see him about to lunge forward and bite the man.

But first Gwendolyn reacted; she wanted to kill the man herself.

Gwen reached over, turned her wrist, grabbed the long sword from Kendrick's second scabbard, and drew it. In the same motion, she stepped forward and held the tip to Baylor's throat.

The cave fell deathly silent as they stood there, Gwen holding the tip to Baylor's throat, he looking down at it, nervous.

"You're not going anywhere," Gwendolyn said firmly.

The cave was as tense as it had ever been, as Gwen felt all eyes looking to her.

"You are not going anywhere," she added, "because I am your Queen and I command it. Those are *my* people that you are trying to lead. They are *mine* to command, not yours. You will not step outside this cave. You will not go anywhere before answering for your crimes."

"What crimes?" Baylor yelled.

"You've attacked this girl," Gwen said, nodding toward the girl still weeping by her feet.

Baylor frowned.

"I shall take anyone I choose," he said. "I might even take you. Now lower that sword and get out of my way, girl, or die here with all your men."

"Yes, I am a girl," Gwen said steadily, her voice steel. "And my father was a King—and his father before him. I come from a long line of warriors, and I assure you my blood is the same as theirs. You, on the other hand, are a scoundrel and a rapist. I *will* stop you because I *am* your Queen—and justice will be done by my hand."

Gwendolyn reached back, and in one quick motion, she plunged the sword through Baylor's heart.

His eyes bulged open and suddenly, he dropped to his knees before her, and fell face first on the ground. As he did, Krohn pounced on him, snarling, tearing open his throat.

Gwendolyn stood there, holding the bloody sword, feeling shocked. Yet she also, for the first time in weeks, felt like a Queen again.

"Anyone who steps past me shall be killed on the spot. You will stay inside because I command it. Because I am your Queen."

The mob looked to her, stunned, not knowing what to do.

Slowly, one by one, they turned and began to filter their way back into the cave. Gwen stood there, holding the sword out in front of her. She was trembling inside, but refused to show it.

Steffen, holding his sword, came up beside her.

"I'm glad to see my Queen back, my lady," he said.

Gwen looked at them all, all those in her inner circle—Kendrick, Brandt, Atme, Godfrey, Aberthol, and the rest—and she could see the new respect in their eyes. And something else: relief.

She looked at them all, filled with a fresh determination. She was determined to go—for their sake. It was time to pick up the pieces. It was time to leave behind her sorrows. It was time to lead.

"They are right about one thing," Gwen said. "It is time to make a decision. It is time to move on."

They all looked at her with silent expectation, all, she could see, waiting to be led.

"Tomorrow," she said, "we march. Live or die, it is time to move on. To find a new home. A real home. Live or die," she said, looking them all in the eyes, "we are going to find the Second Ring."

CHAPTER NINETEEN

Alistair opened her eyes slowly, feeling a deep sense of peace as she lay in Erec's arms in the kingly four-poster bed, on silk sheets, atop a pile of silk pillows, in the newly reconstructed King's chambers. Dawn was breaking slowly over the Southern Isles, visible through their open air bedroom, and birds were already chirping on this temperate day, soft ocean breezes rolling through the window. Alistair could smell the fragrance of all the fruit trees blossoming.

It was another divine day here on the Southern Isles, another day in Erec's arms, the two of them finally happy together, having all the time in the world to spend with each other, and never tiring of each other's company. As she lay there in his arms, his body warm, Alistair thanked the gods for how lucky she was to have finally found peace and contentment in her life. For once, the woes of the world were not intruding on their relationship. She had been given a respite in the endless chaos of her life.

Erec slowly woke, sensing she was awake, as he always did, and he looked at her and smiled. His light blue eyes were shining in the morning sun, and she could feel his love as he stared at her.

"Before the dawn, my love?" he said.

She smiled.

"I am excited," she said. "I am thinking of my dress."

He smiled.

"Our wedding is a week off still, my love," he said. "Try not to weary yourself."

They kissed, and they held it for a long time. Alistair laid her head on his chest.

She could already hear the distant sound of the workers outside her window, already hard at work before the sun rose for the preparations for their wedding to come. The entire island was abuzz with activity. It had given them something to focus on, to be joyous about, at the time they needed it the most. It had given them all something to rally around, to shake off the gloom of the civil war that had happened one moon cycle ago. Now, finally, they could all be united under Erec's kingship. And by their love for Alistair.

Excited, Alistair rose from bed, threw on her robe, and drifted out to the balcony. She stood there, looking out on it all, reveling in it, and enjoyed watching all the preparations, all the banquets being laid out, dish after dish already being rolled out in preparation. Endless rows of flowers were being set and shaped, casks of ail put into place, and the tournament grounds set up. All with a week still to go.

Erec came up beside her, draping an arm around her waist.

"I never thought this day would come," Alistair said.

"Are you sad your family will not be here?" he asked. "Thorgrin?"

Alistair sighed. She had thought about that many times.

"Of course, I would like them all here, Thorgrin, Gwendolyn, and all those we love from King's Court. Perhaps, though, one day we can have a second wedding, in the Ring, in King's Court."

Erec smiled.

"I would like that," he replied. "Very much. In fact, after our wedding, why don't we return? Visit the Ring?"

Alistair's eyes widened.

"Really?" she asked.

"Why not?" he said. "We rushed here to see my father before his death. Now that he is gone, I see no reason why we cannot visit our homeland. We can have a second wedding. King's Court would be thrilled to host us."

Alistair laughed at the idea.

"I can't think of anything finer," she said, "than to be married to you twice."

She leaned over and they kissed again, and Alistair felt so at peace in the world. She was finally exactly where she wanted to be. She loved this place with all her heart, loved Erec even more, could not wait to have Erec's children here, to build a life here. It felt like home to her. For the first time in her life, she felt as if she had really found her home.

There came a sudden bang on the door, the familiar knock of their steward, two short quick knocks, and Erec turned and hurried over to the thick, oak door, opening it.

In marched Erec's chief steward, bowing quickly, looking frazzled.

"Your grace," he said.

Erec laughed.

"It's too early in the morning to be harried," Erec said. "You must learn to pace yourself."

The steward shook his head.

"Too many matters of court pressing, I'm afraid," he replied.

Entering behind him was Alistair's lady in waiting, a kind, portly woman in her fifties.

"Your grace," she said, then turned to Alistair. "My Queen."

"Forgive me, your grace," the steward said, "but there are many pressing matters of court to attend to."

"And what matters can be so pressing before the sun has even risen?" Erec asked.

"Well, let us see," the steward said, checking a scroll. "There are matters of the treasury. Matters of the wedding preparations; matters of the reconstruction; matters of the training grounds; matters of our soldiers and armor and weaponry and supplies; matters of ports; of broken ships; matters of agriculture; matters of…"

Erec put up a hand.

"I shall come," he said. "But I shall not sit in another meeting past midday. I want to get out and plan the Royal Hunt."

"Very well, your grace," the steward said, bowing.

"My lady," Alistair's attendant said, coming up beside her, "there are many queenly matters for you, as well. There are new designs for you to review of all the new buildings and orchards; there are wedding dressed to be examined; there are matters of entertainment—"

Alistair raised a hand.

"Whatever you need," she said, bracing herself for another long day of court matters.

Erec waved them both off.

"Please leave us," he said. "Let us get dressed and we will follow."

They both bowed and hurried from the room, and Erec turned to Alistair with an apologetic smile.

"I'm sorry, my lady," he said. "The days come upon us too quickly."

Alistair leaned in and kissed him, and as Erec turned to get dressed, Alistair turned the opposite way and drifted back out onto the balcony. She stood there alone, at the open-air arched stone entrance, looking out over the island. Standing here, looking down, it was even more beautiful, more perfect, the fresh breeze caressing her face.

I love this place, she thought. *With all my heart, I really do. Please, God, never take it away from me.*

*

"But how do I know he's *genuine*?" came the question.

Alistair turned and saw Dauphine sitting beside her, asking the same question for the third time, as Alistair stood there, arms out, getting fitted for her wedding dress. Attending her were all her ladies-in-waiting, Dauphine and her mother-in-law-to-be among them, getting outfitted in their own dresses as they joined her on this joyous occasion. They all stood on a marble plaza, high up on a plateau overlooking the countryside, all the girls giggling, happy.

"Alistair?"

As Alistair looked back at Dauphine, lost in thought, she marveled at how much their relationship had changed. Every day over the last moon cycle, Dauphine had sought out her company, had nearly clung to her side, having become more than a sister-in-law-to-be: she was now also a best friend. Dauphine confided everything in her, seeing her, clearly, as the sister she'd never had, and oddly enough, Dauphine was now even closer to Alistair than she had been to Erec. They had become nearly inseparable over the last moon, and Alistair marveled over the twists and turns of life. She could not help but remember back to when she had first arrived on the islands, and

121

Dauphine would not even look at her. Now, she not only had Dauphine's respect, she had her love.

"You never answered me!" Dauphine said.

"I'm sorry," Alistair said, snapping out of it. "What was the question?"

Dauphine sighed in exasperation. "Weddings really do make brides air-headed! I'll ask again: how do I know if he's *genuine*?"

Alistair remembered now. Dauphine had been going on about her new suitor, a famed knight from the lower regions of the Southern Isles, who had been wooing her intensely the entire past moon cycle.

"Last night, he took me on a boat ride beneath the moonlight," Dauphine said. "He professes his love for me daily. And now he asks for my hand in marriage."

"And why shouldn't he?" her mother said.

Dauphine sighed.

"Why shouldn't he?" she repeated. "It has hardly been one moon cycle!"

"Any honorable men would not need more than one moon cycle to know if he loves you," her mother said.

Dauphine turned to Alistair.

"*Please*," she implored. "Tell me."

Alistair examined her, seeing how in love Dauphine was.

"Do you feel that he loves you?" Alistair asked.

Dauphine nodded, her eyes aglow.

"With my entire heart."

"And do you love him back?"

Dauphine nodded, tears in her eyes.

"More than I can say."

"Well then, you have answered it yourself. You have a great blessing."

"But isn't it all too soon?" she asked. "How do I know if he's genuine?"

Alistair thought it over carefully.

"When the time comes you won't need to ask the question," she said. "You will know."

"And will you accept his proposal?" her mother asked sharply.

Dauphine reddened and looked down.

"I...don't know yet," she replied.

Finally, Dauphine fell silent, lost in her own thoughts, and Alistair looked out at the countryside, enjoying the views of the vineyards and orchards spread out amongst the cliffs, the distant glimmer of the sparkling ocean. She could not get enough of this place. She felt her attendants wrapping the lace on her wrists and arms, fitting her perfectly, and she was getting more and more excited for the big day.

A sudden cool breeze wisped by, and as Alistair looked out at the horizon, she noticed a darkening of clouds hiding the brilliant sun, a shade passing over all of them, before the sun revealed itself again. Alistair didn't know why, but in that moment, she felt something dark, a premonition, almost a vision. It had to do with her brother. Thorgrin. She suddenly felt him in a very, very dark place. And the feeling chilled her bones.

"Alistair?" Dauphine and asked. "What's wrong?"

Alistair, still staring out at the horizon, shook her head quickly.

"It is nothing," she said. "Nothing at all."

But Alistair could not stop watching the horizon. She sensed danger. She caught her breath, feeling numb with terror, as she sensed dark things on the horizon, and as she sensed her brother, Thorgrin, entering a land of death.

CHAPTER TWENTY

Loti's heart swirled with mixed emotions as she labored in the fields with the others, using her long wooden rake to break up rocks and soil, preparing the Empire fields for planting. It was a monotonous and tedious exercise, one she had done nearly every day of her life, hoisting the long wooden rake high, the shackles around her wrists preventing her from using it as a weapon, and scraping the endless waste of the desert. As she brought it down low, the metal cut into her wrists, scarring them, as they had for years. She had learned to ignore the pain.

But that was not what pained her on this day; as she dragged her rake along the earth, she thought not of her shackles, her scars—but of Darius. She felt awful for having brushed him off the way she had, for not having been more grateful to him for saving her life. An entire moon cycle had passed and finally the shock of it over, she'd had time to process it all. She still could not believe what had happened with the taskmasters, how Darius had saved her from a life of certain hell and slavery and possibly even death. She owed him her life—more than her life. And she had responded with cold indifference.

Yet at the same time, she had been overwhelmed, unsure how to react. She had never seen anyone use a magic power before, and it stunned her to see Darius use it. Her entire life she had been taught by her parents and elders to view magic as witchery, something to be condemned in the strongest possible terms, the only real taboo in their village. It was magic, she had been told, that had led to doom for her people to begin with. And to see Darius use it—well, she did not know how to react. She had reacted impulsively, in a way her parents would have wanted her to.

But now, as she brought the wooden rake down again and again, dragging it into the dirt, she felt terrible for what she had done. She wanted to run to Darius, to apologize to him, to be with him, this boy who had overtaken her heart more than she could have imagined. She had always suspected there was something different about him, though she wasn't sure what it was. He was indeed different from all the others, with his great ability. But even more so, with his big heart. His fearlessness.

Now she had thrown it all away. All because she was afraid, afraid of the condemnation she would receive from her parents and the elders if she were caught with him, if they discovered his power. She was afraid they would not understand; she was not sure she understood herself.

She had also been afraid during this last moon cycle that any day the Empire would arrive and round her and Darius up for having killed those men; each day she expected the bodies to be discovered. Yet that day never came. Perhaps they were so deeply buried beneath that avalanche after all that they would never be found. And as he fear was beginning to dissipate, Loti was beginning to realize, even more, that she had nothing to be afraid of, that perhaps she could even be with Darius—it he would have her back. Perhaps it was already too late.

Loti paused for a moment, took a break as she wiped the back of her brow, looked all about her and saw all the other girls stationed with her on this field, all laboring away. Beside her, she was most happy to see, was her brother, Loc. The taskmasters had added insult to injury by assigning Loc out here in the fields with the girls, and her heart went out to him. Then again, his entire life he had been slighted, all because of his injury, his one leg shorter than the other, and one arm misshaped and shorter than the other. He was even treated as an outcast in his own family, a house full of warriors, where his mother and father looked down upon him as if he did not even exist.

But Loti loved Loc with all her heart, and she always had. She was determined that her abundance of love for him make up for the lack of love he received from the others. Loti projected a tough image, she knew, and on the outside, she was tough; but on the inside, she had a heart of gold. In fact, she loved Loc more than all of her brothers and all of her family. All of them overlooked what she saw front and center in Loc: a big heart, a wide, gracious smile, and more joy and happiness than anyone she'd ever met, even with his circumstances. Loti aspired to be like him, to be as happy as he, to be as kind and compassionate and easygoing and as quick to forgive as he was. She would do anything for him, and she loved his company, so she didn't mind that he was on work detail with her.

"You better keep working, sister," Loc said to her, turning with a smile, "or they'll see you."

Loc picked up his rake with his one good hand and brought it down. His good arm was a strong arm, the arm of a warrior, like his brothers, making up for the other one; yet still, without good balance, it was hard for him. Loc was twice as slow as the girls, and it was hard for him to pull in a straight line, each pull taking great effort. But he never complained, and always set to his work with a huge smile.

"It is *you* who should take a break," she said, still catching her breath. "They assign you with a cruel task. They do it on purpose."

He laughed.

"I've been assigned much worse, my sister," he said. "That is of no concern to me. It is *you* I am worried about. Tell me what has been troubling you. I can see it in your face."

Without responding, Loti raised her rake and went back to work. They toiled together in a comfortable silence as she pondered how to express what was on her mind. She did not have the quick wit that others had; she needed time to think her thoughts through. Loc respected her, not invading her privacy, giving her time and space. That was one of the things she loved about him. She could tell him anything, but if she wanted her silence, he respected that.

They were falling into a steady rhythm, each lost in their own thoughts, when suddenly, Loti heard running footsteps. Loti turned and was horror-stricken to see an Empire taskmaster rush forward, raise his whip, and lash Loc across the back.

Loc cried out in pain, stumbled forward, and fell on his face.

"You fall behind the women!" the taskmaster boomed. "You are no man!"

The taskmaster raised his whip and lashed him again.

And again.

"Stop it!" Loti screamed, rushing forward, unable to stand it.

All the girls stopped working and turned and watched. Loti raced forward, not thinking, not realizing the consequences but unable to control herself. Shackles bound her wrists with a three-foot chain between them, and Loti rushed forward and stood between Loc and the taskmaster just as the whip came lashing down.

Loti took the lash instead, across her shoulder, and she screamed out in pain as she received the blow in place of her brother, who was lying on the ground.

The taskmaster, enraged, backhanded her, and she felt an incredible burn across her face, as she spun.

"You interfere," he said. "I can kill you for that."

He kicked her with his large boot and sent her flying face-first on the dirt and rocks.

Loti quickly spun and looked back to see him walking toward Loc, who still lay on the ground, raising a hand to protect his face.

The taskmaster approached and lashed him again.

"No!" Loti cried.

She jumped to her feet, seeing the cruelty in the taskmaster's face, knowing that he would lash her brother to death.

Loti stood there, the taskmaster's back to her, lashing Loc again and again, Loc covered in blood as he lay there, crying out in pain.

Loti saw red. She could take it no more.

Loti rushed forward, leapt high into the air, and landed on the taskmaster's back. She wrapped her legs around his waist and in the same motion, she lifted her shackles and wrapped the chains around the taskmaster's neck twice—and squeezed.

Loti squeezed and squeezed with all her might, locked in a death grip on the iron chains, knowing that if she let go, it would be her brother's life—and hers. She would not let go; not even the hordes of the world could pull her off of him.

The man was huge, his neck all muscle, a foot wide, and he leaned back and bucked. Yet still Loti squeezed with all her might. It was like holding onto a flailing bull.

The taskmaster reached back, gasping, dropping the whip, and tried to grab her, again and again. He clawed at her, scratching her wrists.

And yet still she held on, squeezing tighter.

127

"You disgusting pig of a man," she cried out. "You know my brother cannot defend himself!"

"Loti!" yelled one of her friends, another woman, running over from her duties, trying to pull her off of him. "Don't do this! They will kill you! They can kill us all!"

But Loti ignored her; nothing would stop her.

The taskmaster flung her about on his back like a wild, crazy horse, throwing her left and right; Loti felt her strength being tested to its limits—but still she held on.

He stumbled forward, then suddenly, he went flying backwards, driving her back, down to the ground, and landing on his back on top of her.

The weight of him landing on top of her nearly crushed her.

Yet still she squeezed.

As she squeezed him, Loti thought of every indignity she'd ever suffered, that every woman had suffered here at the hands of these men. She let her rage loose, coursing out of her hands and arms and shoulders, and she squeezed and squeezed, wanting this taskmaster to suffer as she had. It was her chance for vengeance. Her chance to let the Empire know that she was powerful, too.

Yet still he struggled. He leaned forward and then threw his head back, head-butting her backwards, the back of his skull crushing her cheek—and a horrific pain shot through her head.

Lot, coursing with adrenaline, still did not let go, squeezing her shaking arms, the pain shooting through her head. She did not know how much longer she could hold on. He was too strong for her, and he just would not die.

Loti looked up and saw him lifting his head again. His head came flying back and he head-butted her backwards again, bashing her nose.

This time, the pain was too much, her eyes blinded with the blood of her nose. Involuntarily, she loosened her grip.

Loti knew she was going to die. She looked up, expecting to see the taskmaster about to kill her.

But what she saw surprised her: instead, she saw Loc standing over them, scowling for the first time in his life. She saw, in that moment, the warrior in his eyes.

128

Loc raised his wooden rake high, and he brought the point straight down into the taskmaster's belly.

The taskmaster gasped, leaning forward as Loc brought it down, again and again, cracking his ribs. It was just what Loti needed to regain her grip on the shackles.

Loti grabbed them, doubled her grip, and she spun around, getting on top of him, pinning him face-first in the dirt.

She squeezed all her might, her wrists bleeding from the shackles cutting into them. Blood and sweat stung her eyes, and she lost all sense of time and space as she squeezed and squeezed and squeezed.

It was a long time after he stopped moving that Loti finally realized he was dead.

She looked down. He lay there, perfectly still, all the world perfectly still, and she realized she had just killed the man.

And that nothing would ever be the same again.

CHAPTER TWENTY ONE

Darius slashed and slashed, the click-clack of his wooden sword piercing the air as he blocked blows alternately from Raj and Desmond, each attacking him from both sides. They were driving him back, and he was working up a sweat as he sparred with them, doing his best to fend off one blow after the next. The sun was setting after a long day of labor, and as they had nearly every day during this last moon cycle, Desmond, Raj and Darius sparred, letting out all their aggression for the Empire, all their frustration with their taskmasters, on swordplay.

On the sidelines, Dray sat there, watching every slash, snarling at Darius' attackers every time they landed a blow. Clearly he wanted to pounce, but Darius had finally taught him to sit there and watch patiently. Yet his snarling filled the air, and Darius did not know when he would finally snap and defy his command. He was so loyal to Darius, as Darius was to he, that there was no controlling him.

Over the last moon cycle, Darius and Raj and Desmond had become close friends, the two older boys determined to make Darius a better fighter. It was working. Darius felt his arms and shoulders grow tired, but not as tired as they had been in days before; and while in the past days too many of their blows slipped past, today he managed to block their blows as they attacked relentlessly.

Back and forth they went, Darius blocking side to side, spinning around after blocking one high blow and even venturing to fight back, slashing. He felt himself getting stronger, quicker, more confident. He knew that as their friendship deepened, so had his skills in combat.

Darius was concentrating, finding a weak point in Raj's strike, about to land his first blow—when suddenly, a girl's voice cut through the air.

"Darius!"

Darius, distracted, turned at the sound, and as he did, he lowered his guard and received a mighty blow on the ribcage.

He cried out and scowled at Raj.

"Unfair!" he said.

"You let down your guard," Raj said.

"I was distracted."

"In battle," Desmond said, "your enemy hopes for distractions."

Darius turned, annoyed, and was surprised to see who had been summoning him. To his shock, there was Loti, fast approaching, looking distraught. He was even more surprised to see her eyes were red from crying.

Darius was baffled; he hadn't seen her for the entire moon cycle, and he was certain she never wanted to see him again. He didn't understand why she had sought him out now, or why she was so distraught.

"I must speak with you," she said.

She was so upset her voice broke, and he could see the agony across her face, deepening the mystery.

Darius turned slowly and looked at Raj and blank.

They nodded back, understanding.

"Another day," Raj said.

They turned and walked off, and Darius and Loti were left standing alone in the clearing, facing each other.

Darius walked toward her, and she surprised him by running into his arms, embracing him, and hugging him tight. She cried over his shoulder as she did. He didn't know what to make of it; the ways of women were endlessly mysterious to him.

"I'm so sorry," Loti said, crying, over his shoulder. "So sorry. I am such a fool. I don't know why I was so mean to you. You saved my life. I never thanked you for it."

Darius hugged her back, holding her tight. It felt so good to have her in his arms, and he felt redeemed to hear this, after all they had gone through. All the suffering and anguish and disappointment and confusion he had felt over the last moon cycle began to melt away. She really did love him after all. As much as he loved her.

"Why didn't you—" he began.

But she cut him off, leaning back and raising a finger.

"Later," she said. "For now, I have urgent business."

She cried again, and he looked into her face, wondering, then reached out and held her chin.

"Tell me," he said. "Whatever it is, you can tell me."

She paused for a long time, looking down, then finally she looked up and met his eyes.

"I killed one of them today," she said, her voice deadly serious.

Darius saw the seriousness in her eyes and knew this was no joke. His stomach dropped, realizing.

She nodded back, confirming it.

"They tried to harm my brother," she explained. "I couldn't stand by. Not anymore. Not today."

She broke into tears.

"Now the Empire will come for me," she said. "For all of us."

Now Darius understood why she had sought him out; he pulled her to him, and she held him and cried over his shoulder as he held her tight. He felt sympathy for her, as well as compassion—and most of all, a newfound sense of respect. He admired her actions.

He pulled her back and looked at her meaningfully.

"What you have done," he said, "was an act of honor. Of courage. An act that even men were afraid to do. You should not feel shame—you should feel pride. You saved your brother's life. You saved *all* of our lives. We might all die. But now, thanks to you, we will all die with vengeance, with honor in our lives."

She looked at him, and she wiped away her tears and he could see he had comforted her; yet her face flashed with concern.

"I don't know why I came to you first," she said. "I guess I thought…that you would understand. You among all of them."

He clasped her hands.

"I do understand," he said. "More than I could say."

"I must tell them now," she said. "I must tell all the elders."

Darius took her hand in his and looked at her meaningfully.

"I vow by the sun and the stars, by the moon and the earth below it. No harm shall befall you while I live."

She looked into his eyes, and he could feel her love for him, a love spanning centuries. She embraced him, leaning in close and whispered into his ear, the very words he had been longing to hear:

"I love you."

132

CHAPTER TWENY TWO

Thorgrin, joined by his Legion brothers, walked slowly, cautiously, through the land of the dead, blinked, and wondered what had happened. He felt as if he had lost all sense of time, as if he had been down here for weeks, perhaps even an entire moon cycle, walking through a strange vortex of time and space as he marched through the endless tunnels in the land of the dead. He knew it was not possible to be marching for so many days, yet he felt so weary, his eyes so heavy. Had that much time really passed?

He blinked several times, peering through the reddish vapor that came and went in these massive caves, and looked over to see his companions looking equally disoriented. It was as if they were all finally just now stepping out of the fog, back into the present time. Thor remembered the riverkeeper's warning: *a few steps in this land can last many moons.*

"What has happened to us?" Elden asked the question on all of their minds.

"Have we been marching all this time?" O'Connor asked.

"And yet it feels as if we've just entered the tunnel," Reece said.

Thor looked all around, taking in the surroundings, thinking the same thing himself. He was immediately on guard, squeezing his fist around the hilt of his sword, as he felt a cold draft cling to his skin. Creepy noises filled the gargantuan cave, echoing out of nowhere in this place of blackness. The only thing to light their way were the sporadic fires shooting up from the ground, every twenty feet or so, flaming along the sides of the cave. Occasional geysers of fire shot up, some of them sparking, others slowly bubbling. More so than any place he'd ever been, this place felt like a place of darkness and gloom and death. Thor felt that they had entered another dimension, a place where no human was supposed to travel. He began to wonder if they had made a very big mistake in coming here.

"Guwayne!" Thor shouted.

His voice echoed off the cave walls, returning to him again and again, as if mocking him. He looked about, stopping, listening, hoping for any sound of his child. A baby's cry. Anything.

There came nothing but cruel silence in response. Then, after a long pause, the sounds picked up again—the distant drips and squeals and fluttering of wings, the myriad hidden creatures in the darkness. There also came the distant sounds of hisses, of soft moans, of chains rattling. Endless moans and cries echoed in the air, the sounds of souls in anguish.

"What is this place?" Indra asked, her voice gloomy.

"Hell," Matus answered.

"Or one of the Twelve Hells," Elden added.

Thor walked carefully, avoiding small pools of fire, and he felt a deepening sense of apprehension as he heard a distant roar and rumble of some sort of creature.

"If everyone is dead, what is that?" Matus asked. "What are the rules down here?"

Thorgrin stepped forward, gripping his hilt, and shook his head.

"There are no rules," Reece said. "We left the rules in the land above."

"The only rules here are told by the edge of your sword," Thor said, drawing his sword with a distinctive ring. The others followed, all holding their weapons, all on edge. Reece held a mace, Matus a flail, Elden a sword, O'Connor his bow, Conven his sword, and Indra her sling.

"I don't think these will be of much help," Reece said. "After all, these creatures have already been killed."

"But *we* haven't," Indra said. "Not yet, at least."

They continued marching toward the sounds, deeper and deeper into the cave, the sounds getting louder as they felt themselves enveloped in this other world.

"GUWAYNE!" Thor shouted again.

Again, his voice echoed, this time followed by mocking laughter coming from somewhere deep inside, bouncing off the walls. There came a dripping sound, and Thor looked up to see small drops of lava dripping from the ceiling, sporadic drops, like rain, hissing as they landed.

"OW!" O'Connor shouted and jumped.

Thor saw him jump out of the way and wipe a smoldering flame off his sleeve, slapping it out. They all banded together more closely and hurried down the center, where there was less dripping.

"They said no one leaves," Matus said. "Maybe we will die sooner than we think."

"Not here," Reece said. "As crazy as it sounds, I don't want to die in the land of the dead. I want to die above ground."

Conven stepped forward, looking relaxed, as if he were comfortable here.

"It might just save us a trip," he said.

They marched and marched, the red vapor rising and disappearing, Thor peered into the darkness, some portions of the cave lit by greater flames than others. He looked everywhere for Guwayne.

Yet everywhere he went, there were no sign of him.

Thor heard a sudden rattling, and he looked over and was shocked at what he saw. At first he couldn't process it. But then, the mist cleared and it came clearly into view. He was not seeing things.

There, but a few feet away, Gareth, Reece's brother, appeared out of the darkness. Chained to the wall with iron shackles about his neck, he stared out at them with a gaunt face and hollow cheeks. His arms and legs were shackled by silver shackles, and he had a dagger protruding from his chest.

He smiled at them, blood dripping from his mouth as he did.

"Gareth," Reece gasped, stepping forward, holding his sword out before him.

"My brother," Gareth said to him.

"You are no brother to me," Reece said.

"Do you recognize this dagger in my chest?" Gareth asked. "It is the one I used to murder Father. It has been plunged back into me. For all eternity. Would you take it out for me?"

Reece backed up in horror, staring at his brother, horrified.

Slowly, Reece backed away. He turned, and Thor could see the fear in his face, and then he continued down the tunnel.

The others joined him, all turning their backs on Gareth, leaving him there, chained to the wall, doomed to live out his hell for eternity.

"Please!" Gareth wailed behind them, sounding desperate. "Please free me! Please come back! I'm sorry! Do you hear me, brother? I am sorry I killed Father!"

They marched and marched, and Thor could see the ashen look on Reece's face. He looked shaken.

"I had never thought to see my brother again," Reece said softly as they continued walking.

Thor looked all around and had a new respect for this place; he wondered what might come next.

They passed small caves, recessed into the walls, similar to the one from which Gareth had emerged, and as they did, they were all on guard, wondering who else they might encounter.

There came another rattling of chains, this one more violent, and out of the darkness of one of the small caves there came a figure lunging toward them. They all jumped back and braced themselves, Thor raising his sword, ready to strike.

But the man was stopped by his shackles before he could reach them. He snarled, reaching out at them.

"Come closer," he shrieked, "and I will introduce you to hell!"

Thor looked at the man, horribly disfigured, missing an eye, his face burned and covered in seeping wounds that seemed fresh, and Thor realized, with horror, who it was: McCloud.

"You are the one who attacked Gwendolyn," Thor said, as it all rushed back to him as if it were yesterday. "I had always wished I was there to kill you first. Now I have my chance."

Thor scowled and stepped forward and stabbed McCloud through the heart.

But McCloud stood there, still smiling at him as blood poured through his mouth, looking unfazed.

Thor looked down and saw there were already several swords piercing McCloud's torso.

"Kill me," McCloud said. "You would do me a great favor and end this hell that I'm in."

Thor looked back in wonder, and he realized at that moment that there was justice in the world. McCloud had hurt countless others, and now he was suffering, in his own private hell. And he would suffer forever.

"No," Thor said, retracting his sword. "I won't spare you from any hell."

They kept walking, McCloud's shouts assailing them as they went. Thor was even more on edge now, peering into the darkness, as one by one, figures emerged from caves on both sides of the tunnel, all shackled.

Thor passed men he recognized, men he had killed on the battlefield, most of them foreign enemies. They all seemed to want to try to reach him, to attack, but their shackles held them just out of reach.

Suddenly Matus jumped back; Thor turned and saws his dead father and brothers from the Upper Isles emerge, reaching out for him.

"You let us down, Matus," his father said. "You betrayed us for the mainland of the Ring. You turned your back on family."

Matus shook his head as he stared back.

"You were never my family," he replied. "In blood only. Not in honor."

Reece walked forward, right up to Matus's father, who glowered back at him. He still had the stab wound from where Reece had killed him.

"You killed me," he said to Reece.

"And because of you, the woman I was set to marry is dead," Reece replied. "You killed Selese."

"I would kill her again," he said, "and I would gladly kill *you*!"

He lunged forward for Reece, but he was stopped by his chains.

Reece just stood there and scowled at him.

"I would kill you every day if I could," Reece said, feeling fresh agony for Selese's death. "You stole away from me the person I loved most."

"Why don't you stay down here with us," Matus's brother said to Reece, "and then you can."

Thor turned and led Reece away, yanking him along.

"Come on," he said to Reece. "They're not worth our time."

They all kept marching, passing an endless parade of ghosts. Thor saw all the men he'd killed in battle, faces he hadn't seen in ages, as they walked deeper and deeper into this unholy place.

Thor suddenly felt a chill pervade his system, and he knew, he just knew, that some evil being was lurking in a cave up ahead, obscured behind a cloud of vapor.

Slowly, the figured emerged, stepping forward as the vapor passed, and Thor stopped short, shocked.

"And where is it you march, my son?" came the dark, guttural voice.

Thorgrin's hair stood on end as he recognized that voice, that voice that had caused him such heartbreak, that had caused him endless nightmares. Thor braced himself.

It can't be.

Thor was horrified to see walking out of the blackness, chained by six shackles, his true father.

Andronicus.

Andronicus was stopped by his shackles, and Thor slowly approached, standing before him, staring him back in his face. Andronicus's entire body was covered in wounds, much as Thor had last seen him on the battlefield.

Andronicus grinned back cruelly, seemingly invincible.

"You hated me in life. Will you hate me in death, too?" Andronicus asked.

"I will hate you always," Thor replied, shaking inside.

Andronicus smiled.

"That is good. Your hate will keep me alive. It will keep us connected."

Thor pondered his words, and he realized his father was right. The hatred he felt for Andronicus made him think of him every day; it kept them connected in some strange way. He realized in that moment that he would like to be truly free of him. And that to do so, he would have to let go of his hatred.

"You are nothing to me now," Thorgrin said. "You're not a father. You never were. You're not a foe. You're just another corpse in the land of the dead."

"Yet I live on," Andronicus said, "in your dreams. You have killed me. But not truly. To be rid of me, you would have to conquer yourself. And you are not strong enough for that."

Thor felt a fresh wave of anger.

"I'm stronger than you, Father," Thor said. "I am alive, up above, and you are dead, trapped down here."

"Are you, who dreams of me, truly alive?" Andronicus asked, smiling. "Which one of us is trapped by the other?"

Andronicus leaned back and laughed, louder and louder, a grating noise, his laugh echoing off the walls. Thor looked back at him with hatred; he wanted to kill him, to send him to hell. But he was already in hell. Thor realized it was himself he needed to free.

Thorgrin felt a hand on his shoulder now, and he turned to see Reece, returning the favor, pulling him away.

"He's not worth it," Reece said. "He's just another ghost."

Thor let himself be pulled away, and they all continued walking, Andronicus's laugh echoing in Thor's ears as they continued to weave their way through the endless cave of horrors.

*

They marched and marched, for what felt like moons, twisting and turning their way through endless tunnels, forking more than once, getting endlessly lost in this maze beneath the earth. Thor felt as if they had crossed a desert of blackness, as if he had been marching his entire life.

Finally, they reached what appeared to be the end of the cave. Thor paused, puzzled, as did the others, staring at a wall of solid black rock. Had they reached a dead end?

"Look!" O'Connor said. "Down below."

Thor looked down, and he saw, on the ground at the end of the cave, a wide hole in the earth, a tunnel sloping straight down into the blackness.

Thor walked up to the precipice with the others and looked down; the tunnel seemed to disappear into the earth's core. A warm draft rose up from it, smelling like sulfur. Thor heard a moaning sound echoing deep below.

Thor looked at the others, who all stared back, apprehension in their eyes. He could tell none of them wanted to enter the tunnel, to go sliding straight down into the blackness. He was not sure he did, either. And yet what choice did they have? Had they made a wrong turn somewhere?

As they stood there debating, suddenly, there came a horrific shriek behind them, one that sent the hairs standing on the back of Thor's neck. It was like the roar of a lion.

Thor turned and was horrified to see, standing there, facing them, the most grotesque monster he had ever seen. It towered over them, three times Thorgrin's size, and twice as wide. He looked like a giant, but its skin was bright red and scaly, and in place of fingers it had three long claws. It had hooves for feet and a tall, skinny head, with three eyes at the top and a face that was entirely made up of its mouth. Its mouth was huge, with jagged yellow teeth each half a foot long, and its entire body rippled with scales and muscles, like armor.

"It looks like something that escaped from hell," O'Connor said.

"Or that wants to send us there," Indra said.

The creature threw its head back and roared; then it stepped forward and swiped at them.

Thorgrin jumped out of the way just in time, the beast missing him by inches.

But O'Connor was not so lucky. He screamed out as the beast's long yellow claws slashed him, leaving three slash marks across his bicep, sending him flying through the air and tumbling to the stone. O'Connor, to his credit, rolled as he hit the ground, and, despite his pain, grasped his bow and fired off an arrow.

The beast was too fast; it merely reached up and snatched the arrow from midair. It held it up, examined it, and chewed it, swallowing it as if it were a snack. It leaned back and roared again.

Thor broke into action. He charged forward, raised his sword high with both hands, and brought it down on the beast's foot. With all his might he plunged down, piercing through the skin, through its armor, and down into the bedrock, pinning it to the ground.

The beast shrieked. Thorgrin, exposed, knew he would pay the price, and he did. The beast swung around with its other hand and smacked Thor in the ribs. Thor felt as if all his ribs were cracking as he went flying through the air and crashed into the rock wall on the far side of the cave.

The monster tried to charge after him, but it was still pinned to the ground; it reached down, grabbed Thorgrin's sword, and yanked it from the bedrock and out of its foot.

The beast turned and charged Thor; Thor rolled around, eyes blurry from the collision, and looked up, bracing himself for the attack. He couldn't react in time.

The others broke into action. Matus rushed forward with his flail, swung it wide, and smashed the beast in the thigh.

The beast, enraged, turned, and as it did, Reece attacked it from the other side, stabbing it and making it drop to its knees. O'Connor landed another arrow, and Indra let off several shots with her sling, her stone hitting the beast's eyes, while Elden rushed forward with his ax and brought it down on the beast's shoulder. Conven leapt forward, landing on top of the beast's head, raised his sword high, and brought it down on its skull.

The beast shrieked, beleaguered by all these assaults. It roared, and in one quick motion it rose to its full breadth and height, throwing back its arms and sending Conven flying. It swiped and kicked the others, sending them, too, flying in every direction, smashing into bedrock.

As Thor's vision cleared, he lay there, looking up at it, and realized the beast was impervious. Nothing they did would ever kill it. Fighting it would mean sure death.

Thor realized he had to take charge and make a quick decision if he were to save everyone's life.

"To the tunnel!" Thor commanded.

They all followed his lead, and they looked and saw what he was talking about—the tunnel was their only hope. They sprang into action, grabbing their weapons, racing as the beast charged after them, following Thor as he raced to the tunnel.

Thor stopped before its entrance.

"Go!" he commanded, wanting the others to escape first.

Thor stood there, holding out his sword, blocking the beast's way so that the others could enter. One at a time, Indra, Elden, O'Connor, and Reece entered, jumping down feet first and disappearing into the blackness.

Matus stopped beside Thor.

"I will hold him off for you," Matus said. "You go!"

"No!" Thor said.

But Matus would not listen. The beast charged the tunnel, aiming right for Thor, and Matus stepped forward and slashed down, cutting off two of the beast's long claws as they reached for Thor. Thor slashed down at the same moment, ducking and slicing off the beast's other hand.

The beast shrieked, and Thor and Matus stood there and watched in horror as the hand and claws immediately regenerated themselves. Thor knew that defeating it would be a lost cause.

Thorgrin knew this was their only chance.

"GO!" Thor yelled.

Matus turned and dove into it, and Thor followed, diving in head first, preparing to slide down.

But as soon as he began to slide, Thor suddenly stopped. He felt the beast's claws digging into the back of his leg, puncturing his skin, and he cried out in pain. It was beginning to yank him backwards.

Thor turned and saw the creature yanking him back quickly, right toward its gaping mouth. He knew that in moments he would die an awful death.

Thor mustered his final reserve of strength, and he managed to turn just enough to reach around and slash backwards, chopping off the beast's wrist.

Thor shrieked as he suddenly began to plummet, headfirst, down the tunnel. He tumbled end over end, hurling faster and faster, down into whatever lay beyond.

CHAPTER TWENTY THREE

Volusia sat on her golden throne on the periphery of the arena, surrounded by dozens of counselors and advisors, and looked down, watching with jubilation as an enraged Razif with a flaming red hide charged, lowered its horns, and gouged a slave through the back. The crowd cheered, stomping its feet, as the Razif hoisted the slave high overhead triumphantly, parading its victory, blood dripping down its horns. The Razif spun and spun, then finally threw the corpses, which flew through the air, hitting the ground and tumbling in the dirt.

Volusia felt a familiar thrill; few things pleased her more than watching men die slowly, painfully. She leaned forward, gripping the sides of her chair, admiring the beast, admiring its thirst for bloodshed. She wanted more.

"More slaves!" she commanded.

A horn sounded, and down below, more iron cells opened. A dozen more slaves were shoved out into the arena, the iron gates slamming behind them, locking them in.

The crowd roared, and the slaves, wide-eyed in panic, turned and ran in every direction, trying to get away from the enraged beast.

The Razif, though, was on a warpath, and it was quick for its size. It chased each slave down mercilessly, gorging them through the back, stomping their heads, mauling with its claws, and occasionally, sinking its long teeth into them. Enraged, it didn't stop until every slave was dead.

The crowd went wild, cheering again and again.

Volusia was delighted.

"More!" she called out. The gates opened, to the roar of her people, as yet more slaves tumbled out.

"My lady?" came a voice.

Volusia turned to see Soku, the commander of her army, standing beside her, lowering his head in deference, a concerned look on his face. She was annoyed, distracted from the show. He knew better than to interrupt her while enjoying her afternoon show, and she knew it must be important. No one spoke to her without permission, upon pain of death.

She glowered at him, and he bowed lower.

"My Empress, forgive me," he added, "but it is a matter of utmost urgency."

She looked at him, his bald head bowed low before her, debating whether to kill him or listen. Finally, out of curiosity, she decided to hear him.

"Speak," she commanded.

"One of our men has been killed by a slave. A taskmaster, in a small village north of here. It seems a slave has risen up in an act of defiance. I await your command."

"And why do you bother me with this?" she asked. "There are a thousand slave villages surrounding Volusia. Do what we always do. Find the offender; torture him slowly. And bring me his head as a birthday gift."

"Yes, my empress," he said and, bowing low, retreated.

Volusia turned back to the arena, and she took particular satisfaction as she saw a slave charge forward, stupid enough to try to wrestle the Razif. She watched as the Razif leapt up to meet it, goring its stomach, lifting it high over its head, and slamming it down with all its might. The crowd went wild.

"My empress," came another voice.

Volusia turned, furious at being interrupted again, and this time saw a contingent of Finians, led by their leader, Sardus, all wearing the scarlet cloaks and all with the fiery red hair and alabaster faces of their kind. They were part human, and part something else, no one quite knew what. Their skin was too pale, their eyes a pale shade of pink, and they kept their hands hidden in their cloaks, as if always hiding something. Their bright red hair was distinctive within the capital, and they were the only members of the human race allowed to live freely and not be enslaved; they even held their own seat of power in the capital. It was a deal brokered centuries ago, and held up by Volusia's mother and her mother before her. The Finians were too rich, too treacherous, to cross. They were masters of power and of secrets, traders of all manner of goods and ships that could hamper the city at their whim. They traded in secrets and treachery, and had always managed to gain leverage on the rulers of Volusia. They were a race with which she could not rule without. They were too crafty for their own good, and not to be trusted.

The sight of them made her queasy. Volusia would wipe out the entire Finian race if she could.

"And why should I give my time to a human?" Volusia demanded, impatient.

Sardus smiled, a grotesque smiled, filled with cunning.

"My empress, if I do not forget, you are human, too."

Volusia blushed.

"I am ruler of the Empire race," she replied.

"But human nonetheless. Human in a city where it is a crime to be human."

"That is the paradox of Volusia," she replied. "It has always had a human leader. My mother was human, and her mother before her. But that does not make me human. I am the chosen one, the human crossed with a god. I am a goddess now—call me otherwise, and you shall be killed."

Sardus bowed low.

"Forgive me, my empress."

She examined him with loathing.

"And tell me Sardus," she said, "why should I not throw you to the Razif now, and have your entire race eliminated once and for all?"

"Because then half the power you cherish so deeply would disappear," he said. "If the Finians are absent, then Volusia will crumble. You know that—and your mother knew that."

She looked at him cold and hard.

"My mother knew many things that were wrong." She sighed. "Why do you bother me on this day?"

Sardus smiled in his creepy way as he stepped forward, out of earshot of the others, and spoke in a whisper, waiting for the next roar of the arena to die down.

"You have killed the great Romulus," he said. "The supreme leader of the Empire. Do you think that comes without consequence?"

She looked to him, her face setting in anger.

"I am supreme leader of the empire now," she replied, "and I create my own consequences."

He half-bowed.

"It may be so," he replied, "yet nonetheless, our spies have told us, and we have many, that the southern capital as we speak prepares an army to march our army. An army more vast than anything we have seen. We hear Romulus's million men stationed in the Ring are also being recalled. They will all march on us. And they will arrive before the rainy season."

"No army can take Volusia," she replied.

"The Volusian capital has never been marched upon," he replied. "Not in such force."

"We have ships to outnumber the greatest fleet," she replied.

"Good ships, my lady," he said. "But they will not attack by sea. You have but one hundred thousand men against the southern capital's two million. We would hold these walls for perhaps half a moon before we will be sacked—and all mercilessly killed."

"And why do you concern yourself with affairs of state?" she asked.

He smiled.

"Our sources in the capital are willing to allow us to broker a deal for you," he said.

Finally, she realized, his agenda surfaced.

"Upon what terms?" she asked.

"They will not march on us if you, in turn, accept the rule of the south, accept the southern leader as Supreme Commander of the Empire. It is a fair deal, my empress. Allow us to broker it for you. For the safety of us all. Allow us to get you out of your predicament."

"Predicament?" she said. "What predicament is that?"

He looked back, baffled.

"My empress, you have started a war you cannot win," he said. "I am offering you a way out."

She shook her head.

"What you fail to understand," she said, "what all men have always failed to understand, is that I am exactly where I want to be."

Volusia heard a roar, and she turned her back on him, turned back to the arena, and watched as a Razif gored another slave in the chest. She smiled, delighted.

"My lady," Finian continued, more desperate, "if I may speak boldly, I've heard the most awful rumor. I hear you intend to march to the Mad Prince. That you hope for an alliance with him. Surely you must know that is a futile endeavor. The Mad Prince is aptly named, and he refuses all requests to loan out his men. If you visit him, you will be humiliated, and you will be killed. Do not listen to your counselors. Us Finians, we have lived for thousands of years because we know people. Because we trade with them. Accept our deal. Do the cautious thing, as your mother would have done."

"My mother?" she said, and let out a short, derisive laugh. "Where is she now? Killed by my hand. She was not killed by a lack of caution—but by an abundance of trust."

Volusia looked at Sardus meaningfully, knowing she could not trust him either.

"My empress," he said, desperate, "I implore you. Allow me to speak frankly: you are not, as you think, a goddess. You are a human. And you are frail, vulnerable, like all other humans. Do not start a war you cannot win."

Volusia, enraged, stared coldly at Sardus, who was horrified as all the others witnessed their conversation, all her commanders, all her advisors, all of them watching to see how she reacted.

"Frail?" she repeated, seething.

She was in such a fury that she knew she had to take drastic action, had to prove to all these men that she was the farthest thing from frail. She had to prove what she knew to be true: that she was a goddess.

Volusia suddenly turned her back on them all and faced the arena.

"Open the gate," she commanded her attendant.

He looked at her, eyes wide in shock.

"My empress?" he asked.

"I will not command you twice," she said coldly.

Her attendant rushed to open the gates, the cheer of the crowd much louder as he did so, the heat and stench of the arena coming at her in waves.

Volusia stepped forward, out onto a balcony before stairs heading down, and held out her hands, wide at her sides, facing her people.

As one, all her people suddenly fell silent, shocked at the sight of her, and they all fell on their knees, bowing.

Volusia stepped forward, onto the first step leading down. One step at a time, she descended to the arena, walking down the endless set of stairs.

As she did, the entire stadium grew even more quiet, until one could hear a pin drop. The only sound was that of the Razif, breathing hard, running through the empty arena, anxious for its next victim.

Finally, Volusia reached the bottom and stood before the final gate into the arena.

She turned to the guard.

"Open it," she commanded.

He looked at her, in a state of shock.

"My empress?" he asked. "If I open these gates, the Razif will kill you. It will stomp you to death."

She smiled.

"I won't say it again."

Soldiers rushed forward and opened the gates, and the crowd gasped as Volusia walked through, and the gates quickly slammed behind her.

The crowd stood, in shock, as Volusia walked slowly, one step at a time, into the center of the dusty arena. She walked right to the middle, toward the Razif.

The crowd cried out in shock and fear.

The Razif suddenly set its eyes on her, and as it did, it leaned back and shrieked. Then it charged at her at full speed, horns out, right for her.

Volusia stood in the center of the arena, held out her arms, and let out an enraged cry herself, as the Razif charged at her. Volusia

149

stood her ground and stared back at it, determined, never flinching as it charged and charged, the ground shaking beneath her.

As the crowd cried out, all expecting her to be gored, Volusia stood there, haughty, arrogant, scowling back at the beast. Inside, she knew she was a goddess; she knew that nothing of this earth could touch her. And if she wasn't, if she could be killed by a mere mortal animal, then she didn't want to live at all.

The Razif raced for her, then suddenly, at the last moment, stopped short a few feet away from her. It raised up and reared its legs, several feet away from her, as if afraid of her.

It stood there, not coming any closer, and looked at her. Slowly, it dropped to its knees, then to its stomach.

Then the crowd gasped as the Razif lowered its head and bowed before her, touching its head to the ground.

Volusia stood there, arms out wide to her sides, taking in her power over the animal, her fearlessness, her power over the universe. She knew she really was a goddess. And she feared nothing.

One by one, every person in the arena fell on their knees and bowed their heads low, tens of thousands of people, all of the empire race, all deferring to her. She could feel all of their energy, she sucked in all of their power, and she knew that she was the most powerful woman on earth.

"VOLUSIA!" they cried out.

"VOLUSIA! VOLUSIA!"

CHAPTER TWENTY FOUR

Gwendolyn stood at the entrance to the cave, watching the sun begin to set, preparing. All around her, men were packing up the few provisions they had and bracing themselves to leave this place, to begin the long trek across the Great Waste, on a quest for the Second Ring.

It was time, Gwen realized, to seek out a new home, a permanent home. Her people needed it, and they deserved it. They might all die trying, but at least they would die on their feet, striving for something greater—not holed up here in a cave, cowering, waiting to die. It had taken her an entire moon cycle to realize it, to shake off the depression of missing Guwayne and Thor. That depression still clung to her, yet now, Gwen was able to work through it, to not let it stop her from functioning in the world. After all, giving into her depression would not change her circumstance—it would only make her life worse.

Of course, Gwen felt a deep sense of sorrow and loss in accepting the fact that Thorgrin and Guwayne might not ever return to her. She felt little left to live for. Yet she thought of her father, and his father before him—a long line of kings who had seen great calamity, and who had put their faith in her—and she drew strength from their example. She forced herself to be strong, to focus on the task at hand. She had a people to lead. She had to get them to safety.

"My lady?" came an urgent voice.

Gwendolyn turned and was surprised to see one of the villagers standing there at the entrance of the cave, out of breath, looking at her gravely.

"Why have you come during daylight?" Gwendolyn asked, alarmed.

"We have an urgent matter," he said, in a rush. "You are needed at our village meeting, immediately. All of you."

Kendrick and Godfrey came up beside her, all looking as confused as she.

"Why would you want our people at your meeting?" she asked. "Especially during daylight?"

The messenger, still catching his breath, shook his head.

"It is a matter that concerns us all, my lady. Before you leave, please come."

He turned and ran off, and Gwen watched him go in utter confusion.

"What could they want?" she asked. "They implored us never to show ourselves before dark."

"Perhaps they don't want us to leave," Godfrey said.

Gwen looked off in the distance, watching the messenger sprint back to his village, and she slowly shook her head.

"No," she said, "I fear something far worse."

*

Godfrey hiked with Gwendolyn and Kendrick and the large contingent of Ring members as they all emerged from the cave and hiked carefully down the mountain, clinging to the mountain side so as not to slip and not be detected. As they approached the village, he spotted hundreds of villagers crowded around the village center, and he could sense the chaos from here. All wore disturbed looks, and he sensed something awful had happened.

As they entered the village, Godfrey saw the boy in the center of the crowd, Sandara's brother, the one they called Darius; beside him stood a girl who appeared to be his girlfriend—he had heard her called Loti. They faced the village elders, and the girl looked distraught. Godfrey wondered what had happened.

Godfrey joined Gwen and the others as they silently stood near the center.

"But why did you kill him?" came a voice, panic-stricken, condemning. Godfrey turned to see a woman who must've been Loti's mother, standing beside the elders, yelling at her. "Have you learned nothing? How could you have been so stupid?"

"I didn't think about it," Loti said. "I just reacted. My brother was being whipped."

"So what!?" Bokbu, the village elder, yelled at her. "We are *all* whipped, every day. But none are so foolish as to fight back—much less to kill them. You bring death upon us all. Every one of us."

"And what of the Empire?" Darius yelled out, beside her, defending her. "Have they not broken rules as well?"

The villager, falling silent, looked to him.

"They have the power," one of the elders said. "They make the rules."

"And why should they have the power?" Darius said. "Just because they have more men?"

Bokbu shook his head.

"What you have done today, Loti, was stupid. Very, very foolish. You gave in to your passions, and it was short-sighted. It will change the course of our village forever. Soon they will come here. And with not just one man—with one hundred men, maybe one thousand. They will come with armor and weapons, and they will kill us all."

"I am sorry," Loti said, loudly, boldly, for everyone to hear, "yet I am not sorry. I would do it all again for the sake of my brother."

The crowd gasped in outrage, and Loti's father stepped forward and smacked her across the face.

"I'm sorry I ever had you," he said, scowling at her.

Her father wound up to smack her again. But this time, Darius rushed forward, caught his wrist in midair, and held it.

Loti's father looked to Darius, a look of bewilderment and anger across his face, as Darius locked eyes with his.

"Do not lay a hand on her," Darius threatened.

"You little bastard," her father replied. "You can hang for this. You do not disrespect your elder."

"Then hang me," Darius replied.

Loti's father stared back in rage, then finally he backed away as Darius released his grip.

Loti reached down and quietly took Darius's hand, and Godfrey saw him hold hers back, squeezing it, reassuring her, letting her know he was there for her.

153

"All of this is inconsequential now," Bokbu said, as the people fell silent. "What matters now is what can be done."

The entire village looked to each other in the thick silence, and Godfrey looked at them all, shocked at what had happened. Clearly, this changed everything; it would certainly make it awkward timing for Gwen and her people to just walk out. Yet staying here would be suicide.

"Give the girl up!" a villager cried out.

There came a muted cheer of approval from some villagers.

"March her to Volusia and hand her over!" the man added. "Maybe they will accept her as offering and leave us be!"

There came a few more grunts of approval from some of the villagers—but not from others. Clearly, they were divided.

"You will not touch her!" Loc, Loti's brother, cried out. "Not without going through me!"

"Or me!" Darius yelled.

The villagers laughed in derision.

"And what are a lame man and a long-haired boy going to do to stop us!?"

There came some derisive laughter among a corner of the crowd and Godfrey tightened his grip on his sword, wondering if a fight was going to break out.

"Enough of this!" Bokbu yelled. "Do you not see what the Empire has done to us? We fight ourselves when we should be fighting them! We have truly become like them."

A silence fell over the crowd, as the villagers lowered their faces, humbled.

"No!" Bokbu continued. "We will prepare our defense. We will die either way, so we will die fighting. We will take positions, and attack them as they come."

"With what?" another elder yelled out. "Our wooden swords?"

"We have spears," Bokbu countered, "and their points are sharpened."

"And they will come with steel and armor," the elder countered. "What will your wooden spears do then?"

"We must not fight!" another elder yelled. "We must await their arrival and beg their mercy. Perhaps they will be lenient. After all, they need us for labor."

The villagers all broke out into heated arguing, and chaos ensued as men and women shouted at each other. Godfrey stood there, in shock, wondering how it all could have fallen apart so quickly.

As Godfrey watched, he felt something stirring within him, something he could not contain. He was struck by an idea, and his entire life, whenever he had been overcome with an idea, he'd been unable to contain himself. He'd had to get it out, and now, he felt it boiling over within him. He could not keep silent, even if he tried.

Godfrey found himself stepping forward into the village center, unable to control himself. He stood in the thick of the crowd, jumped up on a high stone, waved his hands, and yelled:

"Wait a minute!" His voice boomed, a deep, loud voice, coming from his big belly, sounding, strangely enough, like the voice of his father, the king.

All the villagers quieted, shocked to see him standing there, with his big belly, a man of white skin demanding attention. Gwendolyn and the others looked even more surprised at his appearance. He clearly was not a warrior, and yet somehow, he demanded attention.

"I have another idea!" Godfrey called out.

They all slowly turned to him, all eyes riveted.

"In my experience, any man can be bought, for a high enough price. And armies are composed of men."

They all looked at him, puzzled.

"Gold speaks in every language, in every land," Godfrey said. "And I have a lot of it. Enough gold to buy any army."

Bokbu stepped forward in the silence, turning to Godfrey.

"And what are you proposing exactly? That we hand the Empire soldiers bags of gold? You think that will send them away? Volusia is one of the riches cities in the Empire."

Godfrey shook his head.

"I will not wait for their army to come," he said. "That is not how men are bought. I will go into the city. I will go myself and bring enough gold to buy whoever needs to be bought. I have conquered men without raising a spear, and I can turn this one back before they even come."

They all stared up at Godfrey, speechless. He stood there, trembling, feeling shocked himself that he had spoken up like this. He did not know what had overcome him; possibly it was the injustice of it all, possibly seeing that poor brave girl in tears. He had spoken before he had even thought it through, and he was surprised as he felt a hand clap him on the back.

A villager stepped forward and looked at him approvingly.

"You are a white man from across the sea," he said. "You do things differently than we. And yet you have an idea. A bold idea and a courageous idea. If you want to enter the city and bring your yellow coins, we shall not stop you. Just maybe, you shall save us all."

All the villagers suddenly let out a soft cooing noise, and spread empty palms toward Godfrey.

"What is that noise?" Godfrey asked. "What are they doing with their hands?"

"It is the salute of our people," Bokbu explained. "It is a sound of admiration. A sound reserved for heroes."

Godfrey felt another hand clap him on the back, then another, and soon the village meeting dissipated, each man going in his own way, their fighting broken up by Godfrey's interruption. At least the tensions had cooled, Godfrey thought, and surely the villagers would regroup to talk strategy in another way.

While he watched them all walk away, Godfrey stood there, a surreal feeling coming over him, wondering what he had just done. Had he really just committed to venturing alone to a hostile city in a hostile Empire to buy off people he did not know? Was it an act of bravery? Or sheer stupidity?

Godfrey looked up to see Akorth and Fulton approach, helping him down from the stone.

They shook their heads, smiling.

"And all this without any drink," Akorth said. "You *are* changing, my friend."

"I suppose you'll want some traveling companions," Fulton said, "someone to share some of those yellow coins you speak of. I

156

suppose we might join you. We have nothing else to do, we're nearly out of drink, and I'm sick of being in that cave."

"Not to mention the brothels we might find," Fulton said with a wink. "I hear Volusia is quite the sumptuous place."

Godfrey stared back, open-mouthed, not knowing what to say, and before he could respond, Merek, the thief from the dungeons who had joined the Legion, came up beside them.

"Any way you go," he said, "you'll want to enter the back alleys. You'll need a good thief by your side. A man as unscrupulous as you. I am that man."

Godfrey sized him up: nearly his age, Godfrey could see cunning and ruthlessness in his eyes, could see a boy who had done whatever it took to scrape his way up in life. It was the type of person he wanted around.

"You'll need someone who knows the Empire as well," came a voice

Godfrey turned to see Ario, the small boy who had joined the Legion, who had trekked alone across the sea from the Empire jungles, after saving Thorgrin and the others, to keep good on his promise.

"I've been to Volusia before," the boy said. "I am of the Empire after all. Yours is a bold mission, and I admire the bold. I shall join you. I will follow you into battle."

"Battle?" Godfrey said, overcome with anxiety as the reality began to sink in.

"Very good, young lad," Akorth said, "but there won't be any battle here. Men die in battle. And we don't plan on dying. This won't be battle. This will be an expedition into the city. A chance to buy ale, some women, and to pay off the right people at the right price and return home unlikely heroes. Right, Godfrey?"

Godfrey stared back blankly, then nodded. Was that what this was? He didn't even know anymore. All he knew was that he opened his big mouth, and now he was committed. Why was it that in times of trouble this streak overcame him, this streak of his father? Was it chivalry? Or impetuosity?

Godfrey looked up to see his sister Gwendolyn and brother Kendrick approach. They stepped up beside him and looked at him meaningfully.

"Father would be proud," Kendrick said. "We are proud. It was a bold offer."

"You've made a friend of this people," Gwendolyn said. "They look to you now. They are relying on you now. Trust is a sacred thing. Do not let them down."

Godfrey looked back and nodded, not trusting himself to speak and not knowing what else to say.

"Yours is both a wise and a foolish plan. Only you might be able to pull it off. Pay off the right people, and choose your people well."

Gwen stepped forward and hugged him, then pulled back and looked at him, her eyes filled with concern.

"Be safe, my brother," she said softly.

With that, she and Kendrick turned and walked off. As they did, Illepra approached, a smile on her face.

"You are no longer a boy," she said. "On this day, you are a man. That was a manly act. When people rely on you, that is when you become a man. You are a hero now. Whatever becomes of you, you are a hero."

"I'm no hero," Godfrey said. "A hero is fearless. Scared of nothing. A hero can make calculated decisions. Yet mine was hasty. I did not think it through. And I am more scared than I have ever been."

Illepra nodded, held a hand to his cheek.

"That is how all heroes feel," she said. "A hero is not born. A hero is made—through one painful decision at a time. It is an evolution. And you, my love, have evolved. You are becoming one."

She leaned in and kissed him.

"I take back all the things I said," she added. "Come back to me. I love you."

They kissed again, and for a brief moment, Godfrey felt lost in that kiss, felt all of his fears melting away. He looked into her smiling eyes as she pulled back and walked away, and he stood there, all alone, wondering: what have I done?

CHAPTER TWENTY FIVE

Thor, bruised and aching, sat beside the strange natural bonfire smoldering out of the bedrock. Reece, Matus, Conven, O'Connor, Elden and Indra sat beside him. The seven of them were exhausted, leaning back against the bedrock, barely able to keep their eyes open.

Thor had never felt so exhausted his life, and he knew it was unnatural. There was something in the air here, having to do with the strange red vapor that rose up and disappeared, making him feel transported. He felt like each step weighed a million pounds.

Thor thought back to the fall they had taken, down that endless tunnel; luckily the tunnel had sloped, the speed of his slide had eased, and at the base, there had been a floor of soft black moss, cushioning the fall. It had saved him from death, but still, the tumbling down had left bruises on nearly every inch of his body. He had been thrilled to discover the others had survived, too. He could not tell how far they had descended, but it felt like miles. He could still hear, echoing faintly, the distant screeching of that monster up above, and he realized how lucky they were to at least be alive.

But now they were faced with new problems. They were much deeper in the earth, and Thor had no idea if they were even heading in the right direction—if there even was a direction in this place. After the fall, they had all picked up the pieces and had managed to march on, deeper and deeper, in this new series of tunnels. Like the tunnels above, they were made of black bedrock, except these were covered in black moss, too. Strange small insects with glowing orange eyes crawled in the moss and followed them as they went.

Finally, they all had been able to walk no further, too weary, too beset with exhaustion. When they'd spotted this natural bonfire emerging from the rock, they all essentially had collapsed around it, knowing they had to take camp for the night, and had to sleep.

As he sat there, silent as the others, his back against the bedrock wall, against the soft moss, Thor felt his eyes closing on him. He felt as if he needed to sleep a million years. He felt as if he had already been down here for lifetimes.

Thor lost all sense of time and distance in this place, did not know if they had been down here for a day or a moon or a year. All he remembered as he stared into the crackling flames, hissing and sparking in this cavernous subterranean level, was Andronicus's face, and their fall, their long slide down. He was beginning to feel that they would never get out of this world. He looked around and realized this might be his final resting place. He could not help but brace himself, unable to relax, wondering what other monster they might meet around the corner. The next time, they might not be so lucky.

Thor looked into the flames and realized they would all spend the night here, however long a night lasted in this place. Would they ever wake up? Would they ever find Guwayne?

Thor felt a wave of guilt as he started to wonder if he had led his brothers down to his own personal hell. He had not meant for them to follow, although he was grateful they had all joined him. Thor felt more determined than ever to reach Guwayne and to find a way to get all of his brothers out of here, one way or the other. For their sake, if not for his.

They all sat in the gloomy silence, each lost in their own world, the only sound that of the crackling fire. He wondered if he would ever see Gwendolyn again, if he would ever see daylight again. His thoughts grew increasingly fatalistic, and he knew he needed to distract himself from this place.

"I need a story," Thorgrin said, surprised by the sound of his own voice breaking the silence.

They all turned and looked at him, surprised.

"Anyone," Thor said. "Any story. Anything."

Thor needed to be taken away, taken some place—any place—else.

A howling draft passed through, and as they sat there, Thor wondered if anyone would speak. If anyone had any energy left to speak.

After an interminable silence, after Thor was certain he would be doomed to his own thoughts, a voice finally cut through the air. It was low, and grave, and exhausted. Thor looked over and was surprised to see that that it was Matus, leaning forward, staring into the flames and speaking.

"My father was a hard man," Matus said slowly. "A competitive man. A jealous man. Not the type of father who took joy in his son's success. Rather, he was the type of father that felt threatened by it. He had to outdo me—in everything. Which was ironic, because I wanted nothing more than to love him my whole life, to be close to him. Yet anytime I tried, he pushed me away. He found a way to create a conflict, to keep me at a distance. It was a long time until I learned that it wasn't me he hated, but himself."

Matus took a deep breath, staring into the flames, focusing, lost in another world. Thor could relate to his words; he had felt the same way about the man who had raised him.

"I felt as if I was born into the wrong family," Matus continued. "Like I didn't quite fit in, at least not to the image of who we wanted me to be. The thing is, I was never quite sure who that person who he wanted was.

"I knew I didn't fit in with the rest of the Upper Isle MacGils. I felt a kinship with the MacGils of the Ring," he said, glancing at Reece. "I envied you all, and I wanted to escape the Isles, to come to the mainland and join the Legion.

"But I could not. I was doomed to be there. My brothers hated me. My father hated me. The only one that loved me was my sister, Stara…. And my mother."

On that final word, Thor detected anguish in Matus's voice. A long silence followed, and Matus finally got the courage to speak again, his voice heavy with exhaustion, as if he were traveling through emotional realms.

"One day," Matus finally said, clearing his throat, "when I was perhaps thirteen, my father called for a hunt. It was a hunt meant for my older brothers, but he challenged me to come along. Not because he thought I would kill anything, but because he wanted to outdo me, to see my brothers outdo me, and to make me look stupid. He wanted to keep me in my place."

Matus sighed.

161

"Late into the hunt, when the day was nearly through, we encountered the largest boar I have ever seen. My father charged, all bravado and aggression, and lacking the fine technique he claimed to have. He threw his spear and missed, enraging it. My two brothers, helpless, missed, too.

"The enraged bore charged my father and was about to kill him. I should have let it.

"Instead, I reacted. My father did not know, but I had spent many nights, long after the others were asleep, practicing with my bow. I fired two perfect shots and landed them in the boar's head. It dropped down right before it had a chance to reach my father."

Matus sighed and fell silent for a long time.

"Was he grateful?" Reece asked.

Matus shook his head.

"He gave me a look I can remember to this day. A look of rage, humiliation, jealousy. Here he was, alive because his youngest managed to fell a bore he himself could not. He hated me even more since that day."

A long silence fell over them, punctuated only by the crackling fire. Thor pondered it, and realized he had similarities with his own father.

Thor was transported by the story, and he thought it was over, when Matus suddenly continued.

"The next day," Matus continued, "my mother died. The storms of the Upper Isles had never agreed with her. She was a frail, delicate woman, transported to those barren isles by my father and his appetite for ambition. She caught a cold and never recovered—though I think what really killed her was the heartbreak of leaving the mainland.

"I loved my mother enough to justify my existence, and when she died, I felt that there was nothing left for me in that place. I attended her funeral with the others at the top of Mount Eleusis. Do you know it?" he asked, looking to Reece.

Reece nodded.

"The first capital," he replied.

Matus nodded back.

"You know your history, cousin."

162

"I was schooled in it since I was a boy," Reece said. "Long before King's Court, the Upper Isles held the seat of power. Five hundred years before, that was where kings ruled. Before the Great Divide."

Matus nodded, and Thor looked at the two and wondered at the extent of their royal education, wondered how much he didn't know about the history of the Ring. He had a desire to learn more, to learn about the ancient kings, the ancient warriors. He wanted to learn the stories of how the Ring had been centuries before, of old wars and battles and heroes and warriors, of old capitals and old seats of power....But now was not the time. Someday he would sit down and learn it all. *Someday*, he promised himself.

"Anyway," Matus said, "on that day, I sat there by my mother's grave and wept; it was too much for me. Long after the others left, I sat there all night long, atop that mount, in the presence of death, and that's when I learned what death felt like. I blamed my father for her death, my father, who would not even attend the funeral. I would never forgive him for that night. He was a selfish man to the last."

Matus sighed.

"Here, in this place, I feel that feeling again, for the first time. A feeling I thought I would never feel again: the feeling of death. My mother is here somewhere. I both dread seeing her, and look forward to it."

His story concluded, they all sat there in the silence, and as they did, Thor looked at Matus with a new respect. The story had transported him indeed, had transported all of them, out of this dungeon and into another place. Would Matus find his mother here? Thor wondered.

And most of all, would Thor find Guwayne?

CHAPTER TWENTY SIX

Darius was awakened from fast, troubled dreams at the first light of dawn by the sound of the village horn—a low, wailing sound that hurt his ears—and he knew immediately that there was trouble. That horn was never sounded except in dire emergencies, and he had only heard it sounded once in his lifetime, when he was a young boy. It was when one of the villagers had tried to escape, and was caught by the Empire, tortured and executed in front of them all.

With a deepening sense of foreboding, Darius jumped out of bed, dressed quickly, and burst out the door of his cottage, Dray beside him, at his heels the entire time. Immediately, he thought of Loti, and of the town meeting the day before. The villagers had all argued endlessly with one another, none agreeing on a clear course of action. They were all bracing themselves for the worst, for an impending doom, the inevitable vengeance the Empire must exact, and as usual, none was willing to attack, to take any decisive action. Darius was hardly surprised.

Yet still, Darius did not expect the Empire to arrive so quickly, the very next morning. He should have known better: the Empire never waited for vengeance.

Darius raced along the dirt path toward the village center, joining a growing crowd emerging from their cottages, men and women, children, brothers, cousins, friends, all swarming the main road for the village center. It grew thicker by the moment.

At his feet, Darius heard Dray following him, nipping playfully at his heels, always game for whatever excitement the town would bring. Darius wanted to explain to him that this was not a game, but Dray, he knew, would not understand.

As Darius went he scanned the faces desperately for Loti, having a sinking feeling this all had something to do with her, with the Empire, and knowing that she needed him now more than ever. They had made an agreement the day before that if something should happen—anything—the two of them would meet by the large tree before town. As all the villagers ran for the village center, Darius turned off and ran toward the tree, hoping she would be there.

Darius was relieved to see that she was. There she stood, scanning the crowd, clearly looking for him, too, panic written on her face.

He reached her and she rushed into his arms, her eyes red from crying. He could only imagine what a long night she'd had, especially in her disapproving household.

"Darius," she whispered in his ear, with an intake of breath, and he could hear the relief and the fear in her voice.

"Don't worry," he said back. "It's okay. Whatever is going to happen, it's okay."

Trembling, she leaned back and shook her head as she looked into his eyes.

"It is not okay," she said. "Nothing will ever be okay again. The Empire wants to kill me. They want vengeance. Our own people want to kill me. A price must be paid."

"Listen to me," Darius said firmly, taking hold of her shoulders. "Whatever happens today, under any circumstance, do not tell them it was you. Do you understand me? Do not volunteer that you did it."

She looked at him, unsure.

"But what if—" she began.

He shook his head firmly.

"No," he said, mustering all the gravity he could. "*Vow to me.*"

She looked into his eyes, and as she did, Darius could see them strengthening, slowly gaining resolve. She nodded, and began to stand a bit straighter.

"I vow," she said softly.

Darius nodded, satisfied, took her hand, and he led her quickly along the path and to the main village.

They rounded the bend, and as they did, Darius saw that his entire village had amassed in the center, as the horn blew once again. As Darius looked up, past their faces, into the breaking light of dawn, his heart dropped at the sight. There, on the horizon, blocking the village road, was a massive Empire force, hundreds of soldiers in full armor. There were rows of zertas, squadrons of soldiers standing before them, wielding all manner of steel weaponry, well-disciplined, standing erect, awaiting the order to kill.

Nothing more needed to be said. Darius looked to his people, and he could see the tension and the fear. His villagers had no real weapons with which to fight back. And it wouldn't be a real fight anyway, not against this professional army.

Darius braced himself for the inevitable attack that would follow, waiting for the Empire to charge. Instead, there came, oddly, a long, awkward silence. The Empire just stood there, facing them, their banners rippling in the morning wind, as if wanting them to sweat it out.

Finally, an Empire commander stepped forward, out in front of his men, flanked by a dozen soldiers, and faced the villagers.

"Blood has been taken," he boomed out, "and blood will be paid. Your people have taken one of ours. You have broken the cardinal rule. Our two peoples have lived in harmony with one another, because you, and the generations before you, have lived by the rules. You knew the price for breaking them."

He paused.

"Blood for blood," he called out. "Our great Empress, Volusia, the greatest of the Volusia Queens, the God of the East and supreme ruler of the sea and all its ships, has, in her abundant mercy, decided not to kill you all. Instead, she will just have us torture and kill one of you, the perpetrator of this unholy act. She's giving you this great grace only once, and only because yesterday was the festival of our gods."

There came a long pause, the only sound that of the rippling of their banners, as the commander let his words sink in.

"Now," he boomed, "the one who did it, you will step forward, admit your crimes, and you will suffer death on behalf of your people. This generous offer will not be made twice. Step forth now."

All the villagers stood there, and Darius looked them over, seeing the panic in all their faces. Some of them turned and looked at Loti, as if debating whether to give her up. Darius saw Loti begin to cry, and he could feel her hand trembling in his. He could sense that she was unsure what to do. He could feel her about to step forward, to confess.

And he knew then and there that, whatever the price, it was something his honor would never allow.

Darius turned to her.

"Remember your vow," he said softly.

Darius, resolved, suddenly stepped forward, taking several paces out before all the others. There came a gasp from his people as he did.

"It was I, Commander!" Darius yelled out, his voice booming in the still morning air.

Darius felt himself trembling inside, but he refused to show it. He was determined to be bigger than his fear, to overcome it. He stood there, chin up, chest out, staring back proudly, defiantly, at the Empire.

"It was *I* who killed the taskmaster."

The Empire commander stared back at Darius sternly for a long time, a tall man, with the typical glowing yellow skin, two small horns and red eyes of the Empire race, with the horns, the massive body structure. Darius could see in his eyes a look of respect.

"You have admitted your crimes," he called out. "That is good. As a gift, I will torture you quickly before I kill you."

The commander nodded to his men, and there came sound of armor and spurs, as half a dozen soldiers marched forward, surrounding Darius, each grabbing him roughly by the arm and dragging him toward the commander.

Dray snarled and leapt up and sunk his teeth into the calf of one of them, and the soldier cried out as he released his grip on Darius. Dray let out a vicious sound as he tugged, drawing blood, the solider unable to shake his grip.

The soldier reached for his sword, and Darius knew he had to act quick if he wanted to save Dray's life.

"Dray!" Darius yelled sharply. "Go home! NOW!"

Darius used his fiercest voice, praying Dray would listen, and Dray suddenly released, turned and sprinted off into the crowd.

He just escaped the slash of the soldier, who swung at nothing but air. They all turned and continued dragging Darius away.

"No!" cried a voice.

They all stopped and turned as Loti stepping forth, crying.

"He did not do it! He's innocent. I did it," she cried out.

The commander, confused, looked back and forth from her to Darius, wondering whom to believe.

"The words of a woman trying to save her husband," Darius called out. "Do not believe her!"

The Empire commander looked back and forth, Darius's heart pounding, hoping, praying the taskmaster would believe him.

"Do you really believe a frail woman could strangle an all-powerful taskmaster?" Darius added.

Finally, the commander broke into a tight smile.

"You insult us," the commander said to Loti, "if you think our men could be killed by a weak woman such as yourself. If that were the case, then I would kill them myself. Silence your tongue, woman, before I cut it out with my sword."

"No," Loti screamed.

Darius saw men step forward and restrain her, yanking her back as she flailed. He was overwhelmed by her loyalty to him, and it touched him deeply, gave him solace before what he knew would be his death.

Darius felt himself yanked forward, and soon he was tied him to a pole, his face against it, his hands and ankles tied to it. He felt rough hands tear the shirt off his back, heard a ripping noise cut through the air, and felt his back exposed to the morning sun and the cool wind.

"Because I am in the mood for mercy," the commander boomed, "we shall begin with just one hundred lashes!"

Darius swallowed, and refused to allow anyone to see the fear on his face as his wrists were clamped down to the wood. He braced himself for the terrible pain that would come.

Before he could finish a thought, Darius heard the crack of a whip, and suddenly every nerve in his body screamed out as he felt an awful pain across his back. He felt his skin rip from his flesh, felt his blood exposed to the air. It was the worst pain of his life. He did not know how he'd recover from it, much less take ninety-nine more.

The whip cracked through the air again, and Darius felt another lash, this one worse than the last, and he groaned out again and clutched the wood, refusing to allow himself to scream.

The lashes came again, and again, and Darius felt himself getting lost in another place, a place of honor and glory and valor. A place of sacrifice. A place of sacrificing for someone else whom he loved. He thought of Loti, of the pain that she would have suffered for this; he thought of her lame brother, a man Darius loved and respected too, and of how she had sacrificed for him. He took the next lash, and the next one, knowing he was taking it for them.

Darius retreated deeper and deeper into himself, into a place of escape, and as he did, he felt a familiar feeling rising within him, felt a heat coursing through his palms. He felt his body willing him to summon his power. It was aching to be summoned. He knew that if he did, he could break free of this. He could overcome them all.

But Darius would not allow it; he stopped himself, preventing it from welling up. He feared to use it. As much as he wanted to, he did not want to be an exile among his people. He would rather die a martyr than be remembered as a magician they reviled.

Another lash came, then another, and Darius struggled to hang on. He gasped for air, and would do anything for water. He was starting to wonder if he would survive this—when suddenly, a voice cut through the air.

"Enough!" came the booming voice. "You have the wrong man."

The crack of the whip stopped and Darius turned weakly, and saw surprised to see Loc, Loti's lame brother, stepping forward out in front of the others.

"It was *I* who killed the taskmaster," Loc said.

The Empire commander stared back, confused.

"You?" he called out, looking him up and down in disbelief.

Suddenly, Raj stepped forward, standing beside Loc.

"No," Raj called out. "It was *I* who killed him."

Desmond stepped forward, beside Raj.

"No, it was I!" Luzi called out.

There came a long, tense silence amongst the crowd, until finally, one at a time, all of Darius's friends stepped forward.

169

"No, it was I!" echoed one voice after the other.

Darius felt so deeply grateful to his brothers, so moved by their loyalty; it made him feel willing to die a million deaths on their behalf. They all stood there, proudly facing off against the Empire, dozens of them stepping forward, all wanting to take the punishment for him.

The Empire commander snarled at all of them and let out a groan of frustration. He marched over to Darius, and Darius felt rough hands behind his back, as the Commander grabbed him tight and leaned in and whispered in his ear, his hot breath on the back of his neck.

"I should kill you, boy," he seethed, "for lying to me."

Darius felt a dagger pressed against his throat, felt the commander pushing it against his skin, and he felt that he just might.

Instead, Darius suddenly felt a tug at his hair, his long, unruly ponytail being pulled back, and suddenly he felt the blade touching his hair—his hair which he had never cut since birth.

"A little something to remember me by," the Commander said, a dark smile on his lips.

"NO!" Darius yelled. Somehow, the idea of his hair being cut affected him more than his being lashed.

The village gasped as, in one clean cut, the commander yanked back his hair, reached up, and sliced it all off. Darius hung his head low. He felt humiliated, naked.

The commander severed the cords binding his ankles and feet, and Darius collapsed to the ground. Weak from the beating, disoriented, Darius felt all the eyes of his people on him, and however painful it was, he forced himself to his feet.

He stood there proudly and faced the commander, defiant.

The commander, though, turned and faced the crowd.

"Someone is lying!" he boomed. "You have one day to decide. At daybreak tomorrow, I will return. You will decide if you want to tell me who killed this man. If you do not, you will all, each and every one of you, be tortured and killed. If you do, then I will only cut off the right thumb of each of you. That is the price you pay for lying here today and for making me return. That is mercy. Lie again, and by my soul, I swear it, you will learn what it means to have no mercy."

The commander turned, mounted his zerta, signaled to his men, and as one, they took off, charging back onto the road from they came from. Darius, his world dizzy, dimly saw his brothers, Loti, all of them rush forward, reaching him just in time, as he stumbled forward and collapsed into their arms. *How much can happen*, he thought, looking up at the sun before he lost consciousness, *before a day breaks.*

CHAPTER TWENTY SEVEN

Godfrey, joined by Akorth, Fulton, Merek and Ario, marched down the dirt road leading to the great city of Volusia, and wondered what on earth he had gotten himself into. He looked about at his unlikely companions, and knew he was in trouble: there were Akorth and Fulton, two drunken slobs, good for witty banter but not much else; Merek, a thief who stole his way through life, cheated his way out of the King's dungeons and into the Legion, good for his back-alley connections and his sleight of hand, but little else; and finally, Ario, a small, sickly-looking boy from the jungles of the Empire, who looked as if he'd be better suited in a classroom somewhere.

Godfrey shook his head as he considered the sorry lot, the five of them a pathetic group, the most unlikely heroes, setting out to achieve the impossible, to enter one of the most barricaded cities in the Empire, to find the right person to pay off, and to convince them to take the gold that even now weighed him down, hanging in sacks on all their waists. And with Godfrey himself as their leader. He had no idea why they put their trust in him; he didn't trust himself. Godfrey would be surprised if they even made it past the city gates, a feat which he still had no idea how he was going to accomplish.

Of all the crazy things he had done, Godfrey did not know how he had gotten himself into this one. Once again, he had stupidly allowed his rare and uncontrollable streak of bravado to take over, to possess him. God knows why. He should have kept his mouth shut and stayed back there, safe with Gwendolyn and the others. Instead, here he was, practically alone, and preparing to give his life for the villagers. This mission, he felt, was already doomed from the start.

As Godfrey marched he reached out and grabbed the sack of wine again from Akorth's hands, taking another long swig, relishing the buzz that went right to his head. He wanted to turn back, more than anything. But something inside him could not. Something in him

172

thought of that girl, Loti, who had been so brave, who had killed the taskmaster defending her lame brother—and he admired her. He knew the villagers were vastly outnumbered and had to find another way. And he knew from his years of fighting that there was *always* another way. If there was one thing he was good at, it was finding another way. It was all about finding the right person—and at the right price.

Godfrey drank again, hating himself for being chivalrous; he decided he loved life, loved survival, more than courage—and yet somehow, he could not stop himself from doing these acts. He marched, sullen, trying to drown out the endless banter of Akorth and Fulton, who hadn't stopped talking since they'd left.

"I know what I would do with a brothel of Empire women," Akorth said. "I would teach them the pleasures of the Ring."

"You would teach them nothing," Fulton countered. "You would be too drunk, you wouldn't even make it to their beds."

"And you?" Akorth countered. "Would you not be drunk?"

Fulton chuckled.

"Aye, I would be drunk enough to know not to enter a brothel of Empire women!" he said, breaking into laughter at his own joke.

"Do those two ever stop?" Merek asked Godfrey, coming up beside him, an exasperated look on his face. "We are walking into death, and they take it all so lightheartedly."

"No, they don't," Godfrey said. He sighed. "Look at the bright side. I've had to put up with them my whole life; you will only have to put up with them for a few more hours. By then we should all be dead."

"I don't know if I can stand a few hours more," Merek said. "Perhaps volunteering on this mission was a bad idea."

"Perhaps?" Akorth scoffed. "My boy, you have no idea how bad it was."

"How did you think you could contribute anyway?" Fulton added. "A thief? What are you going to do, steal Empire hearts?"

Akorth and Fulton broke into laughter, and Merek reddened.

"A thief is quick with a hand, quicker than you'll ever be," he replied darkly, "and it takes far less to slit someone's throat." He

173

looked right at Akorth, meaningfully, as he began to pull his blade from his waist.

Akorth raised his hands, looking terrified.

"I meant you no insult, boy," he said.

Slowly, Merek put his knife back in his belt, and he calmed as they continued marching, Akorth more quiet this time.

"Quick temper, have you?" Fulton asked. "That is good in battle. But not among friends."

"And who said we are friends?" Merek asked.

"I think you need a drink," Akorth said.

Akorth handed him the flask, a truce offering, but Merek ignored it.

"I don't drink," Merek said.

"Don't drink?" Fulton said. "A thief who doesn't drink!? We are truly doomed."

Akorth took a long swig himself.

"I want to hear that story—" Akorth began, but he was cut off by a soft voice.

"I would stop there if I were you."

Godfrey looked over and was surprised to see the boy, Ario, stopping short in the path. Godfrey was impressed by the boy's poise, his calm, as he stood there, looking out at the trail. He peered into the woods as if spotting something ominous.

"Why have we stopped?" Godfrey asked.

"And why are we listening to a boy?" Fulton asked.

"Because this boy is your best and last hope to navigate the Empire lands," Ario said calmly. "Because if you hadn't listened to this boy, and had taken three more steps, you would be sitting in an Empire torture chamber shortly."

They all stopped and looked at him, baffled, and the boy reached down, grabbed a rock, and threw it before the trail. It landed a few feet in front of them and Godfrey watched, stunned, as a huge net suddenly shot up into the air, hidden under the leaves, hoisted by branches. A few more feet, Godfrey realized, and they all would have been trapped.

They looked at the boy in amazement, and with a new respect.

"If a boy is to be our savior," Godfrey said, "then we are in bigger trouble than I thought. Thank you," he said to him. "I owe you one. I will give you one of those bags of gold, if we have any left."

Ario shrugged and continued walking, not looking in them, saying, "Gold means nothing to me."

The others exchanged a glance of wonder. Godfrey had never seen anyone so nonchalant, so stoic in the face of danger. He began to realize how lucky he was that the boy had joined them.

They all marched and marched, Godfrey's legs shaking, and he wondered if this sorry group would ever reach the gates.

*

By the time his legs were trembling with exhaustion, the sun was high in the sky, and Godfrey had emptied a second sack of wine. Finally, after so many hours of marching, Godfrey saw up ahead the end of the tree line. And beyond that, past a clearing, he saw a wide paved road and the most massive city gate he had ever seen.

The gates of Volusia.

Before it stood dozens of Empire soldiers, dressed in the finest armor and spiked helmets, the black and gold of the empire, wielding halberds, standing erect and staring straight ahead. They guarded a massive drawbridge, and the entrance lay a good fifty feet before Godfrey and the others.

They all stood there, hidden at the edge of the forest, staring, and Godfrey could feel all the others turn and look to him.

"Now what?" Merek said. "What is your plan?"

Godfrey gulped.

"I don't have one," he answered.

Merek's eyes widened.

"You don't have a plan?" Ario said, indignant. "Why did you volunteer for this then?"

Godfrey shrugged.

"I wish I knew," he said. "Stupidity, mostly. Maybe a bit of boredom thrown in."

175

They all groaned as they looked at him, furious, then looked back at the gate.

"You mean to tell me," Merek said, "that you've brought us the most guarded city in the empire with no plan whatsoever?"

"What did you mean to do," the boy asked, "just walk through the gates?"

Godfrey thought back on all the foolhardy things he had done in his life, and he realized this was probably close to the top. He wished he could think clearly to remember them all, but his head was spinning from all the drink.

Finally, he belched and replied:

"That is exactly what I mean to do."

CHAPTER TWENTY EIGHT

Reece opened his eyes slowly, feeling groggy from the red vapor drifting in and out of this place, and he looked around in the darkness of the cave. He realized he had fallen asleep, still sitting up with his back to the cave wall; before him he saw the small glowing fire emerging from the stone floor, and he wondered how long they had slept here.

Reece looked about and saw Thorgrin, Matus, Conven, O'Connor, Elden, and Indra all spread out around him, all still lying by the fire. Gently, he leaned over and prodded them, and they woke slowly, one at a time.

Reece's head felt like it weighed a million pounds as he struggled to his hands and knees, then to his feet. He felt as if he'd slept a hundred years. He turned and peered into the blackness as he heard a soft moaning noise, echoing off the walls, but he could not tell where it was coming from. He felt as if he had been down here, in this land of the dead, forever, as if he'd been down here longer than he'd been alive.

Yet Reece had no regrets. He was by his brother's side, and there was no place else he'd rather be. Thor was his best friend, and Reece drew strength from Thor's refusal to back down from a challenge, from his determination to find and rescue his son. He would follow him to the very bowels of hell

It had not been long since Reece had been there himself, to that place of suffering, of grieving over a loved one. He lived with his loss of Selese every day, and he understood what Thorgrin was going through. It was the strangest thing; being down here, Reece felt closer to Selese than ever, felt a strange sense of peace. As he thought of it, he remembered he had been awakened by a dream of her. He could still see her face, smiling at him, waking him.

Another moan rose up from somewhere in the blackness, and Reece turned and tightened his grip on the hilt of his sword, as did the others, all of them on edge. As one, they all began to walk, silently marching on, led by Thorgrin. Reece was famished, feeling a tremendous hunger he could never quell, as if he had not eaten in a million years.

"How long have we slept?" O'Connor asked as they walked.

They all looked at each other, wondering.

"I feel as if I have aged," Elden said.

"You look as if you have," Conven said.

Reece flexed his arms and hands and legs. They felt stiff, as if he hadn't moved in a very long time.

"We must not stop moving," Thorgrin said. "Not ever again."

Together they marched into the blackness, Thor leading the way, Reece by his side, all of them squinting into the dim light of the fires as they weaved in and out of the tunnels. A bat flew by his head, then another and another, and Reece ducked and looked up at the ceiling, and he saw glowing eyes of all different colors, exotic creatures hanging upside down from the ceiling, some on the walls.

Reece tightened his grip on the hilt of his sword, bracing himself for an attack, having a sinking feeling.

As they continued walking, the narrow cave opened, widening into a large circular clearing, perhaps fifty feet in diameter. Before them lay a series of tunnels, caves extending in each direction. The clearing was well lit, fires all around, and Reece was surprised to see it open up like this, to see all the forks in the road.

He was even more surprised, though, at the sight before him.

Reece fell to his knees, overwhelmed, nearly collapsing, as he saw, but a few feet away, his love.

Selese.

Reece, eyes welling with tears, watched in awe as Selese stepped forward and reached out for him. She held his hands, her skin so smooth, smiling down sweetly at him, her eyes shining with love, just as he'd remembered. Gently, she pulled him to his feet.

"Selese?" he said, afraid to believe it, his voice hardly rising above a whisper.

"It is I, my love," she answered.

Reece wept as he hugged her and she hugged him back, each holding the other tight. He was amazed to be able to hold her again, that she was really in his arms. He was overwhelmed at the feel of her, the smell of her, the way she fit in his arms, just as he'd remembered. It was really her. Selese.

Even more so, she didn't hate him. On the contrary, she seemed to still have the same love for him as when he'd last seen her.

Reece wept, overwhelmed, never having had such feelings in his life. He felt tremendous guilt for what he'd done, all brought back, fresh again. Yet he also felt love and appreciation for getting a second chance.

"I have thought of you every day since I last laid eyes upon you," he said.

"And I you," Selese said.

Reece leaned back and looked at her, their eyes locking, and she looking even more beautiful than the last time he had seen her.

Reece spotted something on her arm, and he looked down and saw a lily pad sticking to her sleeve. He peeled it off, confused; it was wet.

"What is this?" Reece asked.

"A lily, my love," she said softly. "From the Lake of Sorrows. From the day I drowned. In the land of the spirits, our methods of death cling to us, especially if self-inflicted. They remind us of how we died. Otherwise, sometimes it is hard to forget."

Reece felt a fresh rush of guilt and sorrow.

"I'm so sorry," he said. "I've asked for your forgiveness every day since you died. Now I can ask you in person. Will you forgive me?"

Selese looked at him for a long time.

"I have heard your words, my love. I saw the candle that you lit, that you sent down the mountain. I have been with you. Every moment, I have been with you."

Reece embraced Selese, crying over her shoulder as he held her tight, determined to never, ever let her go again, even if that meant he could not leave this place,.

"Yes," she whispered, into his ear. "I forgive you. I still love you. I always have."

*

Thorgrin stood beside his best friend Reece, overcome with emotion himself as he watched Reece's tearful reunion with her. He backed away with the others, all of them trying to give them their privacy. Thorgrin had never expected this. He had only expected ghouls and demons and foes; he had not anticipated loved ones. This land, this place of the dead, was so mysterious to him.

Thor barely had grasped the concept when suddenly, out of one of the many tunnels leading from this clearing, there emerged another person, a man Thor knew well. He marched out and stood there proudly, facing the group, and Thor's heart pounded as he saw who it was.

"My brothers," the man said softly, standing there grinning, the shining sword in his belt, just as Thor had last seen him. Thor was amazed. Here he was again, in the flesh, the beloved member of their group:

Conval.

Conven suddenly gasped and rushed forward.

"My brother!" he yelled.

The two brothers embraced, meeting with a great clang, each clasping the other's armor, neither letting the other go. Conven wept as he embraced his long-lost brother, laughing and crying at the same time, and Thor saw his face, for the first time in moons, filled with joy. Conven was more exuberant than Thor had seen him since his brother died. The old Conven, filled with life, was back with them once again.

Thor, too, stepped forward and embraced Conval, his old Legion brother, the man who had taken a blow for him and had saved his life. Reece, Elden, Indra, O'Connor, and Matus each stepped up and embraced him, too.

"I knew I would see you all again one day," Conval said. "I just did not think it would be so soon!"

Thor clasped Conval's arm and looked him in the eye.

"You died for me," Thorgrin said. "I shall never forget that. I owe you a great debt."

"You owe me nothing," Conval said. "Watching you has been repayment enough. I've been watching all of you. Again and again, you've acted with valor. With honor. You've made me proud. You've made my death worth it."

"Is it true?" Conven said, examining his brother, clasping his shoulder, still in shock. "Is it really you?"

Conval nodded back.

"You were not supposed to see me for many years now," Conval said. "But you chose to enter this land. It is a choice from which I could not deter you. So welcome to my home, my brothers. It's bit damp and gloomy, I'm afraid."

Conven broke into laughter, as did the rest of them, and for the first time since entering this place, Thor felt a momentary relief from the tension they had felt every step of the way.

Thor was about to ask Conval more about this place—when suddenly out of another tunnel, there emerged another man.

Thor could hardly believe it. Approaching him was a man who had once meant the world to him. A man he had respected more than any other man. A man he was certain he would never see again.

Standing there was King MacGil.

A wound in his chest where his son's dagger had stabbed him, he stood there proudly, smiling down on them all through his long beard, a smile Thor remembered fondly.

"My King," Thor said, bowing his head and taking a knee, as did the others.

King MacGil shook his head and stepped forward, grabbing Thor's arm and helping him up.

"Rise," he said, his voice booming, the familiar voice that Thor remembered. "All of you, rise. You can stand now. I am your King no longer. Death equals out us all."

Reece rushed forward and hugged his father, and the King embraced him back.

"My son," King MacGil said. "I should have kept you closer. Much closer than Gareth. I underestimated you because of your age. It is a mistake I would never make again if I had the chance."

King MacGil turned to Thor and clasped his shoulder.

"You've made us all proud," he said to Thor. "You have bestowed valor upon all of us. For you, we live on. We live on now through you."

Thor embraced the King, as he embraced Thor back.

"And what of my son?" Thor asked him, leaning back. "Is Guwayne with you?"

Thor was afraid to ask the question, afraid for the answer.

MacGil looked down.

"That is not a question for me to answer," he said. "You must ask the King himself."

Thor looked back, confused.

"The King?" Thor asked.

MacGil nodded.

"All roads here lead to one place. If you are looking for someone here, nothing passes through here without passing through the hands of the King of the Dead."

Thor looked back in wonder.

"I've come to lead you," MacGil said. "One former King can introduce another. If he does not like your petition, he will kill you. You can turn around now, and I can help you find a way out. Or you can march forward and meet him. But the risk is great."

Thor looked at the others, and they all looked back at him in agreement, determination in their eyes.

"We have come all this way," Thor said, "and there is no turning back. Let us meet this King."

King MacGil nodded, approval in his eyes.

"I expected no less," he said.

King MacGil turned and they followed him down a new tunnel, into a deeper and deeper blackness, and Thor braced himself, gripping his sword tight, sensing that this next encounter would determine his life to come.

CHAPTER TWENTY NINE

Volusia rode in her golden carriage, borne by her procession of men, a dozen of her finest officers and advisors accompanying her on this long march to Maltolis, the city of the touched prince. As they neared the gates, the great city unfolding before her, Volusia looked up and wondered. She had heard of the mad city, and of the touched prince, Maltolis, who took his name from the city, like her, ever since she'd been a girl, but she had never laid eyes upon it herself. Of course her mother had warned her, as had all of her advisors, never to venture anywhere near it. They said it was possessed; that all who went, never returned.

The idea excited her. Volusia, fearless, hoping for conflict, looked up at the massive walls, all quarried from black stone, and saw immediately that, as great of a city as Volusia was, Maltolis was ten times greater in scope and size, vast walls soaring to heaven. While Volusia was built on the oceanside, crashing waves and ocean blue visible from everywhere, Maltolis was landlocked, deep in the eastern lands, framed by an arid desert and a field of twisted, black cacti. They were a fitting adornment to herald this place.

They all came to a stop before a stone bridge spanning a moat, twenty yards wide, its deep blue waters glistening, encircling the city. There was only one way in and out of this city, across this arched, black bridge, guarded heavily by dozens of soldiers lining it.

"Set me down," Volusia ordered. "I want to see it for myself."

They did as she commanded, and as Volusia's feet touched the ground, it felt good to stand after all those miles of being carried. She immediately began to march for the bridge, her men rushing to fall in behind her.

Volusia stopped before it, taking in the sight: lining the bridge was a series of pikes, all pierced with the freshly decapitated heads of men, fresh blood dripping down. But what really surprised her was what she saw above it: high above was a golden railing, and from it there dangled the torsos of soldiers, their legs torn off. It was a gruesome sight, and an ominous way to herald the city. It made no sense, as these soldiers all appeared to be the touched prince's men.

"He us rumored to kill his own men," Soku stepped forward and whispered into Volusia's ear, he too gaping up at the sight. "The more loyal they are, the more likely to be killed."

"Why?" she asked.

Soku shrugged.

"No one knows," he replied. "Some say for fun; others say boredom. Never try to analyze the ways of a madman."

"Yet if he is so mad," she countered, "how does he run such a great city? How does he hang onto it?"

"With an army he inherited, vaster than ours will ever be."

"It is said they all tried to revolt when he took power," Koolian said, coming up to her other side. "They thought it would be easy. But he surprised them all. He killed the rebels in the most gruesome ways, starting with their families first. He turned out to be more vicious and unpredictable than the world could have known."

"I urge you again, my lady," Soku said. "Let us stay clear of this place. Let us find an army somewhere else. The touched prince will not lend you his armies. You have nothing he wants, nothing you can give him. Why would he entertain it?"

Volusia turned to him, her gaze cold and hard.

"Because I am Volusia," she said, her voice ringing with authority, with destiny. "I am the Goddess Volusia, born of fire and flame, of wind and water. I will crush nations beneath my feet, and nothing of this world, no army, no prince, shall stop me."

Volusia turned back to the bridge and led the way, her men hurrying to follow, until she reached the base and was blocked by a dozen soldiers lowering their halberds, blocking her way.

"State your purpose here," one said, his face obscured behind his helmet.

"You shall address her as Empress," Aksan said, stepping forward, indignant. "You speak to the great Empress and Goddess of Volusia. Queen of Volusia. Queen of the great city by the sea, and Queen of all provinces of the Empire."

"We let no one pass without the Prince's permission," the soldier replied.

Volusia stepped forward, raised her hand to the tip of the sharp halberd, and slowly lowered it.

"I have an offer for your Prince," she said softly. "One he cannot refuse. You will let us through because your Prince will kill you if he found you turned us away."

The soldiers, unsure, lowered their halberds and looked to each other, puzzled. One nodded, and they all slowly stood erect, making way for her to pass.

"We can bring you to our Prince," the soldier said. "But if he does not like your petition, well…you can see his handiwork," he said, looking up.

Volusia followed his glance and looked up at all the mutilated bodies adorning the bridge.

"Is it a chance you're willing to take?" the soldier asked.

"My Empress, let us leave this place," Soku said urgently in her ear. "Some gates are best left closed."

Volusia shook her head and took the first step forward. She looked out, beyond the soldiers, at the daunting gates, two huge iron doors, each adorned with a grotesque iron sculpture, upside down, one screaming and the other laughing. Those iron sculptures alone, Volusia thought, would be enough to turn away any person in their right mind.

She looked the soldier right in the eye, resolved.

"Bring me to your ruler," she commanded.

*

Volusia walked through the soaring gates of the mad city, taking it all in in wonder. A drop hit her shoulder, and thinking it was rain, she looked down at her golden sleeve, and was puzzled to see it stained scarlet. She looked up and saw a series of ropes crossing the city walls, from which were hanging a collection of limbs—a leg here, an arm there—all hanging like wind chimes, dripping blood. They swayed in the wind, the weathered rope creaking.

Some ropes hung lower and some higher, and as Volusia and her men passed through the gates, she had to brush up against them, swinging against her.

Volusia admired the Prince's barbarism. And yet, she wondered at the extent of his madness. His cruelty did not scare her—but the haphazardness of it did. She loved being vicious and cruel herself, yet she always did it within a rational context. But this...she just could not understand his way of thinking.

They passed through the gates and entered a vast city courtyard, the ground made of cobblestone, the city boxed in by the towering city walls. Hundreds of troops filled the square, their armor clanging, their spurs echoing, as they marched about. Otherwise, the city was oddly silent in the morning air.

As they slowly crossed the square, Volusia felt as if she were being watched; she looked up, and all along the city walls she saw people, citizens, their faces etched with panic and concern, leaning out of small windows and staring down, wide-eyed. Many wore grotesque expressions, some of them smacking their own heads, others swaying, others rocking and banging their heads into the walls. Some moaned, others laughed, and others, still, wept.

As she watched, Volusia saw one young woman lean so far out a window, she fell flying forward, face-first, shrieking. She landed on the stone with a splat, greeting her death fifty feet below.

"The first thing the touched Prince did when he inherited his daddy's throne," Koolian whispered to Volusia, walking beside her, "was to open the gates to all the asylums. He let all the madcaps have free rein in the city. It is said it pleases the Prince to see them on his morning stroll, and to hear their cries late into the night."

Volusia heard the strange moaning and crying and screaming and laughing, echoing off the walls, bouncing off of the square, and she had to admit that even she, undaunted by anything, found it unsettling. She was beginning to sense a feeling of dread. When dealing with a madman, all bets were off. She did not know what to expect in this place, and she had an increasing sense of foreboding that it would not be good. Perhaps, for the first time in her life, she would be in over her head.

Still, Volusia urged herself to be strong. She was a goddess, after all, and a goddess could not be harmed.

Volusia could feel the tension thick in the air as they were marched across the square, and finally, to a soaring golden door. Knockers as big as she were yanked slowly by a dozen soldiers, the immense doors creaking. A cold draft came out and hit her from the blackness.

Volusia was led into the castle, and as she entered this dim place, lit only by sporadic torches, she heard laughter and heckling bouncing off the walls. As her eyes adjusted, she saw dozens of madcaps, dressed in rags, pacing along the floor, some following them, others shouting at them, and one crawling alongside them. It was like entering an asylum. The soldiers kept them at a safe distance, yet still, their presence was unnerving.

She and her entourage followed them all down an endless corridor, and finally into a massive entry hall.

There, before them, Volusia was shocked to see, was the touched Prince. He did not sit on his throne, like a normal ruler, or come out to greet them; indeed, his throne, Volusia was surprised to see, was turned upside down—and the Prince, instead of sitting, stood on it, arms out wide at his sides. Barefoot, he wore nothing but shorts and the crown on his head, mostly naked despite the cold day. He also was covered in filth.

As they entered and he spotted them, he suddenly jumped down.

They all approached, Volusia feeling her heart pounding in anticipation; but instead of coming out to greet them, the Prince instead turned and ran to one of the walls. He ran alongside the ancient stone wall, adorned with the most beautiful stained glass, holding out his palms and running them alongside it. As Volusia watched the precious limestone walls turn red, she realized the Prince's hands were covered in paint. Red paint. He ran back and forth along the walls and smeared this paint along the precious stone, along the stained glass, ruining them; he smeared banners and heralds and trophies, all, no doubt, of his ancestors. And no one dared stop him.

The Prince laughed and laughed as he did so.

187

Volusia glanced at her men, who all looked back with equal apprehension.

It all might have been amusing, had not the chamber been filled with hundreds of deadly soldiers, all standing at attention, perfectly lined up along the center of the hall, surrounding the throne, all clearly awaiting the Prince's command.

Volusia and her men were led down the hall, right up to the Prince's throne, and she stood there, waiting, facing the empty throne turned upside down, watching the Prince run about the room.

Volusia stood there for she did not know how long, growing impatient, until finally the Prince broke free of what he was doing, ran across the room, the jewels on his crown jiggling as he went, raced to his upside-down throne, and jumped on the back of it. He slid down it like a little boy, landed on his feet, laughed and clapped hysterically, and then ran back up and did it again and again.

Finally, on the fifth slide, he landed on his feet and ran toward Volusia and her group at full speed. He stopped abruptly a foot before her, and all of Volusia's men flinched.

But not Volusia. She stood there, resolute, staring back at him, calm, expressionless, as she watched a rainbow of emotions pass over his face. She watched him go from happy to furious to neutral, to happy again, to confused, all in the span of a few seconds, as he examined her. He did not really make eye contact, but rather had a distant gaze to his eyes.

As Volusia summed him up, she realized that he was not unattractive, an eighteen-year-old man, well-built, with fine features. The madness on his face, though, made him seem older than he was. And of course, he needed a bath.

"Have you come to help me paint?" he asked her.

She stared back, expressionless, debating how to reply.

"I have come for an audience," she said.

"To help me paint," he said again. "I paint alone. You understand?"

"I've come…" Volusia took a deep breath, measuring her words carefully. "I've come to ask for troops. Romulus is dead. The great Empire leader is no more. You rule the eastern lands, and I, the shores

188

of the east. With your men, I can defeat the capital, before they invade both our lands."

"Both?" the Prince asked. "Why? It is *you* they are after. I am safe here. I have always been safe here. My parents were safe here. My fish are safe here."

Volusia was surprised by how astute he was; yet he also was mad, and she could not tell how much of him to take seriously. It was a confusing experience.

"Troops are but troops," he added. "They fill the skies. You want to use them. They may use you. I myself don't care for them. I have no need for them."

Volusia's eyes widened with hope, as she struggled to understand his erratic speech.

"We may use your men then?" Volusia asked, amazed.

The Prince threw back his head and laughed hysterically.

"Of course you may not," he said. "Well, maybe. But the problem is, I have a rule. Whenever someone makes a request to me, I must kill them first. Then, sometimes, after they are dead, I grant it."

He stared at her, sneered viciously, then just as quickly smiled, showing his teeth.

"I cannot be killed," Volusia replied, her voice cold as steel, trying to project authority although she was feeling increasingly off guard. "It is the great Volusia you address, the greatest Goddess of the east. I have tens of thousands of men who will die at my whims, and it is my destiny to rule the Empire. You can either loan me your men and rule it with me, or you—"

Before she could finish, the Prince held up a palm. He stood there looking up, as if listening—and the silence was shattered by the distant tolling of bells.

Suddenly, he turned and sprinted from the chamber.

"My babies are waking!" he said, as he ran from the hall. "Time to feed them!"

He clapped hysterically as he disappeared from the hall.

Volusia and her men were directed to follow, as all his soldiers fell in line, beginning to march after him. Volusia wondered where on earth he could be leading them.

189

Volusia found herself led back outside the castle, through soaring gates, and to another arched bridge, leading over the moat at the rear of the castle. They all hurried after the Prince as he stood there alone in the center of the bridge, nearly naked despite the cold, and reached out and held onto a long pole, struggling.

Volusia looked out over the bridge and saw that at the end of the long pole was a rope hanging down; at first she thought he was fishing, but then she looked closely and saw that at the end of it there was a man, with a noose around his neck, dangling in the waters of the moat. Volusia watched in horror as the Prince grasped the pole with both hands, holding on furiously with all his might, his muscles straining.

She heard shrieking, and she looked down and saw that in the moat was a group of crocodiles, biting the man's legs and ripping them off.

The Prince yanked the torso, legs chewed off, up out of the water, the victim's shrieks filling the air. He plopped him down on the bridge, thrashing, still alive.

Several soldiers rushed forward and grabbed the pole and raised the half-eaten man high up in the air, placing him on a hook on the ropes crossing the bridge. The body hung there, the man now moaning, dripping blood and water onto the bridge.

The Prince clapped furiously. He turned and hurried over to Volusia.

"I love to fish," he said to Volusia as he approached. "Don't you?"

Volusia looked up at the body, and the sight, even for her, was too much. She was aghast. She knew that if she were to survive this place, she had to take action, to do something quickly, definitively. She knew she had to relate to him on his own terms, to act crazier than he. To shock him out of his madness.

She suddenly stepped forward and reached up and snatched the crown from the Prince's head. She placed it on her own head and stood there, facing him.

All of his soldiers rushed forward, drawing their weapons—and the Prince himself finally seemed to snap out of it. Finally, she had his attention as he stood facing her.

"That's my crown," he said.

"I shall give it back to you," she said, "once you fulfill my request."

"I told you, anyone who makes a request is killed."

"You can kill me," she said. "But first, grant me my one request before my death."

He stared at her, his eyes darting back and forth, as if contemplating.

"What is that?" he asked. "What is it you want me to do?"

"I want to give you a gift greater than anyone's ever given you," she said.

"Gift? I have the greatest gifts of the empire. Entire armies given to me. What can you give me that I do not already have?"

She looked to him, laying the full beauty of her gorgeous eyes right on his, and she said:

"Me."

He looked back at her, confused.

"Sleep with me," she said. "Tonight. That is all I ask. In the morning, you can kill me. And you have granted me my request."

He turned and looked her for a long while in the heavy silence, Volusia's heart pounding as she hoped he went for it.

Finally, he smiled.

She knew that her powers were greater than any man could resist—not even a touched prince could turn them down. She stepped forward, held his face in her palms, leaned in, and kissed him.

He kissed her back lightly with trembling lips.

"Your request," he said, "is granted."

CHAPTER THIRTY

Thor followed King MacGil as he emerged from the blackest of black caves into a soaring underground cave, its ceilings a hundred feet high, more brightly lit than any other place he'd seen down here. Thor stopped short, as did all the others, in awe at the sight before them. This cavern was lit by massive fires, bubbling lava pits interspersed throughout, and was perhaps a hundred yards in diameter. In its center sat one singular object: an immense black throne made of sparkling granite, one solid piece within the bedrock itself, emerging like a tumor from the ground. Rising thirty feet high and wide enough to hold ten men, its arms ended in huge gargoyles, with sparkling black diamonds for eyes. All around it, bubbling lava pits cast a sinister glow upon it.

But that was not what shocked Thor most. What left him speechless was what occupied the throne: an immense creature, nearly the height of its throne, as wide as three men, with glowing red skin and bulging muscles. Its torso was that of a man's, yet its legs were covered in thick black hair, hanging down low to the floor of the cave. In place of feet, it had hooves. Its face looked almost human, yet it was huge, grotesque, monstrous, its proportions too big, with a jaw wider than Thor had ever seen, narrow yellow eyes and long, black horns which twisted out in circles on either side of its head. The head itself was stark bald, its ears pointy, its eyes glowing. It snarled as it breathed, steam rising all around it, a dark red halo hanging above it, flames shooting out in all directions from behind the throne. On its head sat a shining black crown, made entirely of black diamonds, with a huge black diamond in the center, encased in gold. Like a beast emerging from the bowels of the earth itself, it sat there, steaming, glowing red, exuding rage and death.

It scowled down at them, and Thor felt it was scowling right at him.

Thor gulped, his hairs rising on end, sensing he was looking back at the King of the Dead.

As if all this were not imposing enough, all around the King hovered dozens of creatures, buzzing and flitting about with small red wings, bright red skin, little gargoyles that hung and buzzed in the air. At its feet, on the ground, stood dozens of guards, massively muscular men with bright red skin and horns, standing at perfect attention and holding glowing red halberds, their tips alight with flames. Snakes slithered and wrapped themselves all around the base of the throne.

Thor stared back, knowing he had come to the throne room of death.

Thor felt something crunch as he stepped, and he looked down and saw that the floor was littered with bones, bones and skulls lining the walkway to the throne.

"You have been granted an audience with the King," MacGil said. "You will not be granted it twice. Be strong. Look him in the eye. Do not look away. You will die here, anyway: better to die with honor."

King MacGil nodded back at him reassuringly, and Thor stepped forward, the others by his side, walking down the long, narrow walkway of bones as he approached the King. As he went, on either side exotic creatures, like massive bees, flew near his head, their wings buzzing. They hissed threateningly at him as he went.

Thor heard a moaning, and he glanced around at the periphery of the cave and saw hundreds of humans chained to the wall, huge iron shackles around their necks and wrists and hands. He saw creatures standing over them, lashing them, and heard their screams. Thor wondered what they had done to end up in this place.

Thor had a sinking feeling that he would never leave this place, that this might be his last encounter before he was confined to death forever. He steeled himself, took a deep breath, and marched proudly down the walkway to the throne, MacGil's words in his ears.

Thor came as close as he could, until his path was blocked by the guards, who lowered their halberds. Thor stood there and looked up at the King.

The King looked down at Thor, breathing heavily, a guttural snarling noise coming from its chest each time it breathed, as it clawed the arms of the throne. Thor did not back down, but stood there and looked up, determined.

The buzzing quieted, as a tense silence filled the air. Thor knew this might be the most fateful moment of his life, and he thought of his mother. He wished for her to be by his side, to help give him power to get through this.

Thor felt he had to say something.

"I've come in search of my son," Thor boomed out, his voice filled with confidence as he stared back up at the King of the Dead.

The King leaned forward slightly, looked Thor in the eye, and Thor felt its glowing yellow eyes piercing right through him.

"Have you?" he asked, his voice impossibly deep, ancient. The voice echoed throughout the entire room, and with each word he spoke, the cavern buzzed with the sound of the creatures, hanging on his every syllable. The timbre of his voice was so dark and powerful, it hurt Thor's ears to even hear him speak.

"And what makes you think you shall find him?" he added.

"He is dead," Thor said. "I saw it with my own eyes. I wish to see him. Do not at least deny me this."

"Did you?" the King repeated, then leaned back and looked at the ceiling, emitting a groaning, snarling noise, a gargling in his throat, as he rubbed the arms of the throne.

Finally, he looked back at Thor.

"I would like to have your son here," the King said. "Very much. I had in fact sent my minions off to find and kill him and bring him here. But alas, a very strong energy surrounds the boy. They have failed in their task. He lives, still."

Thor felt himself filling with optimism at the King's words, yet he was in shock and wasn't sure he heard correctly.

"Are you saying Guwayne is not dead?"

The King nodded, ever so slightly, and as he did, Thor felt himself swelling with joy, grinning ear to ear, ecstatic beyond what he could ever imagine. He felt a new life bubbling up within him, a new desire to live.

"It is such a shame that he lives," the King said, "and will never get to see his father, who is now down here with me."

Thor looked up at the King and suddenly felt a fresh determination to live, to leave this place, to find Guwayne and rescue him. As long as Guwayne was alive, Thor did not want to be down here.

"I don't understand," Thor said. "I saw him die with my own eyes."

The King shook his head.

"You saw with your eyes, and your eyes deceived you. You have learned a great lesson. You must see with your mind. And now you must pay the price. You have entered here, but no one leaves the land of the dead. Never. You shall be my slaves down here for all eternity."

"No!" Thor called out, determined.

All the buzzing stopped, as the creatures froze and looked at Thorgrin, clearly shocked. Apparently, no one ever talked to the King that way.

"If Guwayne's not here, I shall not stay, either."

The King of the Dead glared down at him.

"Hold your tongue, Thorgrin," King MacGil whispered urgently to him. "You are down here now, but you can be free to roam about like me. Anger the King, though, and you can be doomed to one of the torture rooms, flayed for all eternity. Don't push it. Hold your tongue and accept your fate."

"I will NOT!" Thor yelled out, a great determination sweeping over him.

Thor studied the room, and as one of the fires died down, he noticed for the first time an amazing sword, plunged into the black granite floor, tip first, its hilt rising up, glowing in the light. It was the most beautiful sword Thor had ever seen, with an intricate ivory hilt made up of what appeared to be bones, and a shining, black blade that looked to be made of the granite in which it was lodged. Adorned with small black diamonds, it gleamed in the light, calling to him. Not since Thor had held the Destiny Sword had he laid eyes on a weapon such as this—or a weapon that called to him so strongly.

"You look at the sword," the King said, noticing. "You look at something you can never grasp. That is the sword of legend, the Sword of the Dead. No one who has passed through here has ever

195

been able to wield it. Only a great king can wield it. Only the chosen one."

Thor let out a great shriek, as he summoned his power, leapt into the air, over the army of guards, and aimed for the throne, for the King of the Dead. He let out a great battle cry as he reached out for the King's throat, fearlessly aiming to kill him.

The King of the Dead didn't even flinch. He weakly raised one palm, and as he did, Thor felt himself slamming into an invisible wall a few feet away, then dropping thirty feet down to the ground, landing hard on his back, winded.

Thor looked up in shock. He had summoned all his power, which had always sufficed to conquer anyone and anything. Even the darkest sorcerers.

"I am not one of your sorcerers, boy," the King seethed, looking down. "I am KING!"

His voice boomed so loudly, it shattered the rocks all around him, small rocks showering down on Thor.

"Your tricks won't work on me. Every dead soul passes through my fingers—and you are not above death. I can confine you to death here for all eternity, and more, to the worst torture you can imagine. Creatures will pry your eyes out and put them back in just for fun all day long."

There came an ecstatic buzzing and cheering amongst the smaller creatures, as they all clearly seemed delighted by the prospect.

Thor scrambled to his feet and looked up at the King, breathing hard, standing beside the others. He did not care for the consequences; he was prepared to fight, to do anything for Guwayne, even if he could not win.

The King leaned forward and examined him, and something seemed to change in his look.

"I like you, boy," he added. "No one has ever tried to attack me before. I admire it. You are more brazen than I thought."

He leaned back and rubbed the arms of his throne.

"As a reward," he continued, "I am going to give you a gift: one chance to leave this place. If you can destroy my legion of warriors, I will do what I've never done before: I will open the gates of the dead for you and allow you to return above. But if you lose, not only will you be confined here, but you and your men will be confined to the worst of the ten hells, an eternity of unimaginable torture. No one has ever defeated my legion. The choice is yours."

Thor looked back at the hundreds of massive warriors facing him, standing straight, holding their flaming halberds, awaiting the King's command; he also looked over their shoulder at the countless buzzing monsters whirling through the air. He knew his odds of winning were slim to none.

He stared back at the King proudly.

"I accept," Thorgrin replied.

The creatures buzzed in delight, and the King looked back at him with a look of respect, clearly pleased.

"But on one condition," Thorgrin added.

The King leaned back at him in surprise.

"A condition?" he scoffed. "You are hardly in a position to be setting conditions."

"I will not fight without this condition," Thor replied, determined.

The King stared back for a long time, as if debating.

"And what is this condition?" he finally asked.

"If we win," Thorgrin said, "then you will grant each of my men one request. Whatever we wish, you shall grant it to us."

The King studied Thor for a long time, and finally nodded.

"There's more to you, boy, than I observed from down below. It is too bad the Druids got a hold of you; if it weren't for your mother, I would have taken you long ago. I would like to have you by my side."

There was nothing Thor could think of that he would like less.

Finally, the King sighed.

"Very well then!" he called out. "Your request is just brazen enough to be accepted! Defeat my legion of warriors, and I will not only allow you to leave, but I shall also grant you each one request. Now let the wars begin!" he shouted.

Suddenly there came a tremendous buzzing in the air, and Thor turned and drew his sword. He saw hundreds of small gargoyle-like creatures flying through the air, swarming right for him and his men.

Beside him Thor heard his brothers draw their swords, too. It felt good to enter battle with Conval back by his side again.

As Thor faced off against these creatures, he felt himself on fire, coursing with a determination stronger than he'd ever felt. His son was up above, alive somewhere, and that was all that mattered to him. He would defeat all these creatures, or die trying.

Thor could not wait. He let out a great battle cry and charged forward to meet them. He used his power to lift himself up into the air, to slash his sword with the strength of a hundred men, and to slice through one red gargoyle after the next. A horrific screeching noise rose up as he slashed their wings from their bodies, and one by one, they fell to the ground.

Thor ducked from their snapping jaws and sharp teeth as they dove down at him, their large yellow eyes aglow. He landed on the ground and immediately turned and swung as the huge soldiers charged him, their flaming halberds out in front.

Thor wheeled and sliced their halberds in half, one after the other. Again and again they came to him, an endless stream, and more than one blow snuck through. Thor screamed out as the flaming tip of a halberd sliced his bicep, leaving a burn mark.

But Thor would not back down; he turned and smashed them in the face with the hilt of his sword, ducked as one jabbed for his head, spun around and slashed another. He summoned every power, recalled his training and summoned every technique he had ever learned, and threw himself into the fray with abandon, fighting hand-to-hand, blow for blow.

All around Thorgrin, his brothers did the same. Conval stepped forward with his great spear and plunged it through two soldiers' throats, while Conven, at his brother's back, swung his mace, taking out three soldiers who tried to stab his brother.

O'Connor raised his bow and fired, taking several gargoyles out of the air, dropping them like flies to the ground before they could attack his brothers. Matus lunged forward with his flail, swinging, and created a wide perimeter around them, taking out all manner of creatures that descended on them from the sky, and more than one of the huge soldiers wielding halberds.

Reece pushed Selese back to safety with King MacGil and drew his sword and threw himself with abandon into the melee, slicing and slashing and blocking left and right. He fought his way right up beside Thor, and more than once, blocked a fatal blow he had not been suspecting. Thor returned the favor, swinging around and using his sword to stop the blow of a flaming halberd right before it plunged into Reece's throat. As Thor held the halberd back, his sword locked with it, his arms shaking, Reece could feel the flames but an inch from his face, nearly searing it. Finally, Reece leaned back and kicked the soldier, and he and Thor both pounced on him each stabbing him at the same time.

Elden charged into the fray with his doubled-handed war ax, swinging great blows that took out two warriors at a time. A gargoyle dove down and landed on the back of Elden's neck, and Elden cried out as it clawed him. Indra drew her sling, took aim, and fired, hitting the creature with a large black stone a moment before it could sink its fangs into Elden's neck. She then hurled three more stones in quick succession, taking out several beasts before they could sink their halberds into Elden's side.

The beasts were powerful, though, and they seemed to never stop coming, and Thor and his men, after their first initial win, began to tire. Matus swung his flail and a beast caught it in his halberd and yanked the flail out of Matus's hand, leaving him defenseless. Another of the King's soldiers stepped forward and stabbed him, piercing Matus's arm with his halberd, making Matus scream out in pain.

The gargoyles, too, flew in a steady stream, and while O'Connor aimed his bow up at them, one of them swatted it from his hands, while three of them descended on him from behind, landing on his shoulders, biting his neck. O'Connor cried out and dropped to his knees, flailing, reaching back and trying desperately to get them off of him.

Elden swung his wide ax and chopped one a beast in half—but the blow left his back exposed, and another beast swung down with the side of his halberd and brought it down on Elden's exposed back, the side of the metal cracking his back, and the shaft splintering in half. Elden, stung by the blow, dropped to his knees.

Indra stepped forward and elbowed the creature in the throat before it could finish Elden off, sparing him; but a gargoyle then descended on her, biting her wrist, making her drop her sling and clutch her arm in pain.

Reece, surrounded and in the thick of the battle beside Thor, slashed and parried every which way, but he could not fight from every side, and soon, exposed, he was pierced in the side by a halberd, and he shrieked out in pain.

Thor, completely surrounded, sweat stinging his eyes, slashed and stabbed furiously in every direction, killing creatures left and right, fighting for his life. But he was running out of steam, struggling to catch his breath. However many creatures he killed, five more appeared. The buzzing filled his ears, as his ranks dwindled, and creatures descended upon him from every possible direction.

Thor knew, even as he fought, that this was a battle he could not win. That he would soon be condemned to an eternal hell of endless grief and torture.

A soldier charged from Thor's blind spot, swung his halberd, and knocked the sword from Thor's hand. It hit the black granite floor with a clang, and Thor was then elbowed in his back. He dropped to his knees, winded, defenseless, closed in on from every direction.

In the chaos, Thor closed his eyes and found a moment of peace. As he felt his life about to end, he retreated to a deeper part of himself. He thought of his mother, of Argon, of all the skills and powers they had taught him, and he knew, deep down, that this was just another test. A supreme test. He knew he was being handed it to rise above all of this. He knew, however impossible it seemed, that he had the power deep within him to overcome all of this. Even here, in the land of the dead, below the earth. The universe was still the universe, and he still had dominion over it. He knew that he was denying his power, once again.

A realization suddenly flashed over him:

I am bigger than death. I only die if I choose to die. If I want to live, if I truly want to live, I can never die. All death is suicide.

All death is suicide.

Thor felt a sudden burning coursing in his palms, between his eyes, and he leapt to his feet with an enormous amount of strength, more than anything he'd ever encountered. He leapt up twenty feet in the air, just missing the halberds as they struck for him, flying over their heads, and landing on the other side of the hordes.

Thor found himself landing right before the sword—the Sword of the Dead. He looked at it, immersed in the rock, and felt its power. He felt as he'd felt that day he had drawn the Destiny Sword. He felt that it was his. That it was *always* his. That he was meant to wield more than one special weapon in the life—he was meant to wield many.

Thor reached forward and with a great cry, grabbed the Sword of the Dead, his hands wrapping around the smooth ivory hilt, and yanked it up with all his might.

To his amazement, it began to move. With a sound like that of the earth tearing apart, stone being torn in two, the ground trembled, and the sword slowly rose.

Thor held the sword high overhead, feeling triumphant, feeling its power course through him, feeling one with it. He felt that his power was limitless. Even over death.

Thor noticed the King of the Dead stand up in his throne, looking down on him in shock and awe.

Thor turned and threw himself into legions of beasts, moving faster than he'd ever had, reaching back and slashing with the sword. He found that the sword, instead of slowing him, despite its weight actually made him faster, as if it were slashing on its own—as if it were an extension of his arm. Thor found himself cutting through beast after beast, taking out one soldier after the next, cutting through them like they were not even there. Shrieks rose up all around them as he felled one creature after the next, on the ground and in the air alike. He drove scores of soldiers back into a lava pit, screaming. He blocked their blows as they charged him with their halberds, the sword so powerful that it sliced the halberds in two, as if they were twigs. In the same motion, Thor swung around and took out a dozen soldiers in a single blow.

With a fierce battle cry, Thor charged whomever remained of the beasts, slashing with all his might, killing them left and right, going

201

faster and faster in a chaotic blur. His shoulders no longer felt tired—now, he felt invincible.

Soon, Thor found himself standing there alone, facing no more enemies. He did not understand what happened. All was still. The floors were covered with corpses, and there was no one left to fight.

Thor stood, his heart hammering, and faced the throne.

In the silence, the King of the Dead, a grave look on his face, looked down at him in disbelief.

Thor could not believe it.

He had won.

CHAPTER THIRTY ONE

Darius sat beside the fire at sunset, hunched over, his back raw, stinging, the pain worse than anything he'd experienced. It felt as if his skin had been ripped off his back, and it hurt to breathe, to move, to sit up. Dray sat loyally by his side, whining, his head in Darius' lap, unwilling to leave his side. Darius offered him small pieces of food but Dray, downcast, would not accept it. He gritted his teeth and grunted as Loti, kneeling at his side, placed a cool rag on his back, doused in ointments, running it along his skin as she had been doing for a while now, trying her best to ease his pain. As she did so, he noticed tears in her eyes, and he could see how guilty she felt.

"You did not deserve this," she said. "You have suffered for my actions."

Darius shook his head.

"You have suffered for *all* of our actions," he corrected. "It should not have fallen on you alone to have to stand up to the Empire. What you did for your brother, for all of us, was an honorable thing; what I did for you was the *only* thing."

Loti cried softly as she rubbed his wounds, wiping her tears with the back of her hand.

"And now?" she asked. "What was it all for? They'll return in the morning. They will take me, and maim us all. Or worse—they will kill us all."

Darius shook his head emphatically.

"I will not let them take you," he said. "I will not see them offer you up to save all of their lives."

"Then we shall all die," she stated.

He looked at her, her face grim, severe.

"Perhaps we shall," he said. "But are there not worse things? At least we shall die together."

He could tell by her expression how touched she was, how loyal she was, how grateful.

"I shall never forget what you did for me today," she said. "Never. Not as long as I live. You have my entire heart. Whether we die tomorrow or not, do you understand me? I am yours. I will love you from now to the end of eternity."

She leaned in and kissed him, and he kissed her back, a long meaningful kiss, and Darius felt his heart beat faster. She pulled back, her eyes glazed, and he could feel her sincerity. Her kiss took away the pain of his wounds; he would do it all again gladly for her, despite all the pain, despite all the suffering.

The village horn sounded, and all around the village fire, there gathered near Darius and Loti the Council of Elders, along with hundreds of villagers. Darius could sense the anxiety in the air, could see the panic across all their faces as they all swirled about, mumbling loudly, arguing with each other, a sense of desperation in the air. Darius could not blame them—after all, this could be their last night on earth. Tomorrow, a wave of mutilation or destruction was coming for them, and there was little that they could do about it.

The horn sounded again, and the villagers quieted as the chief elder, Bokbu, stepped forward, raised his palms, and faced them. He looked down sternly at Loti and Darius.

"Your actions have endangered our people," he said slowly, his voice grave. "But that matters little now. What matters," he said, looking out at the people, "is the choice that lies before us. At daybreak, what will we choose? Execution or maiming?"

A loud grumbling arose, villagers arguing with each other.

"We'll take maiming over death any day!" one shouted.

"I shall not be maimed!" yelled Raj. "I will die first!"

More grumbling erupted, everyone seeming to feel differently about it, and no one happy. Darius was shocked; even with faced with maiming, his villagers still wouldn't stand up, wouldn't all agree, as one, to fight back. What more did they need? Had their spirits been crushed so deeply?

"It is not a choice," one of the elders said, as the crowd slowly quieted. "It is not a choice that any man can make. It is a horror, a curse open us all."

The crowd fell deeply silent, somber, for a long time, all that could be heard was the whipping of the wind.

"We *do* have a choice!" a villager yelled. "We can hand the girl over to them!"

There came a muted cheer of approval amongst some villagers.

"She's endangered us all!" he yelled. "She broke the law. She is to blame! She must pay the price!"

There came a louder cheer of support among the crowd, mixed with arguing. Darius was amazed to see his people at such odds with each other, so willing to give her up.

"There is another choice!" another elder yelled out, raising his palms as the crowd grew silent. "We can offer them the girl and plea for our lives. Perhaps they will relent. Perhaps they shall not maim or kill us."

"And perhaps they should do both!" another crowd member yelled out.

There came a cheer, and the crowd once again broke into an agitated murmur, long and intense—until Bokbu stood and raised both of his palms. As he did, all eyes turned to him with respect, and finally, there was silence.

He cleared his throat, his presence grave, commanding authority and attention.

"Because of the actions of this one girl," he boomed, "our entire village has been put in an impossible situation. Of course we cannot accept death. We have little choice but to accept life as the Empire wishes us to have it, as we always have. If that requires handing over the perpetrator to them, then that is what we are compelled to do.

"As much as it pains me, sometimes one must sacrifice for the sake of the whole. I see no other way out. We must accept their sentence. We shall be maimed, but not dead. Life will go on for us, as it always has."

He cleared his throat as the crowd remained silent, and he turned and fixed his gaze on Darius.

205

"Tomorrow, at daybreak, we will do as the Emperor commands and you, Darius, as they requested, will represent our village and present our offer to them. You will hand over the girl, we will accept their punishment, and we will move on. There shall be no more talk of this. The elders have spoken."

With that, Bokbu reached out and slammed his staff on the hollow wooden log, making a definitive sound, the sound always used to mark an important ruling. It meant the ruling could not be changed, could not be argued.

One by one, the villagers dissipated, drifting back to their homes, despondent. Darius's friends, Raj, Desmond and Luzi came over, along with several of his other brothers, as Darius sat there, numb, in shock. He could not believe that his people would betray Loti, betray him, like this. Were they that afraid of death? Were they so desperate to cling to their pathetic little lives?

"We can't hand her over," Raj said. "We can't go down like this."

"What are we to do?" asked Luzi. "Shall we fight? Us against ten thousand men?"

Darius turned to see his sister, Sandara, approaching, joined by that Queen of the white people, Gwendolyn, and her brothers. He saw the concern across Sandara's and Gwendolyn's faces. As Darius looked at Gwendolyn, he could see the warrior in her eyes; he knew that she was their best hope.

"How are your wounds, my brother?" Sandara asked, coming over and inspecting them, her face lined with concern.

"My wounds are deep," he replied meaningfully. "And not from the lashing."

She looked at him, and she understood.

"You cannot fight," she said. "Not this time."

"You have not lived here," Darius said. "Not for years. You cannot tell me what to do. You don't understand what our people have suffered."

Sandara looked down, and Darius felt bad; he hadn't meant to be so harsh with her. But he was feeling desperate, furious at the world.

Darius turned and looked at Gwendolyn, who also looked down at him with concern.

206

"And you, my lady?" he asked.

She looked back at him questioningly.

"Do you plan to leave us now?" he added.

Gwendolyn stared back, expressionless, and he could tell she was consumed by that very decision.

"The choice is yours," he added, "to leave or to stay. You still have a chance to get out. The Empire does not know you are here. Of course, the Great Waste might kill you, but at least it is a chance. We, though—we have no chance. Yet if you stay, if you stay here and fight by our side, we would have a greater chance. We need you, you and your men, and their armor and their steel. Without you, we have no chance. Will you join us? Will you fight? Do you choose to be a Queen? Or do you choose to be a warrior?"

Gwendolyn looked back and forth from Darius to Sandara to Kendrick, and he could not read her expression. She seemed under a cloud, and he could see how much she had suffered. He could see that she was weighing the future of her people, as Queen, and he did not envy her her decision.

"I'm sorry," she said finally, her voice broken, filled with sadness. "I wish I could help you. But I cannot."

*

Gwendolyn, on her way back to the caves at sunset, passed through the village, all the people agitated, a panicked energy in the air, and her mind swirled with mixed emotions. On the one hand, she thought of Sandara's people, of their predicament, and her heart went out to them. She knew how cruel the Empire could be—she had experienced it firsthand. Her first impulse, of course, was to rush to their aid, to throw her people into their fight, to give up all of their lives for their cause, for their freedom.

On the other hand, she was a Queen now. She was not her father's daughter, not a teenage girl, but a Queen, with responsibilities for her people. They all looked to her and their lives all depended on her. She could not make the wrong decision on their behalf. After all, what right did she have to give up their lives for someone else's? What kind of Queen would that make her?

Gwen had seen her people suffer so much, too much, and she had suffered so much herself. Did they deserve to be thrown into another war, to end their lives this way, far from home, here in this dusty village? The villagers would be terribly outnumbered in the morning, all of them maimed or worse. She knew the right thing to do, not as warrior, but as a *leader*, was to round her people up and, at the first light of sun, march them in the opposite direction, into the Great Waste. To begin the great journey to find the Second Ring. It might just be a fantasy, she knew, and they would all likely die out there in the Great Waste—but at least they would be striving for something, striving for another life. Not walking into instant death.

Regardless of what *she* wanted, *she*, Gwendolyn, the individual, that was her job as Queen demanded, wasn't it? To protect her people?

Gwen's heart broke for the villagers. She believed in their cause, and it was a cause she shared. Yet, even the villagers were divided, and even they didn't have the heart to fight. Few of them had the warrior spirit—few except for Darius. Could she fight a battle for them that they did not wish to fight themselves?

"As Queen, surely you cannot be considering their predicament?" Aberthol said as he walked beside her. "True, they are a good people. A kind and fair people—"

"And they took us in," Gwen added.

Aberthol nodded.

"They did," he replied. "But they do not fight our wars for us. We have no obligation to fight theirs for them. Not that we could win anyway. It is not, you see, an invitation to join them in battle—but an invitation to join them in death. Those are two vastly different propositions, my lady. Your father never would have approved of that. Would he have sacrificed all of his people? For a fight they do not wish to fight, and a fight they cannot win?"

They continued to walk, falling into a comfortable silence as Gwen pondered his words.

Kendrick and Steffen walked alongside here, and they did not need to say anything; she saw the compassion on their faces. They understood, all too well, what it meant to make a hard decision. And they understood Gwendolyn, after all this time, all these places together. They knew the decision was hers to make, and they gave her the space to make it.

All of which made Gwendolyn feel even more tortured by it. She could see both sides of it; yet her mind felt muddled. If only she had Thor here, by her side, with his dragons—that would change everything. What she wouldn't give to see her old friend Ralibar appear in the horizon, swoop down with his familiar roar and let her take a long ride.

But he was not here. Nor would he come. None of them would. She was, once again, on her own. She would have to make her own way in this world, just as she had done so many times before.

Gwendolyn heard a whining noise, looked down and saw Krohn walking at her feet, and was reassured by his presence.

"I know, Krohn," she said. "You would be first to attack. Just like Thor. And I love you for it. But sometimes we need more than a white leopard cub to win."

As they hiked all the way to the base of the caves, Gwen stopped and looked up the hillside, to the small cave in which Argon lay. Steffen and Kendrick stopped and looked at her.

"Go ahead," she said to them. "I will join you shortly. I must ascend alone."

They nodded and turned away, understanding, and Gwen turned away from them. As the sun was setting, its last rays caressing the hillside, she turned and hiked up the hillside, going to the one person she knew might be able to give her answers, who had always been able to give her solace in times of need.

As she hiked, she felt something at her heels, and looked down to see Krohn.

"No, Krohn, go back," she said.

But Krohn whined and stuck to her ankles, and she knew he would not be deterred.

They hiked up the mountainside until she reached Argon's cave, and she paused at the entrance. She prayed he would be able to help her. He had not answered her the last several times she'd visited, still more out of consciousness than in it. She did not know if he would answer now, but she prayed he would.

As twilight fell, the last glimmer of light illuminating the sky and the first of two moons rising, Gwen took one long look at the countryside, beautiful in a barren sort of way, then turned and entered the small cave.

There lay Argon, alone, in this small cave, as he had requested. There was a heavy energy in the air; when she was young, she remembered an aunt she'd had who'd laid in a coma for years. The air in this cave felt like that.

Gwen walked over and knelt beside Argon. She reached down and felt his hand; it was cold to the touch. As she held his hand, she felt more confused than ever, more in need of his counsel. What she wouldn't give for answers.

Krohn walked over and licked Argon's face, whining; but Argon did not stir.

"Please, Argon," Gwen said aloud, unsure if he could hear her. "Come back to us. Just this once. I need your guidance. Should I stay here and fight with this people?"

Gwen waited a long time, so long, she was sure he'd never answer.

Just when she was ready to leave, she was shocked to feel him squeeze her hand. He opened one eye and stared at her, his eye shining dimly.

"Argon!" she said, overwhelmed, crying. "You live!"

"Barely," he whispered.

Gwendolyn's heart lifted to hear his voice, however raspy. He was alive. He was back with her.

"Argon, please, answer me," she pleaded. "I'm so confused."

"You are a MacGil," he said, finally. "The last of the MacGil Kings. The leader of a nation without a home. You are the Ring's last hope. It is up to you to save your people."

He fell silent a long time, and she didn't know if he would continue; yet finally, he surprised her by going on.

"Yet it is not a land that makes a people; it is the heart that beats within it. What they are willing to live for—and what they are willing to die for. You might find land beyond the Great Waste, you might find safe harbor, a great city. But what will you give up for it?"

Gwendolyn knelt there, struck by the gravity of his words, waiting, hoping for more. But there was no more. He fell silent again, closing his eyes, and she knew he would not stir.

Krohn lay his head on his chest and whined, and Gwen knelt there, all alone in her thoughts, as a gale of wind ripped through the cave.

What will you give up for it?

What mattered more, she pondered: honor? Or life?

CHAPTER THIRTY TWO

Godfrey stood at the edge of the woods, Akorth, Fulton, Merek, and Ario beside him, and stared out, watching the gate, trying to think clearly as he felt the strong wine going to his head. As he stood there, he wondered for the millionth time how on earth they could ever get inside. It was easy, he realized, to volunteer for a mission; executing it was the hard part. He wished he could just volunteer and let someone set out for him.

"Are we just going to stand here all day?" Akorth asked.

"Or are we going to walk up to those soldiers and ask if we can walk through?" Fulton added.

"Maybe give them some flowers while we're at it," Akorth said. "I'm sure that would do the trick."

"We could always overpower them," Fulton said.

"Right," Akorth said. "I'll take out the thirty on the right, and you take out the thirty on the left."

They snickered.

"Shut up, all of you," Godfrey said.

He couldn't get his head clear, between the wine and their banter in his ear. He was trying to concentrate, to think clearly. They had to get into this place, and they couldn't wait here much longer. He just did not know how. Force had never been his way, and force would be ridiculous in this case.

As Godfrey stood there, running through all potential schemes, all the ways to trick the guards, suddenly, he heard the distant sound of horses' hooves.

He turned and looked out at the road behind them, leading to the gate, and saw in the distance, rounding a bend, coming into view amidst a cloud of dust, a huge caravan of slaves. There came one horse-drawn wagon after the next, a small army of Empire taskmasters and, behind them, an endless rope of chains and shackles, hundreds of slaves being brought into Volusia. It was a chaotic parade of people, the slaves far outnumbering the soldiers.

Suddenly, Godfrey was stuck with an idea.

"That's it," he said, excited, watching the caravan.

The others all looked at him, then at the caravan, confused expressions on their faces.

"We'll hide among the slaves," he added.

Godfrey turned as he heard the sound of a gate creaking, opening, iron being raised slowly, and saw the drawbridge being lowered and saw the city gates being opened. He knew this was their chance.

"Do you see there," he added, "where the tree line meets the road?"

They all turned and looked.

"That group of slaves in the rear," he said. "On my count, we run for it. We'll blend in with them. Keep your heads low and your chins down and get as close to those slaves as you can."

"What if we're caught?" Akorth asked.

Godfrey looked him in the eye, and suddenly, inexplicably, he felt a certain strength overcome him; for a moment he was able to throw off his fears, and to look back at him as a man. He made a commitment, and he was going to follow through.

"Then we'll die," Godfrey answered flatly.

Godfrey could hear in his own voice the authority of a ruler, a commander, and he was surprised to hear something like his father's own voice coming through him. Was this what it felt like to be a hero?

The caravan passed, the dust rising in his face, the sounds of the shackles all consuming. With the wagons just a few feet away, he could smell the sweat of men, the horses, the fear.

Godfrey stood there, heart pounding, as he watched a taskmaster pass right before him. He waited a few more seconds, wondering if he had the courage. His knees felt weak.

"NOW!" he heard himself say.

Godfrey broke into action, running out in front of the others, away from the tree line, his heart pounding as he gasped for breath, sweat stinging his eyes, pouring down his neck. Now, more than ever, he wished he was in better shape.

Godfrey raced for the rear of the caravan, shuffling in and joining the group of slaves quickly, to the puzzled expressions of the slaves. None of them, luckily, said anything.

Godfrey did not know if the others would follow; he half expected them not to, to turn around and head back into the woods and abandon this crazy mission.

Godfrey was surprised as he turned to see all the others joining him, cramming in to the center of the group of slaves, brushing up against him. They all marched with their heads lowered, as he had instructed, and in the thick of the group, they were hard to detect.

Godfrey glanced up, just for a moment, and saw the massive gates to the city before him, the high spiked iron portcullis. His heart pounded as he kept on marching, passing underneath it. At any moment he expected to be caught, to be stopped.

But he never was. To his own amazement, within moments, they were inside the city walls.

There came a definitive slam behind them, iron meeting iron, reverberating in his ears, and Godfrey felt the finality of it.

They had achieved the impossible.

But now, there was no turning back.

CHAPTER THIRTY THREE

Alistair held on for dear life as she rode the dragon, grabbing its slippery scales, flying in and out of clouds as it circled over the Ring. She did not understand how she got there, but she cried out and grabbed on as it dipped down lower, breaking through the clouds, offering her a bird's-eye view of the countryside.

Alistair looked down, and as she did, she was horrified to see her homeland, her beloved Ring. It was not the homeland she once knew. It was up in flames, the entire Ring one huge conflagration, burning higher and higher to the heavens.

Everywhere she flew there was fire.

Suddenly, the flames disappeared.

As Alistair flew lower, she saw, in place of the flames, ash and rubble and ruin. The Ring had become a wasteland. She flew over her beloved King's Court and saw not a single wall left standing.

They covered more and more countryside, and as they did, Alistair looked down and saw millions of troops, Romulus's men, marching systematically, occupying the Ring from every corner. All the people she had loved and knew were gone, dead. Everything that had once been so familiar to her, destroyed.

"No!" she cried.

The dragon made a sudden sharp move, and Alistair couldn't hold on. She found herself plummeting, flailing through the sky as she shrieked, heading down to the scorched earth below.

Alistair woke screaming. She sat up in bed, breathing hard, and looked all around, disoriented.

Slowly, in the first light of dawn, she realized it had all just been a dream. She was sitting there, safe and sound, in the luxurious Queen's chamber, in a down bed, covered in fine silks. Beside her lay Erec, safe and sound, yet startled. He sat up, too.

"What is it, my lady?" he asked.

Alistair sat on the edge of the bed, her forehead cool and damp, and shook her head. It had seemed so real. Too real.

"Just a dream, my lord," she said.

215

Alistair stood, draped her silk robe around her, and walked out to the open-air balcony, past the billowing drapes.

She stood outside, breathing in the warm ocean air and immediately felt at ease. She stared out at the gorgeous vista, the steep cliffs, the rolling hills, the endless vineyards, the blossoming trees planted along the steep slopes. She smelled the fresh orange blossoms, heavy in the air, and she felt deeply at home. She felt that nothing could be wrong in the world, that this place had the power to wipe out her nightmares. There was something about this place, something about the way the sun struck the sea, lit everything with a glow that made the world feel glorious.

Yet this time, try as she did, Alistair could not shake the nightmare from her mind's eye. It felt like more than a dream—it felt like a message. A vision.

Alistair heard a fluttering of wings, a screech, and she looked up, startled, to see a falcon descend from the sky. She could see it held a message in its claws, a small, rolled up piece of parchment.

Alistair put on the silver gauntlet, crossed the balcony, and held out her wrist; the falcon spotted it and swooped down, landing on her wrist.

Alistair took the message tied to its claw and lifted her wrist, sending it on its way. She stood there and examined it, afraid to open it. She had an ominous feeling and did not want to read whatever message it bore.

Erec walked out onto the balcony, joining her, and stepped up beside her.

Alistair reached out and handed the scroll to him.

"Don't you want to open it?" he asked.

She shook her head. After her nightmare, she sensed with certainty that it was a message informing them of the destruction of the Ring. Her vision had already shown it to her; she did not need to read the message.

Erec unrolled it and read, and she could hear him let out a soft, involuntary gasp.

She turned and looked at him, and his expression told her all she needed to know.

216

"I fear it is grave news, my lady," he said. "The Ring has been destroyed. Romulus's men occupy it. Our brothers and sisters have all fled. Exiled. They have crossed the open sea, fled to the Empire. It is a message from Gwendolyn. This falcon has crossed the sea. She asks for help."

Alistair looked out on the landscape, and she felt a desperation welling up inside her. She knew it, and yet still it pained her to hear the words. She knew what this message meant: it would change all of their lives, forever. They would have to leave this place at once, of course, and go after their people.

"Is there word of Thorgrin?" she asked, immediately thinking of her brother.

Erec shook his head.

Alistair looked longingly at the beautiful landscape, and felt torn inside to have to leave it. She sensed they would be going on a long voyage, across the sea—and even worse, that they might not ever return here again.

Alistair looked down in the distance at all the wedding preparations below, and imagined what a beautiful ceremony she would have had. She would have been Queen here, and they would have lived their lives in peace and harmony. They would have had many children here, and raised them in this beautiful place. Finally, after a life of chaos and strife, she would have had peace.

Instead, they were about to embark on a life of travel and battle and danger and strife. Alistair breathed deeply and shook her head, trying to make it all go away.

She finally turned to Erec, holding back tears, and nodded stoically.

"I already knew, my lord," she said.

"You *knew*?" he said. "But how?"

"A dream. A nightmare. More like a vision."

"We must make preparations," Erec said, looking out at the horizon meaningfully, his voice already morphing to that of a wartime commander. "We must help them at once."

Alistair nodded.

"Yes, we must."

217

He looked at her, softening.

"I'm sorry," he said gently, following her gaze down to the wedding preparations. "We shall wed another time. In another place."

She nodded, holding back tears, and smiled at him, as he took her hand and kissed it.

With that, he turned and marched off, walking purposefully into the morning, into the life they were about to lead. She watched him go, and she knew that the life she had once dreamed for herself was gone forever. And that life would never be the same again.

*

Alistair took the familiar path she took every morning, barefoot on the cool stone, as it wound its way through a beautiful orange grove, the trees providing shelter and privacy as she wound her way from the royal grounds to the reflecting pools. While Erec gathered the fleet, there was still but a sliver of time left before she packed up to leave this place—and she wanted her final memory here to be a fond one. She had looked out in longing at the hot springs, hidden in the plateaus, and she wanted one more chance to soak in them before she said goodbye to this island.

The sun began to warm as it rose on the islands, and it shone down on her as she emerged from the forest onto the small, hidden plateau perched at the edge of a cliff, hidden by trees. She removed her silk robe and, naked, slipped into the small hot pool.

She floated in the natural spring waters, floating on the edge of a cliff, looking out, seeing the entire island spread out before her, the cliffs, the sparkling blue sea, the endless sky. Birds sang high above her, the branches swayed and rustled, and she floated, relishing every moment here, relishing this deeper peace than she had ever found in her life.

Alistair prayed to god that her brother was safe, that all her people were safe. That they would reach them in time, rescue them from whatever troubles they were in.

Alistair tried to reach a deep sense of peace, floating here, as she always did. But today, with all the troubles on her mind, she was just unable to.

She rose from the waters and prepared to dress herself in her robe, when suddenly, as she stood there on the stone, she spotted something that made her think twice. She saw the broad, white leaves of the acylle tree, hanging low beside the pool, and she recalled what her mother-in-law had told her: that leaf could tell you if you were with child.

Alistair did not know why she looked at the leaf now, but something inside her drew her to it. It had only been a moon since she had been with Erec, and she knew the chances of her being pregnant were remote. Yet still, she wanted to try.

Alistair's heart beat faster as she walked over to it, tore off a large white leaf, held it up, and placed it to her breast, as her mother-in-law had instructed her. She placed a palm over it and held it there for a good ten seconds, the leaf cool on her skin. Finally, she removed it and held it up in the light. If she was pregnant, it was supposed to turn yellow.

Alistair's heart fell to see that it was still stark white.

She knew it was silly to try, so soon, yet still she began to worry: would she ever be able to have a child? There was nothing she craved more to bring her closer to Erec.

Alistair set the leaf down on the stone and dressed quickly, pulling back her hair, tying it tight, and turning to leave. As she did, as she was about to enter the forest trail, she glanced back one last time and took one last look at the leaf.

She did a double take.

Sitting there on the stone, she watched in disbelief as the leaf slowly changed colors before her eyes.

She walked over to it, and held it up to the light with trembling hands. As she did, her entire body froze, numb with shock.

She was with child.

CHAPTER THIRTY FOUR

Volusia opened her eyes, as the first light of dawn broke through the window, and looked over to see herself lying in the Touched Prince's arms, her cheek on his chest, both of them naked beneath the silk covers. They lay asleep in his kingly chambers, in his luxurious four-poster bed, on the finest bedding she ever felt, and as she realized where she was, she woke with a start, immediately raising her head, on guard.

It all came rushing back to her; sleeping with the Prince had been a different experience than any man she'd ever been with. He was so truly mad that it had taken her hours just to get his clothes off, and he had resisted her most of the time.

But finally, after a certain point, she had tamed him, had made him hers. She did not enjoy it, not a second of it. But she could tell that he did—and that was what mattered. This was all a necessary means to an end, as all men had been in her life. She would climb the rungs of power in any way necessary, whether that required killing her own mother or sleeping with a thousand men. Nothing would ever stand in her way.

Nothing.

Volusia had a way of turning off a switch in her mind, creating a sense of detachment, carrying herself away to a faraway place. It was this cold detachment that allowed her to sleep with her worst enemy, or torture someone just for fun. The touched prince was an evil, sadistic man, who also happened to be mad. But in Volusia he had met his match: she could be more sadistic than anyone—even someone like him.

Volusia thought of their agreement, her vow to let him kill her only after she had slept with him. She smiled as she thought of it. She loved making vows.

And she loved breaking them even more.

As she sat up, the Prince opened his eyes and sat up, too. He turned to her, and as he looked at her, she saw something different in his eyes this time. There was a clarity she had not seen before, as if his madness had been calmed.

"My lady," he said.

His voice surprised her. Now it was clear and cool, not filled with the erratic madness she had heard before.

"You have done something to me," he said. "Sleeping with you…I can't explain it. I feel different than I ever have before. I don't hear the voices. I feel calm. Normal. Back to the self I once knew."

Volusia stood, putting on her robe, and studied him, surprised. He stood, too, and put on his robe, lacking all of the erratic movements and behavior he had shown the day before. He walked around her, took both of her hands in his, and looked her in the face. She was baffled. Was this just another act of madness? Or had something really shifted within him?

She had not foreseen this—and it was very rare in her life when Volusia did not foresee something.

"You have given me life again," he said sweetly, softly, holding her hands. "You have made me *want* to live."

Volusia looked into his eyes, and she could that he was indeed a different man. She was speechless, and did not know how to react.

"My lady, stay here with me," he said. "Stay by my side. Let me make you my queen. I will cherish you. My armies are vast, and I will give you all my troops to do with as you wish. Anything—it shall all be yours. Whatever your heart desires. Just stay by my side. *Please.* I need you."

She looked into his eyes as he leaned in and kissed her, a soft gentle kiss, filled with lucidity. Volusia's mind raced, as she tried to contemplate this turn of events.

In the distance, Volusia could hear a soft chanting. It gradually rose, greater and greater, and the Prince smiled and turned toward his open-air arched balcony.

"My people," he explained. "It is how they greet the day—they chant my name. They worship me. Be by my side, and they will worship you, too."

He took her hand and led her gently outside, onto the spacious balcony, right up the trail. Volusia looked down over the edge and her

221

stomach dropped as she saw the steep drop below. Down below, the courtyard was already packed with thousands of people, on their hands and knees, bowing, all chanting.

"Maltolis! Maltolis!" they chanted.

He smiled and turned to her.

"Like you," he said, "I take the name of my city."

Volusia took it all in, and she could see that he was right: his people really did see him as a god. They worshipped him. Tens of thousands of people, a greater army than she would ever have.

He turned to her.

"We shall unite, and we shall rule the empire together," he said.

Volusia smiled back at him, leaned in, and kissed him.

They held hands as they turned and faced his people together, all of them cheering wildly. Volusia knew that if she accepted his offer, all of it would come to pass. She would have everything handed to her that she needed to rule the Empire.

Yet as she stood there, Volusia felt something rising within her. It was a sense of resentment. She did not want to rule the Empire together. She did not want to rule an army together. She did not want to have the Empire handed to her. Everything in her life thus far she had taken. By force. By force of will. With her own two hands. Nor did she want the love of a man, mad or not, or a union to one. She did not want to be loved—not by a man, not by anyone. And if she wanted love, she would take it for herself.

"You offer is a generous one, my lord," she said, turning to him. "But you're forgetting one thing."

"And what is that?" he asked.

In one quick motion, Volusia reached back, grabbed him by the back, and suddenly, unexpectedly, used all her might and threw him, head-first, off the balcony.

There came a horrified gasp from his thousands of people, as Maltolis fell through the air, shrieking, flailing, head over foot, until finally he hit the ground, a hundred feet below, with a smack.

His neck broken instantly, he lay there in a pool of blood, dead.

"I am the great Goddess Volusia," she said proudly, down to his dead body, "and I share power with no one."

CHAPTER THIRTY FIVE

Thorgrin stood facing the King of the Dead, the Sword of the Dead still dripping blood in his hand, and all the King's dead creatures at his feet. Thor felt numb with victory.

The King stood on his throne and looked down at it all with an amazed expression.

"They said that you would come one day," the King said, looking at Thorgrin. "The man who would defeat the darkness. The man who would wield the sword. The King of the Druids."

The King looked Thor over carefully, and Thor did not know how to respond. Could it really be true? Would he one day be King of the Druids?

"Let me tell you what it means to be a King," he continued. "It means to be alone. Utterly alone."

Thor stared back, his heart still pounding from battle, beginning to process it all. He looked around and saw with relief that his men, while wounded, were still alive.

He turned back to the King, remembering.

"You promised to open the gates," Thor said. "If I defeated your creatures, you vowed to let us go."

The King smiled wide, a grotesque image, his face collapsing in a million folds and wrinkles.

"A King does not always keep his promises," he said, laughing, his voice deep, echoing off the walls, the tone of it hurting Thor's ears.

Thor stared back, crestfallen. He tightened his grip on his sword, and was about to respond, when the King continued.

"In this case," the King said, "I will. But it is not quite so simple. The Land of the Dead exacts a price. You don't just walk out of here. Seven of you entered, and for each exit, there must be a price. The price you will pay will be seven demons."

"Seven demons?" Thorgrin asked, not understanding, but not liking the sound of it.

The King turned, and as he did, a huge secret door, made of solid stone, slid open in the cave wall. It opened up slowly with an awful sound of stone scraping stone, revealing spiked iron gates behind it. Beyond the gates, Thor saw a vast purple sky, the sun setting over an ocean; he heard the howling of the wind, and felt a cold breeze rush into this place.

"Beyond the gates lies the world above," the King said. "You will return to your precious world, but your release will also release seven demons, free to roam the world. These demons will plague you, each of them, at some point in place and in some time you'll never know. You will receive seven tragedies, one from each demon. When you least expect it. The tragedies might strike you—or they might strike someone you love. Do you still want to leave?"

Thor looked at the others, and they stared back at him with an amazed expression. Thor turned and looked back at the massive iron gates, each bar two feet thick, glowing red, and he watched seven black shadows, looking like gargoyles, suddenly appear and fly through the air, slamming their heads into the gates again and again, as if waiting to be released.

Thor thought of Guwayne, of Gwendolyn, of all the people he knew and loved up above; he thought of his brothers who had come down here for his sake. He knew he had to return, if not for his own sake, then for everyone else's. Whatever the cost.

"I accept your price," Thorgrin said.

The King stared back, expressionless, then finally nodded. He began to motion to his men to open the gates, but before he did, Thorgrin stepped up and called out:

"And what about you? You made me a promise. You vowed that if I defeated your creatures, you would give each of us one request."

The King studied him.

"Indeed, I did. And what is yours?" he asked.

Thor looked deeply into his eyes, staring back with all the seriousness he could muster.

"I request that you, King of the Dead, not take my son. Do not allow Guwayne to die, at least not until I have had a chance to hold him in my arms, to look into his eyes, to be reunited with him. That is all I ask."

The King pondered Thor's words, then finally nodded.

"Your request shall be granted."

The King next looked to O'Connor.

"And what is yours?" he asked.

O'Connor replied: "I request to be reunited with my sister before my death. That you not take her until we've seen each other again."

The King nodded and turned to Matus.

"I, too, request you do not take my sister until I have had a chance to see her again."

Elden stepped forward.

"And I wish to be reunited with my father."

"And I with my people," Indra said.

The King turned and looked at the remaining two Legion brothers: Reece and Conven.

Reece stepped forward solemnly, looked up at the King, and said: "I request that you release Selese from this place. Let me take her with me. Release her. Return her to the land of the living."

The King of the Dead scrutinized Reece.

"Such a request has never been made," he said. "A difficult request. If she returns to the land of the living, she cannot be as she was. For once you're dead, you can never truly live again."

"I will give anything," Reece said, clutching Selese's hand.

"Is this your wish, too?" the King asked Selese.

She nodded, tears falling from her eyes she gripped Reece's hand.

"I would give anything to be with Reece again," she said.

After a long pause, finally, the King of the Dead nodded.

"Very well," he said. "You shall return to the land of the living. For now. Rest assured we will meet again."

The King turned to the last of them, Conven, who stepped forward proudly.

"I request that my brother, too, be released and allowed to join us in the land of the living."

The King shook his head gravely.

"That is not possible," he said.

Conven looked outraged.

"But you allowed Selese to return!" he protested.

"Selese can return only because her life was not taken by someone else's hand. Your brother, though, was murdered. I'm afraid he cannot return. Not now. Not ever. He will be here for the remainder of his days."

Conven's eyes welled up as he looked to Conval, then back to the King of the Dead.

"Then I change my request!" Conven called out. "I request to be allowed to stay here, with my brother!"

Thorgrin gasped, as did the others, horrified.

"Conven, you cannot request such a thing" Thor said hurriedly, as they all came up to him.

"You must not!" Reece added.

Conven shook off their hands, though, and stepped up proudly.

"If my brother cannot be free," he said, "then neither shall I. I request it again!"

Conval grabbed Conven's arm.

"Conven," he said, "don't do this. We shall be together again, one day."

Conven stared back at him, serious, undeterred.

"No, my brother," he said. "We shall be together again now."

The King stared at them long and hard, then finally said: "A brother's love is not easily broken. If you wish to be here before your time, then your wish is granted. You are welcome here."

The King nodded, and suddenly the massive gate began to rise. Slowly, higher and higher, it revealed the open air, the blood-red sky. When it was high enough, the seven demons, looking like shadows, flew out and into the open sky, letting out a horrific shriek as they did so. They immediately dissipated in seven different directions.

Thor and the others walked to the edge, looked out at the world before them, the open twilight sky, the fresh air. He looked down and saw the ocean spread out before them, heard waves crashing far below.

226

Beside him was Reece, holding Selese's hand, along with the others. He turned and saw behind them Conven, standing there with his brother, looking back at them sadly; yet at the same time, somehow, finally, Conven seemed satisfied, seemed to have the peace that had eluded him on earth.

Thor turned and embraced Conven, hugging him tight, and Conven hugged him back.

One by one, they each embraced Conven, their eyes welling up, feeling the pain of leaving their Legion brother behind, this man who had been with them from the very start.

Thor looked him in the eye, clasping his shoulder.

"One day, we shall be united again," Thorgrin said.

Conven nodded.

"Yes we shall," he replied. "But not, I hope, one day soon."

Thor turned and looked out at the open sky, saw their boat rocking in the waves below, and he knew that soon they would be back at sea, sailing across the ocean, seeking out Gwendolyn, Guwayne, and all their people. Soon, they would be united again.

He looked up and as he did, he watched the seven demons, black shadows in the distance merging with the twilight, spread out in seven directions, preparing to blanket the world. Finally, they disappeared from view. Thor heard the last of their screeching, and he wondered: *What have I unleashed on the world?*

CHAPTER THIRTY SIX

Guwayne looked up at the sky as he flew through the air, through the clouds, feeling himself grasped in the gentle claws of a baby dragon, a baby like himself. The dragon's screeching somehow comforted Guwayne, as it had for days. He felt he could fly like this forever.

Guwayne had lost all sense of time and place, his entire world this dragon, looking up at its belly, its chin, its jaws, mesmerized by its flapping wings, by the way its scales shimmered in the light. He felt he could soar with it forever, wherever it should take them.

Guwayne felt the dragon gradually diving downward, lower and lower, for the first time since he had lifted him up into the air. As they turned slightly, Guwayne saw the endless ocean spread out below.

The dragon flew lower and lower, through the clouds, and for the first time since they set out, Guwayne saw land: a lone small, circular island, surrounded by nothingness as far as the eye could see. The island rose out of the ocean, straight up, tall and vertical, surrounded by straight cliffs, like a geyser shooting up from the seas. At its top was a wide plateau of land, to which they dove.

The dragon screeched as they went lower and lower, and then finally, it slowed, flapping its wings as their speed reduced.

As the dragon nearly came to a stop, Guwayne looked down and cried as he saw the face of a stranger, a lone man standing there, in bright yellow robes, with a long, yellow beard, holding a gleaming, golden staff, a single diamond sparkling in its center. Guwayne did not cry out of fear—but out of love. Already, just seeing the man, he felt comforted.

The dragon came to a stop, flapping its wings, holding them still, as the man reached out and the dragon placed Guwayne gingerly in his arms.

The man held Guwayne gently in his arms, wrapping him in his cloak, and slowly, Guwayne stopped crying. He felt safe in this man's arms, felt a tremendous power radiating off of him, and he sensed that he was more than just a man. The man had sparkling red eyes, and he stood up straight, and raised his staff to the heavens.

As he did, the world thundered.

The mysterious man held Guwayne tight, and as Guwayne looked into his eyes, he had a feeling that he would be here for a very, very long time.

CHAPTER THIRTY SEVEN

Gwendolyn marched at the head of her huge convoy of people as dawn broke over the desert, leading them away from the village, toward the Great Waste. Kendrick, Steffen, Aberthol, Brandt, and Atme marched behind her, Krohn at her heels, as they all slowly wound their way out of the caves, up to the top of the mountains, and looked out west and north, toward a vast, empty desert.

As they reached the top, Gwendolyn paused for a moment and looked out at the purple and red sky, the first sun rising, the endless trek that lay ahead of them to a place that might not exist. She turned and glanced back at the village down below, in the opposite direction, all quiet and still in the early morning. Soon, she knew, the Empire would come. The village would be surrounded. They would all be wiped out.

Gwen turned and looked at her people, all that she had left of the Ring, these people who she loved so much. Not far from her stood Illepra, holding the baby girl Gwen had rescued from the dragon's breath. The baby cried in the morning air, shattering the silence, and Gwen wondered: *what have I saved this child's life for if I do not protect it now?* Yet a conflicting thought arose immediately after: *what is the purpose of this child's life if it cannot be a life of valor?*

Gwen had remained awake all night, tormented by her decision. The villagers had encouraged her to move on; her own people wanted her to move on. The time had come. She could not, in good conscience, lead her people to a sure death. That was not what Queens did.

Yet as Gwendolyn stood atop the cliff, looking out, something stirred inside her. Something was calling her. It was, she felt, her lineage, her ancestors, their blood pumping through her veins. The seven generations of MacGil Kings, she knew, were with her, whispering down into her ear. They would not let her walk away.

She had a duty and an obligation to her people, to guide them to safety. That was what it meant to rule as a Queen.

230

Yet a Queen, she realized, also had another obligation. For honor. For valor. To bring out the best in her people. To define who her people were. Even in the face of death—perhaps *most of all* in the face of death. That, after all, was when it mattered most.

Gwendolyn heard her father's voice ringing in her ears:

One day you will be faced with a choice that torments you. Every part of your rational mind will pull you one way; yet your ideals will tug you another. That torment, that is what it is all about. That is when you will know what it means to rule as a Queen.

Gwen turned back and looked down, seeing the small village in the vast countryside below, watching all the villagers beginning to rise, to face the dawn, to face a certain death. They rose proudly. Fearlessly.

She looked up, and in the distance, on the horizon, like a storm brewing, she could already detect the Empire forces, stretched as far as the eye could see.

As she looked down one more time at the villagers, pondering her choice, feeling her people behind her, waiting here at this crossroads, she realized: yes, it is the duty of a Queen to shepherd her people; yet it is also her duty to shepherd their spirit. To embody their spirit. And the spirit of her people was to never run. To never back down. To never turn your back on those in need.

Safety meant nothing when it came at the price of someone else's harm.

Gwendolyn faced the village, the horizon, the gathering Empire army, and she knew there was but one choice she could make:

"Turn our people around," she commanded Kendrick.

Gwen turned and marched forward in the opposite direction, heading down the slope toward the village, toward the Empire army. She led her people, and she knew, as a shepherd knows its flock, that they would follow.

She knew they were marching to their deaths. Yet that mattered little now. Everyone died—but not everyone really lived.

What mattered most, she knew, was that they were marching to glory.

CHAPTER THIRTY EIGHT

Darius stood with all his brothers and villagers as dawn broke over the village, Loti at his side, Dray at his heels, all the elders around him, and he looked out at the sight before him: there was the strength of the Empire, hundreds of soldiers returning, line up on zertas, facing them. The day of retribution had come.

Darius stood there, his back still raw, killing him, feeling hollowed out. Knowing what his village demanded of him, he hadn't slept all night, tormented. He stood there now, bleary-eyed, knowing they demanded he give up Loti so his people could go on living.

But Darius knew that if he did that, if he did what they asked, then he himself could not go on living. Something inside him would be dead; something inside all of them would be dead. This, this self-preservation, might be the way of his elders, but it was not his way. It would *never* be his way.

The Empire commander came forth on his zerta, leading an entourage of a dozen soldiers, his hundreds of soldiers lined up in rows behind him in the early morning light, and he stopped but fifty feet away from Darius. He dismounted and walked forward in the dirt, his spurs jingling, heading right for Darius.

Dray began to snarl, and Darius lay a hand on his head, and turned, squatted and looked him in the eye.

"Dray," he commanded urgently. "Remember what we talked about. You are to stay here. Do you understand?"

Finally, Dray fell quiet, and as he looked into Darius' eyes, Darius felt that he did indeed understand.

Darius turned and glanced at Loti, and he could see the fear in her face as she looked back at him. She nodded at him, squeezed his hand with a firm grip.

"It's okay," she said. "Give me up to them. I wish to die. For you. For all of you."

He shook his head quickly, and leaned down and kissed her hand.

232

Then he turned and walked off, alone, one man to face the Empire.

The commander stopped, waiting, as Darius walked up to him and stopped before him. Darius glared back at him with hatred, feeling the lashes on his back, feeling the cold breeze on the back of his neck where his hair had been chopped off. He felt hatred. Yet he also felt like a new man, reborn.

He stood a few feet away from the Empire commander, who glared down at him mercilessly.

"It is a new day," he boomed to Darius and the villagers. "You have one chance now. You will name the victim of this crime, we will maim you all, and you all shall live."

The commander paused.

"Or," the commander boomed, "you can remain silent, and we will kill you all, torturing each one of you slowly, beginning with you."

Darius stood there, staring back, resolute. He felt the gentle wind of the desert as his world narrowed, came into focus, his heart thumping in his ears. As all grew silent, in the distance he saw a small thorn bush roll along the desert floor. He heard its rattle, a strangely soothing sound. Time slowed as he sensed every detail in the world. Every detail which he knew could be his last.

Darius nodded slowly back at the commander.

"I am going to give you exactly what you came for," he said.

Darius knew that if he did not hand Loti over, if he defied them, it would be a battle they could not win. He would give up his life for loyalty, for honor. For justice. He would defy the law of his elders. He would defy them all.

The Empire commander smiled wide, bracing himself.

"So who among you was it?" he demanded. "Which one of you killed our taskmaster?"

Darius stared back, his heart pounding, expressionless, yet shaking inside.

"Come close, Commander, and I will tell you his name."

The commander took a step closer, and in that moment, Darius's entire world froze. With trembling hands, he reached down, pulled a dagger from his belt, a steel dagger, real steel, which the smith had

233

given him and he had hidden away. He lunged forward, and he could hear the horrified gasp of his elders, his people, as he plunged the knife, up to the hilt, deep into the commander's chest.

The commander, wide-eyed with shock, dropped to his knees, as if unbelieving that such a thing could happen.

"The offender's name is a name you shall never, ever forget," Darius said, sneering down. "His name is Darius."

COMING SOON!

BOOK #14 IN THE SORCERER'S RING

Books by Morgan Rice

THE SORCERER'S RING
A QUEST OF HEROES
A MARCH OF KINGS
A FATE OF DRAGONS
A CRY OF HONOR
A VOW OF GLORY
A CHARGE OF VALOR
A RITE OF SWORDS
A GRANT OF ARMS
A SKY OF SPELLS
A SEA OF SHIELDS
A REIGN OF STEEL
A LAND OF FIRE
A RULE OF QUEENS

THE SURVIVAL TRILOGY
ARENA ONE (Book #1)
ARENA TWO (Book #2)

the Vampire Journals
turned (book #1)
loved (book #2)
betrayed (book #3)
destined (book #4)
desired (book #5)
betrothed (book #6)
vowed (book #7)
found (book #8)
resurrected (book #9)
craved (book #10)
fated (book #11)

About Morgan Rice

Morgan Rice is the #1 bestselling author of THE VAMPIRE JOURNALS, a young adult series comprising eleven books (and counting); the #1 bestselling series THE SURVIVAL TRILOGY, a post-apocalyptic thriller comprising two books (and counting); and the #1 bestselling epic fantasy series THE SORCERER'S RING, comprising thirteen books (and counting).

Morgan's books are available in audio and print editions, and translations of the books are available in German, French, Italian, Spanish, Portugese, Japanese, Chinese, Swedish, Dutch, Turkish, Hungarian, Czech and Slovak (with more languages forthcoming).

Morgan loves to hear from you, so please feel free to visit www.morganricebooks.com to join the email list, receive a free book, receive free giveaways, download the free app, get the latest exclusive news, connect on Facebook and Twitter, and stay in touch!